MAIDEN OF
CANDLELIGHT AND
LOTUSES

THE ZHENINGHAI CHRONICLES

MAIDEN of
CANDLELIGHT
AND
LOTUSES

THE ZHENINGHAI CHRONICLES

ANASTASIS BLYTHE

MAIDEN OF CANDLELIGHT AND LOTUSES

Hardcover ISBN: 978-1-960606-00-6

Cover design by Moorbooks Design.
Interior Design by Dragonpen Designs.

FOR NANA. I MISS YOU.

CHAPTER
1

L IENA DIDN'T THINK it was a crime to complete the tasks
assigned to her. Thus, it took her a few minutes to figure out
why Ma would have her *I'm Furious* look when she came charging
out of their hut.

Liena swiped the sweat from her brow, wincing from the sun,
and straightened. She gauged the distance between her and Ma and
decided she could probably harvest a few more heads of millet in the
time it took Ma to reach her.

It was only after she'd turned back to work that she realized why
Ma was angry.

"Oh!" she cried, immediately stopping and spinning back toward
Ma, who was flailing her arms and gesturing much more wildly than
necessary. She cupped her hands over her mouth and shouted, "I'll
finish this row and come back to the house!"

"Come *now!*" came Ma's wailed response. "Or we'll be late! And
then what ever will become of us?"

Liena chewed the inside of her cheek, glancing up at the sun again. They still had two hours, and it wouldn't take her that long to get ready.

But Ma would not be put off.

Heaving a sigh, she picked up her basket, hefted it to her shoulder, and trudged back toward the house.

"I don't think we need two hours to get ready," she said calmly to her mother when she caught up. "And if we don't finish this harvest—"

"We'll starve, I *know*," said Ma flippantly. "But if you don't find a husband, then you'll definitely starve."

Which was worse? Starving now, or starving in fifteen years?

Liena kept silent.

"Lao Lao prepared a bath for you," Ma continued prattling as they returned to the hut. "You look wretched. I know you think it'll only take fifteen minutes to get ready, but you've got miles of grime caked to your skin!"

Liena could see the top of Pa's lanky form peeking over the stalks of millet in the left field. Her heart clenched a little tighter. If she was gone all day at the matchmaker's, then he would have to work extra hard. And that would take a tremendous toll on his bad hip.

If only Liena had been a son. Or better yet, three sons!

"Oh! Look, it's Wu Lan!" said Ma in a hushed whisper, grabbing Liena's arm and smiling toward the roadside where a boy around seventeen years old strode by. Liena had known him for her whole life from a distance—he was the son of their local butcher, and in her mother's words, was *a rather nice boy*. She'd never spoken to him though.

"Just think, if you could marry the butcher's boy!" said Ma once he'd past them. "Do you think they eat meat regularly? Imagine the luxury! You'd be set for life. We need to hurry so we're not late for the matchmaker!"

The matchmaker would never match a butcher's son and a farmer's daughter. Liena was too far below him. But that didn't stop Ma from

2

dreaming. It didn't stop Liena from sighing as she dumped her basket of millet heads onto the waiting pile.

The moment the door swung open to their hut, she should have expected it. She should have dodged or timed her entry better. But she was lost in thought, lost in a last forlorn glance over her shoulder at the work she'd abandoned, when the cane descended upon her prone arm.

"Ow!" Liena cried, jerking back and glaring down at the scowling set of wrinkles before her. "You'll bruise me for the matchmaker!"

Lao Lao's cane tapped the dirt floor threateningly, her face severe and completely unremorseful. "What's wrong with you girl? Forgetting all about the matchmaker!"

"We're not late!" Liena protested.

But Ma was already hustling her into the corner where Pa had set up the tub. When Ma said that Lao Lao had prepared the bath, what she *meant* was that Lao Lao had sat outside the hut caterwauling until Pa had come to do her bidding.

The water was tepid, and she was glad it wasn't icy like the streams. Ma stripped off Liena's robes so fast she didn't have time to be embarrassed before she was shoved into the small wooden tub.

"I hate how this thing leaks," said Lao Lao, tapping her cane disapprovingly on it.

"Ma, why are you washing me? You haven't helped me wash since—"

"Yes, well, today is different. Now quit your squawking and hold still."

"Don't you want me to help?"

Whap!

For someone as old and slow as Lao Lao, her cane sure moved like lightning. Liena gasped and pulled her stinging hand in to her chest.

"Listen to your mother!" Lao Lao snapped.

"I wasn't—"

"And no talking back!" Lao Lao waved her cane threateningly.

Liena swallowed her protests, grumbles, and eyerolls in quick succession. She'd vexed Lao Lao and there was nothing she could do but feign penitence until Lao Lao forgot why she was angry.

"If only we had more money for proper paint!" Ma whined as she helped Liena out of the tub and into a borrowed set of robes.

"Charcoal works just as well as any of that fancy stuff," said Lao Lao, whacking the makeshift fireplace.

"What's all this fuss?" came a new voice from the door.

All three pairs of eyes turned at Pa's silhouette against the noonday sun. Liena finished tying off the sash at her waist, leapt away from her mother's charcoal smeared fingers, and ran to him.

"Save me!" she cried, flinging her arms around him.

He laughed, starting to wrap one dirty arm around her.

"Don't touch her!" shrieked Ma and Lao Lao at once.

Pa's eyes twinkled, but he stepped back so he wouldn't muss her, chucking her chin affectionately. "You be a good girl for your Ma and grandma."

"Be a good girl for the matchmaker!" growled Lao Lao. "Doesn't matter if she's a wretch here."

"Well, Liena is not a wretch here, so she won't be at the matchmakers," said Ma, with a warning glance that completely contradicted her words. If Liena didn't know that her mother was just a fusser, she might have been offended.

"If you get yourself a respectable match today," said Pa, "then I'll let you sleep in tomorrow."

"Sleep in? I couldn't possibly! I'm not being helpful at all today!" Liena wrung her hands around her too-big sleeves.

He leaned in and planted a kiss on her forehead, smiling as he did so. "Going to the matchmaker's is the best thing you can do today, little dove."

Because if Liena found a good husband to marry, one with a way to support his family, then she would ensure her parents were well-taken care of in their sunset years. But still! If they didn't finish this harvest before the first frost, then they would starve this winter.

And what was the point of having an auspicious husband-to-be if she starved before she could marry him?

"Liena?" said Pa, his voice sounding strangely faraway. "What's the matter?"

She looked up at him, but he began drifting away from her. A wave of heat washed over her, one so potent it made her want to rip off these unfamiliar robes and jump into the nearest icy stream.

"Liena?"

"Liena!"

She opened her mouth to tell them she was fine, just suddenly feeling a little strange, but then she hit something hard. The ground— she'd hit the ground. Had she fallen? Her limbs seemed to be sucked by some otherworldly force down, down, *down*. Into the earth, into an undug grave.

The world grew darker.

Was she dying?

Before she could crawl to her feet, lavender light burst all around her. It swallowed the hut, swallowed the noonday sun shining through the doorway, swallowed herself. She lost control of her body, lost control of everything.

Everything, save her heart-pounding fear.

Was she truly dying?

Then, the all-encompassing lavender light clarified, and Liena saw something. Not a family member's worried face, the wooden tub in the corner, or Lao Lao's cane. No, something entirely different. Something like she had never seen before.

She stood in a dark, unfamiliar room. The edges glowed lavender, rendering the entire picture blurry. She could make out no details except the window she faced. It opened into the night, and a full moon hung low in the sky. Silhouetted against that moon was a tall, distinctly masculine figure.

"I'll be back for you. Be ready when I come."

Desperate anger and a deadly sort of love stabbed into her core, and she reeled backward, gasping. The image fled, leaving her in blinding, pulsing, lavender light. Even after the image was gone, she felt it. Those strange, pinpricks of impressions that plucked at her mind, insistent. She was lost to the snarling forces around her, could think of nothing but how much she pitied the hazy man as he leapt out of the window and was swallowed by moon and shadows.

She had no idea why she felt those emotions—the anger, the love, the pity. Some of those emotions seemed to come from herself, but others seemed to come from elsewhere. From him?

The lavender light eased slightly, enough that she could hear screams and shouts filling her mortal ears. There was a strange scraping sound. Odd, buzzing chatter. Fearful.

With each breath, the light faded, and Liena became more aware of her body. Realized the screams she heard came from her own mouth. Despite her attempts to stop, her straining vocal chords continued to shriek of their own accord. But she could feel the screams now, feel how her body arched with them. Her arms flung, mostly flailing in air, but sometimes connecting with something solid.

Abruptly, the last bit of light dissipated, leaving her voiceless. Her entire body sagged with relief, weakness, and released strain. For a long moment, she could do naught but lie on the dirt floor, her nice, borrowed clothes now bedraggled. Her hair had come loose of its scarf, and she sucked strands into her mouth with every heaving breath.

She'd never felt so weak in her entire life.

"Liena! Liena!"

"Liena!"

"LIENA!"

She was surrounded. Blinking against exhaustion so sheer she almost gave into death that very moment, her gaze cleared. There—Ma, Pa, Lao Lao.

"Liena, wake up! What has happened to you?" Ma cried, dragging Liena's limp arms up in a fruitless attempt to help her sit. Liena only fell back heavily, caught and arranged by Pa so her head rested in his lap.

She looked up, parting her lips. Her tongue cleaved to the roof of her mouth; her throat was dry. Her voice was hoarse, brittle like the ginger candy she had only seen children eat in the markets and never tasted herself. Yet she spoke, focusing all her attention on her Pa's wide-eyed worry.

"I saw a vision."

Liena was still wearing the borrowed robes, sitting on the floor of the hut, as her parents and grandma chattered incessantly about this new development.

She apparently wasn't going to the matchmaker today, after all.

"Oh, my dove, your magic is such a gift! Such an unexpected, sudden, gift!"

"Just think, if everything goes well at the Academy, we might not need to be farmers anymore. You can get a wonderful appointment, have a *salary*, Liena! No more digging in the dirt, no more sowing and harvesting. You can make something of yourself!"

"You could make an auspicious match!"

"You could have powerful, magical children! Think of what this could mean for your children. We could give you nothing but life as a poor farmer's daughter, but *you*, you could give your children so much more!"

Through the barrage of plans and the sudden explosion of dreams for the future, Liena only managed to ask, "What if I end up being appointed to hunt *mó guǐ*?"

Lao Lao immediately scoffed, chomping her gums loud enough to echo through the entire hut. "Hunt monsters, dear girl?" She lifted her cane and tapped Liena's wincing head with it. "Oh no, you're a seer. Your magic is not battle magic! You'll end up in the capital—maybe even the palace!"

"The palace!" Ma exclaimed. "Imagine the auspicious matches available *there*!"

It was decided that the entire family must go to the village to help Liena buy enough food for the journey south to the capital, where the Academy was. She found herself insisting that no, she did not need sticky buns—they would be entirely too impractical. No, she did not need jewelry, even "for the occasion."

"Remember," Liena said to her mother, "they provide clothes for me. What I have is suitable for the journey."

"And show up to those handsome Academy boys wearing this?" Ma sniffed as she pinched the sleeve of Liena's threadbare robes.

"I'm sure it won't—"

"Oh! Oh, there is Xu Da! Come, come, let us go tell her the news!"

"She has likely already heard—"

"Nonsense!"

Pa had disappeared into the crowd, doubtlessly to brag to his acquaintances. Ma dragged Liena after her toward a short, severe-faced woman who regarded Liena with several upraising glances. As if to say, "This *is a seer?*"

It seems I have become a prized cow, Liena thought to herself as her cheeks were pinched and patted, as strangers, half-acquaintances, and friends alike studied the length of her. Every so often, someone would chime, "One of my relative's sons had a friend who had magic! Turned straight up out of nowhere like this!"

This was such a waste of time. She could have made the trip by herself, could have avoided her parents spending far more than necessary of their very meager funds for food, and could have escaped notice. With all the attention her Ma and Lao Lao garnered for her, she could be an entire traveling circus act all by herself.

The day waned before Liena's eyes. They were still at the market, still strutting around like peacocks, and they hadn't bought even half of what they came for—yet somehow they'd spent twice the amount of money necessary. Every clink of a copper tangu sent her wincing and pleading that they should not spend their money so frivolously.

The family celebration would not be dimmed. Magic in the family changed *everything*.

"Oh, just this once, my dear!" Ma kept saying.

Meanwhile, Liena's thoughts were a tight ball of anxiety. They'd left the crops for too long! How would they ever catch up on all this lost time? How would her family manage without her? What if something happened to them—what if they couldn't finish the harvest in time—and what if she didn't hear about it for months or even years? Would she even be able to see her family again . . . ever?

Lao Lao skittered across the market, scattering squawking chickens and accidentally thumping her cane on unsuspecting toes. She held something up in one hand, a large and gummy grin splitting her weathered face.

"Look, girl, look what I found for you! It's perfect!"

Ma gasped behind her, prodding Liena forward even as she insisted, "I'm sure it's perfect, but I don't think—"

Lao Lao smacked Liena's knuckles with her cane. "Stop your sniveling, child! It's *perfect*, you hear?"

Liena clutched her smarting hand to her chest, but she shut her mouth and nodded with furrowed brows. Ma squealed as Lao Lao held out a beautiful, beaded necklace on a leather cord. It couldn't have been very expensive, but it was still frivolous. What use had she for decorations and ornaments? It was better spent on yams and rice to fill bellies.

But then her grandmother pressed the beads into Liena's hand and her own eyes widened as she saw the smooth, painted wood beads. On the centermost one, painted so tiny it was almost unrecognizable, was a blooming lotus. Despite everything, despite her dominating practicality, she exhaled softly as she studied it and ran her finger over that center bead.

She knew the many wives of the emperor wore jewelry far finer than this, but somehow she couldn't dream of seeing anything more beautiful. She couldn't help her smile or her honest admission. "I love it."

"I knew you would," Lao Lao said with a wink. "It has your namesake."

"Put it on!" Ma cried. "Put it on!"

They stayed at the market until well after sundown, mingling with the good folk there, retelling the well-known news of Liena's magic. She tried to hang back as much as possible, but her fingers kept finding her necklace and touching the lotus bead.

There was no time for Liena to voice the thoughts swirling through her mind. *Am I too old? Too late?* Would her family survive without her? What if this was all some wild mistake?

CHAPTER
2

H ERE'S A NEW student."

"Better be the last," came the responding growl.

Liena blinked, clutching her small bundle of belongings to her chest, and stared at the figure on the opposite side of the office.

It was a dark room, with crimson curtains drawn over the windows, and a low ceiling. The air was full with the smell of musty tea leaves and other things that she'd never smelled before. Smells she guessed were associated with the stacks of scrolls on the squatty desk, in a basket nearby, and on shelves along the far wall.

A woman was scribbling away at the desk, her back straight even as she bent over her work. She was cross-legged on her mat, her long, gray-streaked hair pooling on the floor behind her.

"Now that I've gotten you here, I'll be off," said the short man who had greeted her as she trudged up, exhausted and wide-eyed, to the

Academy gates. All he'd done was ask what she was doing, frowned as he looked her over, then escorted her inside. He didn't seem to care that she gawked at the large complex, the expansive sandy area that must be what they called "the pits," and the curved arrangement of the buildings.

"Where are all the students?" she had asked.

"In class, of course," he had said.

He abandoned her now.

Liena tried not to shuffle her feet awkwardly, but despite her best efforts, her fingers found the sash of her robes. She twisted it fretfully.

Why did the woman before her not turn around? Was Liena supposed to say something?

When in doubt, stay silent.

"Name?" came the sharp word from the woman. She didn't turn, only dipped a quill into a pot of ink and kept scribbling.

Would Liena learn to read and write here? The thought sent a thrill shooting all the way to her toes, enough to nearly quell the suffocating homesickness and sense of misplacement.

"Song Liena," she said.

"What? Speak up girl!"

Liena straightened, drew a deep breath, and enunciated, "Song Liena."

The quill stopped. Liena forced her hands back down to her side. *Don't be nervous.*

The woman turned.

Liena sucked in a breath and bit her tongue in surprise.

Where the woman's left eye should have been, there was an empty socket. A long scar ran from the middle of her forehead down to her ear. No eye-patch or scarf or anything to hide the visage. Her one good eye, however, was narrowed to a slit.

"How old are you, girl?"

Liena found her voice with difficulty. "I am sixteen, ma'am."

"Master. Not ma'am. *Master.* Master Gu. And why, pray, have you come to the Academy so late?"

"My magic has only now just developed. I came as soon as it did."

"What is your magic, girl?"

"I am a seer, ma'—Master."

"Hmmph. Not surprising. Low magic, I presume?"

"Low magic?"

"Can you control your magic?" Master Gu snapped. "Did you conjure your first vision? Or did it come out of nowhere?"

"I did not conjure it."

"Low magic, most likely then. We'll have to test it just in case."

Liena's eyes flew wide as her hands fisted in the fabric of her travel-worn robes. "Test?"

"Oh, not *that* Test. Don't look so terrified girl. Besides, if you're going to succeed here, you will need to conquer a fear of pain."

At this, the woman stood up from her mat, rising to an impressive height. Liena tried not to crane her neck backward as she approached and stared her down with one narrowed eye. She stopped a mere foot from her. Liena swallowed.

Her rational mind told her not to be frightened. After all, Master Gu had no reason to hurt her. These were just intimidation tactics—nothing more.

They worked anyway.

"Rice farmer?" asked the woman.

"Millet."

"From the north?"

Liena nodded.

Fast as lightning, the woman's hand darted out, snatched her chin, and tilted her face to the side. Liena tried not to flinch.

"Your accent betrays your heritage," said the woman. "Part barbarian, are you not?"

Was that a problem? Or uncommon here, so far from the border? Of all the things Liena expected them to criticize about her, her parentage was not one of them. "I am," she said only.

"Hmm," came the displeased response.

Heat crawled up her neck, but she forced calm and even breaths through her nose. If they turned her away, she would simply . . . How *could* she get home? She had used up all of her supplies and money to get here.

She would think of something. Later. If it came to that.

Right now, she had to keep herself from staring into the empty socket of the intimidating woman before her.

Master Gu released her grip. "I see you are alarmed by my eye. Do you care to know what happened to it?"

Yes, but also no. Liena said nothing.

"A dragon tore it out," she said without preamble. "And *ate* it. Then I ran my sword through its neck and tore out both of its eyes. Now, the *mó guǐ* sits on my wall."

For a horrible moment, Liena expected to see a pair of bloodied eyes pinned to the wall when the woman gestured behind her. But instead, hung above the desk she'd been writing at a few minutes ago, was a scaly, amethyst hide. She wouldn't have guessed it had once been a dragon.

She shuddered.

"Do you know the kind of world you're getting into, girl?"

Liena shook her head honestly.

There was a self-satisfied smirk and huff, then Master Gu proceeded, gliding toward the purple dragon skin on the wall. Her black robes trailed behind her. "Most of our students come between the ages of five and seven. The vast majority graduate by twenty. Then they receive their career appointments. Some stay here in Suguan to work at the palace, or in the bureaucracy. But most take their appointments in the military, or in cities around the empire. They are the wielders of the empire, and they protect our people. What do they protect our people from?"

"From the *mó guǐ*."

"And?"

"Invasions."

14

"And?"

Liena blinked, searching for another response. "Um . . . crime?"

Master Gu snorted but didn't correct her. "For our wielders to withstand such trials, do you think they come here to be coddled for their talent?"

Liena shook her head.

"No indeed. We work our students *hard*. They face dangers here they would face on the field. In fact, we push them so hard that some of them don't survive."

The woman fixed her with a heavy stare now, as if expecting Liena's knees to buckle beneath the weight of her fear. But though her heart skipped a beat inside her chest, though ice swept down her spine, she kept her expression as solemn and neutral as she could.

"We had five die last year," the woman continued. "All bright, talented individuals. One died of exhaustion and strain. She had a health condition she didn't know about, and her body couldn't handle the rigor."

A stone dropped into Liena's gut.

"Two died in the pits while battling an opposing student. The fourth wasn't paying close enough attention in his Poisons and Foreign Substances class. And the last died from a *mó guǐ* attack during a Hunt. Not to mention the student who almost died because of . . . *issues* in detention."

Her head suddenly felt like it was a fluffy cloud, floating away from her body. But now was *not* the time to faint.

Judging by the tiny smirk playing at the edges of Master Gu's mouth, Liena's face had probably gone green or white. She swallowed, pressing her sweaty hands to her sides. Anything to keep them from twisting her sash.

"This isn't a nice little boarding school, girl. This is *the* Academy. It is the most rigorous school in the entire empire, and the most rigorous experience you will ever endure. And you're about ten years behind."

CHAPTER
3

A NOTHER MASTER CAME to collect her from Master Gu. When Liena peered up at him, she found a warm smile awaiting her. It was set in a pleasant face, one with surprisingly soft lines and a welcoming light in his eyes.

The tension flowed like water out of Liena's limbs. Bolstered by his kindness, she smiled back.

"I'm Master Zhong," he said. "I am here to guide you to your dormitory. Please follow me."

Behind her, she could feel the eye of Master Gu on her back. Felt the weight of a sightless stare. She pushed away her premonition, telling herself that she was only grateful that she was still allowed to attend the Academy.

"We do not typically have students come at your age," said Master Zhong. "You're a special case."

Something about his words made her feel a little taller, like she could stand straighter. Everything seemed wrong about all of this, but this master reminded her that not long ago, she thought she was just another ordinary girl. Now, she was officially a magic-wielder of the empire.

Perhaps things could be better for her. For her family.

She reached up and touched the beads at her throat.

Perhaps things wouldn't be as bad as the Master made it seem. After all, Liena was no stranger to hard work. She grew up on a farm; she knew rigor. She was no soft lord's daughter. Her hands were strong and callused, her limbs and body toned.

Finding her voice, she said, "I know I am late, but I am prepared to work hard."

She meant it, too.

"Keep up that attitude. It will serve you well here. You're behind, but with effort and determination, I'm sure you will do just fine."

She smiled, reassured again, and felt lighter with each step. This wouldn't be that bad. "At least, when I get my appointment"—Such a weird thing to say! She had never thought *she* would get an appointment—"I won't have to fight *mó guǐ,* since I'm a seer."

The master's steps slowed, his smile fading immediately. He glanced at her, then looked away.

"What?" she said, quietly, suddenly afraid. "Shall I be appointed to fight *mó guǐ*?"

He let out a great gust of a sigh. Before he answered, he beckoned her down the hallway. A hallway that was brilliant crimson, with sunlight pouring through latticed screens and catching on the gold detail on the sapphire paint of the ceiling, swept out before her. It was the grandest thing she'd ever seen.

If the Academy was this fine, how majestic must the palace be?

"Sweet girl," said the master gently, "you are one of the most likely candidates for monster fighting. You do not have battle magic and you are a low magic-wielder. You will likely be given a post in a village, and you will be little more than a deputy, fighting crime and monsters alike. When you have visions, you will be required by law to submit them for review. Is it the most practical matching of magic and skill to an appointment? No. But that's the way things are."

Suddenly, everything felt larger and more intimidating, and she felt smaller. The ceiling seemed to soar higher above her, the weight of the air pressing down on her shoulders.

A *mó guǐ* hunter?

She bit her lip but forced down the sudden flare of panic. *Everything will be alright.* She simply needed to be rational about this. There was no reason for her to worry about her appointment now when she needed to be focused on catching up on the years she had missed.

One of the doors ahead opened, and a tall young man strode out. He was wearing white robes, like the ones that Liena held in her arms. He wasn't just tall, but broad as a mountain, with shoulders whose breadth stretched the fabric of his robes. His black hair was coiled up on his head, half falling out of the fastening pins. His face was slicked with sweat, beads of it sliding down the cut of his jaw.

He was easily the handsomest man she'd ever seen.

He strode past her without a glance.

A master in black scurried after him, slamming the door closed in his hurry. "Highness!" he called after the young man.

"Thank you," replied the young man crisply. "But I am well capable of fulfilling the emperor's summons on my own. I won't lose myself if that's what you're worried about. You are dismissed."

The master gawked after him, and Liena swiveled her head to watch the young man march down the corridor. His gait was one of purpose, of authority, as if he was the master of these walls.

She didn't mean to gape, but when she finally glanced back at her escort, she realized her mouth was hanging open.

"The dormitories are just around the bend here," said Master Zhong.

"Was that one of the princes?" she asked.

"Indeed. The Crown Prince himself."

She paused, trying to decide if she should ask more questions or leave it be. "His magic . . . He's a fire wielder?"

"Indeed." The master seemed brisker now, as though he was made uncomfortable by her questions. He walked faster, his head faced forward unlike hers, which kept craning back to peek another glance.

She decided to drop the subject, but that didn't stop her curiosity from bubbling up to the surface. She tried to clamp down on that too. *Snap it together, Liena! He may be handsome, but that doesn't mean . . . It doesn't mean anything!*

She drew herself taller, straighter, and decided she wasn't going to think about him. Her grandma's words to find a husband here rang through her mind. There would be plenty of other young men.

Plenty of other handsome men.

And if Liena was being realistic, she now knew that her magic was not going to raise their position in society much. As much as she hated to admit it, her best chance would be to find a husband with stronger magic who would have her.

As if anyone would want to wed a half-barbarian millet farmer.

Beggars couldn't be choosers. Handsome wasn't something she could care about.

"Here's your dorm. Your dormmate will be back soon once she's done with class. You have time to wash up for supper, change, and get settled. Do you see that hallway? Take a left, head down that hallway until you exit the building. Then just follow the crowd of students to the mess hall. Do you have any last questions before I leave you?"

So many. "No but thank you."

Perhaps she could ask her dormmate later once she'd gotten to know her better. She glanced around the tiny room, the patterned, paper-thin walls, and noted the two mats on either side of the room. She set down her bundle on the floor next to the mat, then poked at the plush head cushion.

MAIDEN OF CANDLELIGHT AND LOTUSES

There was no water, so it took her a bit of wandering around to find the communal washroom where she could clean herself up.

The white robes she donned were the finest things she had ever seen or touched. Except . . . Carefully, she ran her fingers over the beaded necklace at her throat. It was a little dusty, so she eased it off and wiped each bead, focusing special attention on the lotus bead.

CHAPTER
4

THE MESS HALL was loud.

There were hundreds of students in identical white robes funneling into the small mess hall. She was immediately caught in a tidal wave of white, nearly losing herself in the throng.

Feeling small and insignificant was not a pleasant feeling, but it was accompanied by a sense of invisibility, which she was glad for. She was invisible until she bumped into someone who apparently thought it was a good idea to wriggle her way upstream through the crowd of people.

"Hey!" said the girl. Her brow was darkened, furrowed with irritation. But then she stopped once she saw Liena. Her eyes swept over her, landing on the sash at her middle. "Hey," she said again in a completely different tone, a slow smile curving up her lips. "You're new, aren't you? What's your name?"

23

Why did Liena immediately bristle? The tone was by no means unkind. Surely she wasn't made uncomfortable by the fact that the girl was beautiful, with long, fluttering lashes and a tall, willowy form. That would be petty of her.

"My name is Liena," she said, mustering enough courage to smile.

"What a pretty name! Unusual too. Mine is Mao Shu." She paused, letting her eyes drift over Liena again in assessment. "So, you're new—at your age?"

Liena tried not to get shuffled by the crowd as Shu stared at her with a brimming smile, heedless of how she stopped the flow of traffic.

"Yes, my magic just developed."

"Fathers, I didn't know people could develop magic so late!" Shu exclaimed with a too-bright smile that flashed a row of white teeth. "What's your magic? I bet your family was very excited. Oh! Sorry, please excuse me, I've got to go!"

Liena followed the trail of the girl's attention to see a tall figure moving through the crowd parallel to them. Her stomach immediately knotted up, and she bit her lip to keep from gaping again at the Crown Prince.

"Let me know if you need anything!" said Shu. "My sister over there has been here for a couple years. I'm sure she'd be glad to help! Bye!"

With that, Shu scurried off after the prince, and Liena felt a pang of jealousy. She glanced toward where the girl had pointed and found that said sister was about ten years old, sitting cross-legged at one of the long rows of tables, laughing with a crew of ten-year-old friends.

Liena bit her lip again, her hands moving unconsciously to her necklace. She just had to find a place to eat. It didn't matter that she didn't know anyone yet. She would get to know people soon enough.

Students were taking seats, arranging themselves at the long, low rows of tables ladened with bowls of food. Liena marveled at the ease with which the young people of both genders interacted, mingling together like it was completely normal. She would have been fodder for gossip back home if she'd dared address a boy!

It appeared things were done differently here. And if she didn't sit down somewhere, she'd be the only one still standing. Her cloak of invisibility would be gone, and everyone would notice the awkward new student.

But sitting down among strangers was almost as terrifying of an option.

She scoured the mess hall, trying not to gape at the beautiful ceiling designs, until she happened to spot a lone figure sitting on the far side of the room. He sat at the very end of the farthest table, near a white and red ornamental screen and a life-sized replica of a phoenix.

It was a young man, his head tilted down with his elbow propped on the table. His hair was tied back in a long queue, as typical. She couldn't get a good view of his face from here.

With a deep breath, she gripped her robes with both hands and marched toward him. He might turn her away, certainly. Might send her off to sit with someone else. But something about the set of his shoulders and something else she couldn't name made her think he could use a smile. If that was the case, then perhaps another lonely soul could brighten his day a little.

If he didn't growl at her to leave him alone.

She approached him purposefully but cautiously, waiting for any sign that he'd seen her and didn't want her to come. He didn't look up. Not until she was standing before him on the opposite side of the table did he slowly swivel his face up to hers.

He was just about her age. Sixteen or seventeen, slender and lean, with long limbs that betrayed his height. His dark eyes were softer than she'd expected, though his mouth was turned down in a frown. His brows cocked half in question, half in confusion. The latter was revealed by the little furrow between his eyes.

His mouth was full of food, his cheeks bulging out one side.

He wasn't exactly handsome, but there was something about his face that she liked. Something that made her smile tentatively and say, "Hello. I'm Liena. May I sit with you?"

His chopsticks stopped halfway between his bowl and his mouth. "With me?" he blurted, then shoved his hand toward his mouth as he choked on his food and set into a fit of coughing.

"Oh! Forgive me!" Liena cried, dropping to her knees, and casting about for some water.

But he had already guzzled down his cup and was smacking his fist against his chest. "No, no, it's just me being"—*Cough!*—"stupid, is all. Name's Liena?"

She nodded, offering up a tight-lipped smile. "Song Liena. Yours is. . .?"

"I'm Fang Zedong."

"Can I sit with you?"

He shrugged. "Won't stop you."

Taking that as invitation enough, she situated herself opposite him and began scooping food from the steaming platters into her own bowl. Her mouth immediately watered, and she could hardly believe the fragrant smells that wafted up to her nose. Academy students ate like this? There was rice enough to feed an army—though she supposed this *was* an army of sorts—and there was all variety of cooked vegetables and even multiple types of fish. At first, she thought she should be polite and take little, but her growling stomach overcame her mind's rationale. She heaped her bowl full, barely managing to keep her mouth closed so she didn't drool.

"Hungry?" Zedong asked with a smirk.

She blushed, her chopsticks slowing their return to her bowl. "I don't mean to—"

"Dragons, just eat. There's more than enough. Here, try this. It's really good."

She winced at the swearing but smiled when he snapped up a chunk of broiled fish with his chopsticks and set it atop her heaping bowl. She glanced around, noting how everyone was already eating.

"Do . . . do people say blessings here? Before they eat?" she whispered, leaning over the table.

Zedong shrugged. "Maybe some do. I don't know."

"So, it's alright if I say one?"

He waved his hand. "Do whatever you want."

She smiled again, lowered her chopsticks, and—despite how hungry she was—mumbled a blessing under her breath with her eyes closed. It wasn't long or elaborate, just something that her mother had taught her.

"So," Zedong said once she'd finished. "What kind of magic do you have?"

She could hardly bring herself to answer before she tucked into her food. "Seer. You?"

He wrinkled his face, reaching back one hand to rub his neck. "My magic is . . . weird."

"Oh?"

"It's kind of complicated."

"I'm listening."

He chuckled. Was it her imagination, or did his eyes shine a little brighter than they had a moment ago?

"I can hear nonarticulated exchanges of information. *Sometimes.*"

"You can hear what?"

"It just means that . . . Well, you know how some people can communicate with looks? If I'm nearby, and *if* my magic decides to work"—The words were laced in bitterness—"then I can understand it. Even if I don't know anything about the people."

Liena chewed on this information as she ate. "That seems . . . complicated."

"It is. And it's next to useless, even if it wasn't so spotty."

"Why is it useless? It seems rather handy to me."

"Because most nonverbal communication isn't verbal because it doesn't *need* to be verbal."

"I'm sure there are plenty of circumstances where it is useful."

"I'm awaiting the day," he said grumpily, stabbing his chopsticks into his food. "It's so unpredictable that it took me a while to even know that I had magic, and when my parents and I finally realized that I did, we couldn't prove it. I had to undergo the Test before I could set foot in the Academy."

Liena's eyes went wide. "You had to do the Test?"

He nodded solemnly, then rolled up his sleeve. Punctuating the skin up his forearm and bicep were tiny white scars. Liena's stomach twisted. What he must have gone through . . .

"There's more scars too," said Zedong.

He didn't offer to show her those.

A shrill whistle sliced through the din of the mess hall. Everyone fell quiet. A sidelong glance at the students further up the table from her revealed that they'd set down their chopsticks too. She followed suit.

Zedong kept eating.

"Students of the Academy!" boomed a voice from the front of the room.

Liena craned her neck to get a better view.

"Headmaster," Zedong whispered around a mouthful of rice.

She gave him a grateful smile before returning her attention to the tall master in black robes. It was hard to get a clear view of him over all the shoulders and heads of her fellow students, but she caught a glimpse of a bald head, gray beard, and gray eyebrows.

"Students of the Academy," said the headmaster again. To Liena's surprise, he actually inclined his head toward them in a bow. "The hope of Zheninghai."

Her lips were suddenly extraordinarily dry. She licked them, glancing at any of the other students to see if this was normal. No one else seemed to bat an eye. Most even straightened in their seats, though Zedong rolled his eyes and kept eating.

"In this room are the greatest talents of the next generation. It is not long before you will wear the mantle of Zheninghai's protection. It is not long before you will be Academy masters, high government officials, city wardens, warriors in our military, generals, even territory guardians. Our empire will rest on your shoulders. That is why our curriculum is so rigorous, why we demand everything of you."

Liena stared at the bowl before her that had been so appetizing only moments ago. Now the thought of eating another bite sent her stomach turning.

A sharp crack sounded. Her head shot up just in time to see the master lift his fist from the table he'd just pounded.

"Headmaster Table Breaker," muttered Zedong.

"You are the future," said the headmaster, impassioned. "And we will *not* leave the future in uncapable hands. Apply yourselves diligently, and there will be a future for you. Make your families proud. Some of you come from nothing. *This is your chance to be something.* Some of you come from the proudest families in the empire. This is your chance to *fight* for your legacy. Don't let it die. Don't be the shame of your family. Your place in Zheninghai, whether high or low, is not determined by birth, but by your magic, and how well you succeed here at the Academy. Rise up, you magic-wielders of Zheninghai. Fight for honor, for the honor of your family, for our empire's future."

Whatever Zedong was grumbling across from her, the headmaster was right. This was Liena's chance to raise her family out of poverty, out of the constant cycle of sowing and harvest, with their entire livelihoods dependent on whether it rained or frosted.

She was ten years behind, and about as disadvantaged as possible. But could she still fight for her family?

As hard as this would be, she wasn't going to waste this opportunity to *be* something more. If it took every ounce of strength she had, so be it. She needed to graduate as quickly as she could, with as high marks as she could, so she could get her family out of poverty before they starved.

"Class at the eighth watch tomorrow," said the headmaster. "As you were."

CHAPTER
5

LIENA LOST HERSELF trying to find her dormitory.

She poked around the corner outside, seeing the maze of covered paths and dozens of potential doors. Why hadn't she paid more attention when she came out earlier? She had been so focused on finding supper that she had lost her dormitory.

A burst of laughter sounded nearby. Instinctively, she ducked behind the corner, then chastised herself for appearing so suspicious. She just needed to act normally, and no one would realize she was new. She would blend in, and all would be fine.

Except that these people seemed to have an eye for noticing new people. Even in a crowd, Shu had realized she was new.

She drew in a deep breath and fortified herself. She would just walk around the corner like nothing was wrong and like she wasn't anxious out of her mind in this new place.

One more deep breath. It would be fine. She was overthinking this.

She forced one foot out before the other, making her way around the corner. She intended to keep her head down and not look up as she passed a laughing group of students. But then one called out, "Hey, Liena! It is Liena, right?"

Her eyes widened, and she lifted her head to find herself the subject of five pairs of staring eyes. She tensed.

Most of the faces she didn't recognize. Except Shu—who was the one who'd called out to her—and *oh!* Her heartrate kicked up several notches, and her breath snagged in her lungs. It was the prince! And he was . . . he was looking at *her*.

Her throat went dry as dirt. She couldn't even answer the question. All that she could manage was a tiny smile that probably looked utterly terrified.

"First day of class tomorrow? Man, you're in for a rude awakening!" said Shu with a laugh and a slightly unsettling twist of her lips.

The others snorted. All except the prince, who wrinkled his face into something like a glare at Shu. "Are you *trying* to frighten her?" he asked.

Shu rolled her eyes at him, then gave a nonchalant wave of her hand toward Liena. "You'll be fine, but it'll probably be a *lot* at first. I mean, you're . . . How old are you?"

Why did Liena feel weird about answering the question? "I'm sixteen."

"Sixteen! I had no idea magic could develop so late."

"And I had no idea Shu apparently doesn't have a single ounce of tact," said the prince, lifting up both hands in exasperation, fixing a glare on Shu.

One of the other young men with patchy stubble snorted. "Shu? Tact? Pfft. Where have you been all our lives, Nianzu?"

The others laughed while the prince rolled his eyes, crossing his arms over his chest. Liena had to work to keep her smile in place as she slowly inched away. She was ready to bolt the moment their attention turned away from her. For a brief moment, she thought she was free.

But Prince Nianzu's gaze shifted to hers, his dark eyes full and potent, set in his handsome face. Suddenly her feet wouldn't budge, rooted into the ground by the weight of his attention. One of his eyebrows seemed to quirk slightly, and she had the distinct impression he was measuring her.

"Best of luck to you tomorrow," he said, eyes not leaving hers for several heartbeats.

One of the others called out, "You'll need it!"

"Fathers, you all are wretched!" cried the prince. He swiveled his attention away from Liena toward his cackling friends.

That was her cue to flee.

Biting her lip, she hurried past them numbly. She simultaneously wanted to cry and grin, and the mixture was so stupid and confusing that she could only blink and keep walking. Trying to parse out that exchange would only confuse her more.

She was just overthinking and overanalyzing.

It took a while of poking around before she worked up the nerve to ask a friendly-looking girl where the dormitories were. The girl gave a funny look, one that Liena quickly answered with, "I'm new."

"Oh! Um, the girls' dormitories are over there."

The dormitories were full to the brim with girls getting ready for bed. A few were standing by the door, stretching themselves out at unnatural angles. Liena tried not to stare, especially at the girl who was literally wound around one of the awning support beams, her knees somehow twisted above her shoulders.

They were all very young.

Young, as in they were anywhere from seven to twelve years old. Liena blinked, suddenly wondering if she'd gone to the wrong dormitory. But no, this one was hers, and this room . . .

Her dormmate came up to her chest.

"Oh, hello!" came the chirped greeting.

"Um . . . hi," said Liena with a tight smile. "Is this—"

"Yup, you're in the right place! My name is Jia. I heard you're new. I lost my dormmate last year, so I didn't have anyone, and I guess they thought since you were new, you'd need to stay with someone who had been here for several years to help you out!"

Liena smiled, still tight-lipped, down at the little girl. "How many years have you been here?"

"Five years."

Liena blinked.

"I came here when I was five. So, half of my life is here and half was at home!"

Ten years old.

"Your old dormmate . . . you said she was lost? What do you mean?"

"Oh, I mean on the Hunts. She got lost and no one ever found her, so they assumed a *mó guǐ* got her."

Liena blanched. *One of the five students.* Somehow, it felt like bad luck to take this girl's cot in her absence.

"How . . . old do you have to be to go on Hunts?"

She shrugged. "It depends. You go when the masters decide that you're ready, but that's usually around nine."

A kernel of hope blossomed in her chest. What if the masters deemed her unready for the Hunts? Perhaps she could avoid it this year.

What even *were* the Hunts?

"You should get some sleep," said the girl. "Training is first thing tomorrow morning."

"Training?"

"Yup."

"Training in what?"

"Combat, of course. In the pits."

Combat. Of course. Right. *Naturally.* Liena shook her head, as if it would make her brain sort through all of this information.

34

She should just go to sleep. She would wake up early, be at the pits before dawn, and then she would be able to process it all better. Exhausted minds and bodies were no good to anyone.

The girl wasn't going to sleep yet. She began going through a stretch routine, and it looked so painful that Liena couldn't help but gawk. Though the girl's body was slender, it was strong and lined with muscle. When she had balanced her entire body upside-down on her forearms, she didn't wobble.

How in the world was Liena going to catch up?

She curled up on her cot, resting her head on the cushion, and was almost instantly asleep.

Liena intended to be the first out by the pits. That way, she could thoroughly prepare herself for what was ahead. As it turned out, it seemed like the entire Academy was there before her. She was almost late! She had thought that half fifth watch would be plenty early, but apparently not.

Was there a group she was supposed to join? The beginners group for combat?

She looked around, spying everyone else wearing the same simple tan training tunic and coarse trousers that she did, and realized that there didn't seem to be much structure. In fact, as she watched, people peeled off into pairs and groups of three or four to begin fighting with one another.

It was unintentional—the way her eyes picked out that tall, broad form across the pits. She didn't *mean* to notice him. It was entirely unpractical to do so. But she did anyway. Once she saw him, she almost couldn't drag her eyes away.

The prince was grinning, holding a wax wood staff in both hands and fending off a barrel-chested opponent. She didn't know the names of his moves, knew nothing about any of this, but she could tell that he was good. Better than good. He moved with the lightness of someone half his size, but the power behind his blows was unmatched.

He was standing over his opponent in a matter of seconds, grinning triumphantly.

Why in all the seven valleys was she blushing?

Stupid, stupid, stupid.

"Hey."

Liena whirled, forcing away the heat crawling up her neck. "Zedong!" The relief must have been evident in her voice, because he gave her a sleepy smile.

"Want to practice with me?" He yawned.

"Yes!" she said immediately, desperately.

"Now, you've got to know that I'm not very good, and I came late too, but I know a few things."

The next two hours dragged by. Liena tried not to get frustrated, or to give up because of how exhausted she was. It wasn't even that Zedong was a hard master—he wasn't—but that no one else was stopping. Everyone kept drilling their battle skills until the sun was hot overhead.

She was used to manual labor from dawn to dusk, but somehow even life on a farm hadn't prepared her for this.

All around them, magic flared and weapons crashed together. She startled when a wild boar charged toward a student, then nearly screamed when it shifted into a leopard and went to pounce. Zedong kept telling her to focus on him, that the others weren't going to come charging toward them, but she couldn't help her reflexes when a roar or a sizzling snap sounded close behind her.

By the end of practice, all Liena had to show for it were a few defensive maneuvers he'd taught her with a wooden practice sword.

Finally, it was time to be done. Sopping wet with her own sweat, she trudged back to her dormitories only to discover the long line for the washroom. She peeked outside at the lotus pond and thought it strange that only a fortnight ago she would have not hesitated to bathe in it. Now, not so much. She grabbed her white robes and waited in the line of girls nearly half her age.

First day of class.

She was determined to do the best she could.

After washing and breakfast, everyone dispersed to their classes, obviously knowing exactly where to go. Liena fidgeted off to one side until a master was sent to rescue her and guide her to her classes.

She was put with the first-year students for her academics. The five- and six-year-olds.

She was only a millet farmer, so it wasn't like she had much in the way of pride. This stung even so.

There is no use in embarrassment. Just do your best, she told herself.

She sat cross-legged on her mat, feeling like a giant. Which was an entirely new sensation. The master's smile faltered into confusion, then realization, when he saw her. She tried not to wince. Behind her, children whispered unintentionally loudly.

"She's so old. Why is she with us?"

"I heard she's new!"

"She's got to have low magic then."

What kind of five-year-olds talked like this? It seemed like everyone here, except maybe Zedong, was a prodigy of sorts. Not that it mattered. She would simply do her best. There was nothing else she could do.

She couldn't expect to be a genius if she was ten years behind.

The moment that Liena realized this first class was reading and writing, she forgot all her wounded pride. Forgot all except the beautiful character the master drew for them.

"Academy," he said, pointing at it.

In that instant, it was like a new world of possibilities opened up in her mind. She didn't mean to grin, but she couldn't help herself. Around her, fellow students bent over their little scrolls and drew the character in gloppy black ink.

Holding a writing utensil in her fingers was strange and electrifying. Her hand shook as she drew the character once, then again and again. Already, her hand seemed to take an affinity to the tool, and she kept grinning as she continued writing.

Writing.

When she finally looked up, she realized the master had drawn three more characters. Glancing around quickly, she saw they'd all moved on past that first character.

Class went by way too fast. One minute, she was frantically sketching the characters, and the next the master was saying to practice those characters on their lunch break and come back tomorrow with them memorized.

An idea entered her mind, and though Liena was not an impulsive person, she gave into this impulse. Gathering her things up in her arms, she approached the front of the classroom as the other students filed out.

"Master?" she asked timidly.

He looked up and cocked his head to one side. "Yes?"

She bit her lip, then held out her board. "Could I . . . have a few more?"

The day went by in a flash. All her fears, stresses, and doubts that she had about coming to the Academy were gone while she was in the classroom. She didn't care anymore that she was in the children's classes. All of this was just so *new.* So thrilling! She felt like a dying field of crops during a thunderstorm. Drinking in every drop of knowledge.

Perhaps succeeding here wasn't too out of reach for her.

But then the bell rang again, and when she walked into her next classroom, it wasn't a classroom at all. It was a large training room, unusually plain for the typically ornate Academy. It had square wooden pillars surrounding the matted training area. Sunlight streamed through the papered windows, and at the front of the room were wooden plaques fastened to two pillars with a painted character on each. She couldn't read them yet, but she took a stab in the dark and guessed they meant something like *strength, discipline, determination,* or *endurance.*

This must be her first combat class.

CHAPTER
6

B ALANCE—" THE master began.
"—is sustained, not created," replied all the students except Liena.

She blinked, glancing at the students around her, surprised to find they were of varying ages and sizes. Maybe this was the class for struggling or new students?

She wasn't expecting to be tossed a wax wood staff, told to prepare herself, and immediately confronted by the master. He went down the line of students like a whirlwind, his staff slicing through air and smacking soundly, knocking students off their feet.

Once they were all on the ground, the master planted the heel of his staff into the floor and stared them down as they groaned and pulled themselves to their feet. Liena's shoulder ached from the blow she'd taken, but she forced herself not to rub it and blinked away the tears prickling the corner of her eyes.

"See where you are now?" said the master. "By the end of your time at the Academy, you will be *almost* as good as I am. This is a class for magic-wielders who don't have battle magic, which means your magic cannot be used in combat. Your training will be different from the others, and will focus more on fighting skills than magic honing."

To her relief, they put the staffs away and the rest of the class ended up being mostly lecture and stretches. Even if she was about as flexible as a head of millet—meaning, not at all—she could stretch and listen to the masters drone on about the importance of balance in fighting and in the empire.

What made her suddenly concerned was when the lecture turned from talk of balance to talk of pain.

"Pain is in the mind," said the master, tapping his temple. "Pain is *all* in the mind. Learn to control your mind, and you will be undefeatable. Nothing will hurt you if your mind is made of steel."

This wasn't boding well for future combat lessons.

At dinner, Shu came over. Liena told herself there was no reason to be wary, no reason to grit her teeth. She made herself smile widely and greet her, even though she had been heading toward where Zedong sat by himself again at the end of the farthest table.

"Hey Liena!" said Shu. "How was your first day?"

"It was good!" she said. *Except combat training.* That was stressful.

"Really? I'd have thought it would be *diyu* for sure!"

"Oh. Well, I thought it was very interesting. I learned a lot."

"Did they put you with the children?"

There was that strange light in Shu's eyes that raised Liena's hackles. That strange *something* that made her feel like she wanted to hear that Liena was struggling.

But that made no sense. There was literally no reason Shu should care at all what happened in Liena's life beyond a friendly care for the newcomer.

"Yes," Liena admitted.

"Yeah, don't worry about that; usually older people skip ahead quickly enough. They just have to see if you know *something* or *nothing.*"

At Shu's words, a stunningly beautiful girl next to her spewed out her water on the ground and set into a fit of choking laughter.

Shu cast a glance at the girl, grinning.

Liena forced another tight-lipped smile, watching as the laughter and snickers built around them while the beautiful girl laughed and wiped up the mess. "Yeah, thanks."

"Lei! What was so funny?" asked a boy another table down.

Lei whacked her chest, drew in a deep breath, coughed again, and opened her mouth to speak. Then she burst into another round of giggles. More people were leaning over now, asking what was so funny.

"It wasn't *that* funny," said Shu, even though she was clearly very proud of herself.

She was right. It *wasn't* that funny. Liena made her escape, drawing away and hurrying to settle down next to Zedong. He was rolling his eyes.

"I hate her," he said.

She shrugged. "I don't think she means to be . . . the way she is."

"She definitely does."

After supper, she headed back to the dormitories. Just like the night before, she heard the laughter before she rounded that dreaded corner. Was there another way to her dormitory? Did she have to skirt around Shu and her crew again?

And the prince.

Her stupid heart was fluttering again, sending her palms into a sweaty frenzy. This was so *dumb.* She never thought herself the type to have her head turned by good looks.

She hurried around the corner, but this time, Shu didn't stop her. No one stopped her. She scurried by like an invisible fly, hoping that the prince didn't notice her. The latter was mixed with a desperate and wholly idiotic desire for him to notice her anyway.

She needed to get her head screwed back on straight.

Laughter rang behind her, and it sent something like a knife through her chest.

If she was going to succeed here, she had to work *hard*.

She paused when she reached her dormitory, seeing all the young girls talking and laughing together as they completed their ridiculous stretches. Their white robes billowed in the waning sunlight as it dipped behind the mountain above them, casting dancing shadows everywhere.

Liena didn't enter her dormitory. Instead, she turned and kept walking down the path.

A familiar form loitered outside what was presumably the boys' dormitories. Or one of them. He sat on the red painted railing, his legs dangling as he picked at his lip and stared into nothing.

"Hey!" Zedong called, spotting her. He straightened on his perch, leaning forward. "Are you lost? Your dormitory is back that way."

"I'm not going to my dormitory," she said. "I'm going to the library. Want to come?"

He looked surprised, but then he shrugged. "Um, sure. I guess."

"Perfect! Because I don't know where it is."

He gave another shrug before hopping down from the railing. "I'll show you."

When Liena and Zedong arrived in the library, it was eerily dark. Not completely dark, as there were a few candles. But somehow the candles seemed to be fighting against the oppressive darkness, and they weren't succeeding as well as they should like. It had a very musty smell, one that seemed to dry out her nose with each inhale.

Liena picked up one of the candles by the door, surveyed the tall shelves and the low desks surrounded by mats, and sat down at a desk in a corner. Away from a few other students who were already there.

"What are we going to do?" Zedong asked, sitting across from her.

"Study, of course. Don't you have anything to study?"

He shrugged. "Not really."

"*Nothing*?" She frowned, inspecting the ink wells and quills already set on the desk. "I have to practice the characters I learned today. And if it's alright with you, I'd like to recite to you what I remember from my history class. So I don't forget it."

He blinked.

"What?" she asked. "Do people not normally do this?"

He squinted, rubbing the back of his neck. "Well . . . I suppose lots of other people do it. It's just that *I* have never done it."

"You've never studied? And you've been at the Academy for years? Are you very smart?"

Zedong snorted, then covered his mouth and glanced around the library to make sure no one was annoyed by the sound. "I'm not smart," he said bluntly, and perhaps a little bitterly. "In fact, I'm failing most of my classes."

"Failing!" Liena cried. "And you've never come to study? Of course you're failing! Don't you want to learn?"

He was grinning now, shaking his head. "You make it sound so easy and obvious."

"Of *course* it's easy and obvious! Here, we'll start with you. Tell me what you remember from one of your classes today."

"What? I don't remember anything!"

"That's impossible," said Liena.

Slowly, bit by bit, she coaxed out of him a few tidbits from his class. It was almost agonizing work, but she was determined. He was smiling by the end. Smiling in disbelief.

"I suppose . . . I do remember some things."

"Alright," said Liena, straightening her spine and fixing him with her most authoritative stare. "You need to pay attention tomorrow in class and find out what you need to be studying. It'll do you a world of good. Now, can you help me?"

He started to nod, but stopped, his eyes flitting up from her to beyond her shoulder. Liena waited, then twisted around.

There, standing in the darkness shrouded by the library door, was a tall form. A woman's form. And by the sparse candlelight, Liena could see a scarred, empty eye socket. Her mouth opened.

Master Gu stared back at her. At her and Zedong.

Liena turned around, bowing over her parchment and quill. Occupying herself for several long minutes, she refused to give Master Gu the satisfaction of turning around and acknowledging her presence again.

"She's gone," said Zedong.

Liena let out a gust of pent-up breath. "Why in the seven valleys was she watching us?"

He shrugged. "I don't know. She's weird."

"Something seems off to me about her."

"Something's off for sure. Did she show you that dragon hide she has in her office?"

Liena nodded, unable to help her little snicker. "Does she show everyone?"

"Every single new student," said Zedong, leaning over the table and whispering around a shielding hand. "It's not even that big of a dragon."

"You've seen a dragon?"

"No. Just heard from some of the other students who have that it's small."

"Why do you think she acts like it's such a big deal? Do you think it's because she is ashamed of her eye?"

"Or her magic," snorted Zedong.

"Her magic?"

"Yeah. Her magic was feral."

"Was?"

"*Is,* I suppose. But she's here at the Academy because it doesn't work as well anymore, now that her eye is gone. She lost her position in the military after that incident."

"Wait . . . what's feral magic?"

"It's—eh, I call it animal magic. It means you were born with augmented senses and abilities. She had night vision and something else. Something that made her really good at running enemy raids at night. But then the encounter happened with the dragon, and she lost her eye, so she cannot see very well anymore. I think something about the event made her supervisors mad too, so they demoted her to working at the Academy."

"Are all the Academy masters demoted?"

"Oh no! Just a few of them. Most of them are retired and were very important a while back."

"That makes more sense."

They studied late into the night, until Liena was nearly falling asleep sitting up. At breakfast the next morning, she was barely awake enough to scoop food into her mouth.

Until a student's shout echoed through the mess hall.

"Arena battles have been posted!"

CHAPTER
7

L IENA'S HEART GAVE a little sputter, and her hands wound up in the folds of her sash, crept up to touch the beads at her throat. Across from her, Zedong began frantically shoveling food into his face as he stood.

He made a garbled sound at her that, paired with his gesture to follow him, she took to mean, *"Let's go check!"*

"I'm not going to be on there, right?" said Liena, catching up to him. The potent smells of fish-topped congee and baozi, which had once been so appealing, now turned her stomach.

Zedong's response was distorted again, his cheeks so full he looked like a chipmunk. She had no idea what he said until he shrugged.

She had just gotten here. No use fretting over a battle she was almost certainly not going to fight.

She tripped over the lip of the next hallway. She caught herself quickly, but not before a few snickers sounded from the crowd crammed around the huge sheets of character-filled parchment nailed to the wall by the pits.

Zedong elbowed his way through the front, dragging her along behind him.

"Dragons," said Zedong, swallowing his mouthful. "I'm paired with Tai. He'll beat me so bad."

"You haven't lost yet," said Liena. "Maybe you'll beat him this time."

"Hey, you're on here too!"

The blood drained from her face. "*I'm* there?"

"Yeah! They have you competing against . . . Wei Ling? Hm, I haven't heard of her. At least that means she's probably not that good."

"But . . . but . . . but I can't fight!"

"Get out of the way!" a student barked from behind them. "The rest of us want to see!"

"Sorry!" said Liena, just as Zedong made a rude face at the bigger student. "Zedong!" she hissed. "Don't provoke him!"

The other student shot Zedong a look, but Liena dragged him away before anything could escalate.

"I can't fight!" Liena said again, drawing Zedong's attention to her so he didn't keep glaring over his shoulder at the other student. "How am I supposed to—"

"Sure, you can fight," said Zedong. "We've been practicing every day for the last week, and you've been going to your combat classes each day."

"I'm doing terribly in that class!" she wailed. "I thought they would give me more time! I've only been here for a week!"

"Don't freak out, it'll be okay. If worst comes to worst, you'll just take a blow or two and then it'll be over."

A blow or two? How hard were these blows? Would she be injured? Memory of Master Gu's words made unease crawl up her spine. About the student who died in the arena battles.

"Zedong? Um . . . Master Gu said that there was a student who died in the arena last year. Aren't the masters supposed to keep that from happening?"

"Well," he said. "It's very rare. The masters do intervene to keep that from happening, but they can't stop everything. Sometimes there are accidents, and sometimes there are *accidents*." He wiggled his eyebrows as if she should know exactly what he meant.

"What do you mean, *accidents*?"

Liena found herself gripping the railing with white knuckles, looking out at the sandy pits and the few students who were squeezing in more practice before class. Most were still clumped around the posting like a flock of white doves in their uniforms, ready to fly south for the winter.

"That student who died last year," said Zedong, leaning his elbows on the railing and letting his hands dangle over the edge. He squinted against the rising sun. "Well, the other student really had it out for him, and the masters didn't know. The students did. They knew how much they hated each other. So, when they were paired in an arena battle, the masters didn't think anything of it. They just thought they were fighting extra hard. But a lot of us students saw it for what it was." Did his jaw just tick? "It was too late by the time the masters realized the same thing." He blinked, shook his head, and his tone sounded perhaps just slightly too casual to be convincing. "You're safe though, because you don't have any enemies."

No enemies. Right.

It wasn't as comforting as Zedong intended it.

"It'll be fine," he said, reaching out and giving her shoulder a squeeze. "You still have until tomorrow."

That wasn't very comforting either.

"I've done some research for you," said Zedong, catching up to her in the mess hall later that day. "Your opponent is another seer, so you don't have to worry about magic. Plus, she's only twelve."

"What is better, being beaten by someone your age, or someone several years younger?" asked Liena sourly.

Zedong laughed, and it only made her frown more. "You never know what is going to happen! These battles are kind of crazy. Things happen all the time and the underdog wins."

"You stink at offering comfort."

He looked sheepish. "Sorry."

"Instead of studying after supper, can we practice more?"

He shrugged. "Sure."

When they went out to practice after supper, the pits were already full. Why did everyone have the same idea as her? She trudged behind Zedong to the armory, which flanked the pits. Inside, the low-ceilinged, darkened room held all manner of weapons and practice weapons. A master with his head tilted back, and a long beard trailing down past his waist, stood at the entrance and watched their perusal of *jiauns*, broadswords—both wooden and real—knives, and wax wood staffs.

It was very orderly. Liena had already had several classes now on weapon respect and care. They'd been admonished in strong language to honor these weapons, both in their training and when they went to return them. There was even a table to one side with tools for sharpening and cleaning.

"You're going to be fighting with a wax wood staff," said Zedong, grabbing two from the rack. "It's good for defense." He tossed one to her.

She fumbled to catch it, then glanced self-consciously at the narrow-eyed master watching. She straightened, biting the inside of her cheek, and gripped the staff in both hands. "How do they even decide who wins?" she asked as they left the armory and entered the pits.

"They have to incapacitate you."

Liena's eyes widened in alarm.

"Not like *that*," said Zedong, growing impatient. "They have get you like . . . Here, fall over."

"I'm not falling over."

He shot her an exasperated look. She glared back.

"Fine, *I'll* fall over," he said. He crouched on the ground, then laid himself flat in the sand. "Now grab your staff and stand over me."

She stood next to him.

"You just beat me in a fight. *Act* like it. Shove the staff in my face or something."

She poked his belly with it.

He huffed and contracted his abdomen, knocking aside her staff and rolling into a sitting position. His brow was lowered. "You're useless. You've got to show that you've gained mastery over your opponent. You'll never win if you act like *that*."

Was he genuinely upset with her? She wasn't sure.

What she really wanted to ask him was if he'd ever won an arena battle before. Because, no offense to her friend, but she wasn't sure he had, and imagined that if she was going to get better, she would probably need another instructor.

But he was flicking sand out of his hair, and she didn't want to anger him further.

"How do I fight?" she said.

"You've got to get your stance right. See, look how easy it is for me to knock you off balance?" He brought his staff up in both hands and knocked it against the underside of hers, forcing her back several steps.

"What's the proper stance?"

A new voice entered. "You're asking *him* about proper stance?"

Laughter.

Liena gritted her teeth into a smile and lifted her gaze to Shu, standing with arms crossed a few feet away. Two girls flanked her, and one was so beautiful that Liena had to struggle to not stare. She wasn't tall, but toned and curvy, with glossy black hair and full lips. Liena recognized her as the laughing girl from the mess hall—had someone called her Lei?

"Would you like to show me?" Liena asked Shu, forcing her smile sweeter.

"Oh sure!" said Shu, oddly cheerfully. She snatched the staff from Zedong's hands, making the girls behind her snicker. She approached Liena swiftly, like a tiger about to pounce on its prey.

Liena could immediately see the skill difference. She couldn't say exactly *what* was different, but the overall impression was one of alarming proficiency.

"Like this," said Shu, grinning. She adjusted her stance, not pointing out the particulars.

Then she came, staff swooping in a deadly arc through the air, for Liena.

Liena barely got her own staff up in time, squeaking. Her arms buckled on impact. But Shu cut underneath her raised arms, simultaneously sweeping her feet behind her knees, and knocking her to the ground.

Then Shu was crouched on top of her, pinning her legs with one knee and her elbow with the other foot. She gripped Liena's wrist, pressing it into the sand, and held the staff above her head with her free hand.

She gave Liena a sunny smile. "One bash with the end of this thing, and you're dead."

Liena gritted her teeth against the pain. "Thank you for showing me," she muttered, trying not to sound too sour.

"Any time!" said Shu, hopping up and offering her a hand. She turned to Zedong with a smirk. "Want me to show you proper stance too?"

He shook his head, his ears scarlet.

One of the girls snickered. Lei buckled over in full on laughter. Shu tossed Zedong back his staff and winked. "See you both tomorrow! Hope you do well!"

They left. Liena glanced over at Zedong to find him staring at the ground, his hands clenched into fists.

"Who are you fighting?" asked Liena.

There were no classes today. It was only arena battles all day. Barriers had been erected in the pits, making little arenas that people could crowd around and watch the fighting.

Zedong pointed to a boy she'd never seen before. He was lean, like Zedong, but far more muscular. He stretched on the side, then worked through a series of sword moves.

"He looks pretty fierce," said Liena.

"Yeah. And he's a shifter too. Shifters are the worst. They're high energy, vicious, and they fight so hard. They're not *careful* fighters. They just throw themselves into the fray like wild animals, even if they're super disadvantaged. And then they turn *into* wild animals and it's just the worst."

"Are you going to be alright?"

He shrugged. "Yeah, I'll be fine. Let's go find your opponent."

The first battles started while they were working their way through the crowd. The moment they did, she almost couldn't keep moving. Her steps slowed as she stared wide-eyed.

They were vicious. Sometimes the spectators had to duck to keep from being slammed by magic or taken out by a blow. Her feet rooted to the spot as she watched, mesmerized and horrified as her fellow students fought each other mercilessly.

"Are they trying to kill each other?" she said, pointing to two students fighting in one of the nearest arenas. They were young, but Liena had no doubt that they could win a fight against anyone in her village back home, even the grown men.

"Nah."

"Are you sure?"

"Totally."

"See? That blow was meant to knock them to the ground, not kill."

"It sure looked like it was meant to kill."

He shook his head. "You know nothing."

She shot him a look.

"See how they're not talking? Usually if they're good friends or bitter enemies, they talk. But they're just focused on the fight. Plus, my magic sometimes randomly works on arena battles. I can usually tell pretty well if they're trying to kill each other."

"If you say so."

"Yes, I say so. Besides, they're not even using magic. Ye Min is a mind-reader, so she can't use her magic in the arena. Same with Pen Tao there, who's a high seer. One of the only ones, actually. The scariest battles are the ones where they can't even have them in these arenas. Like today, one of those dirt movers—think her name is Na?—is going to battle Xian Hanying, who's a river-bender. They're taking that battle out into the wilderness later."

"Are you going to go watch?"

"Nah. Seen enough of them."

He was quiet, his attention suddenly sucked into the battle.

She glanced at him then, watching him curiously. In the entire last week that she'd been here at the Academy, she'd never seen Zedong speak to someone other than herself unless he absolutely had to.

Was she his only friend? Did he have no friends before she came?

It certainly seemed the case when she arrived and found him sitting in his own corner of the mess hall.

Her attention was ripped away from him as her periphery recognized a familiar form. She swiveled her head to the arena at her right.

It was the prince. He faced off a block-shaped student who was already growing a beard. They circled each other in the arena, and

Liena drifted closer. She wasn't the only one either; a whole herd of students congregated around the arena to the point she almost couldn't see what was happening.

It appeared that this was one of the "big" fights happening today.

She stood on her tiptoes, trying to get a view over the two tall students in front of her. Peeking around one's elbow, she was in time to see vines explode out of the ground by the prince's feet. He leapt aside just barely, slamming a wall of fire into the earth. The vines all but exploded with the impact of the fire. His opponent used that opportunity to strike, running forward with his swinging broadsword.

Liena's chest seized up.

The prince deflected the blow, and *grinned.*

It is just a battle, she told herself. They weren't trying to kill each other.

Zedong appeared at her side, apparently finding this fight more interesting than the other one.

"Who is the boy fighting the prince?" she asked him.

"That is Zuan Wan. He's the only plant wielder alive right now. One of the top students."

"He looks very fierce."

Zedong scoffed. "You say that about everyone. Do you not think the prince looks fierce?"

She considered the prince in the arena, launching a volley of fireballs at Wan that were narrowly dodged. His brow was knit, the tightly corded muscles of his forearms straining with the force of his magic. "He looks very fierce too."

The ensuing battle was riveting. Wan kept trying to catch the prince with his vines and restrain him. The prince kept burning his way out. She watched, biting her nails.

Despite how engrossed she was, she gradually became aware of a few girls nearby talking.

"He's holding back."

"Who? Zuan Wan?"

"No, Prince Nianzu. They say he's the most powerful fire wielder to be born. *Ever.*"

That was probably an exaggeration.

"His magic is so powerful that he could incinerate entire armies with the sweep of his hand!"

"And who told you this?" came the skeptical reply. "Have you seen it?"

"I haven't, but Shu has. She said it was the most impressive thing she'd ever seen. See, he's holding back his magic so Wan can have a fair fight."

It sure didn't look like he was holding back, and Wan certainly wasn't. In the end, it was the prince who stole the victory.

Then it was her turn in the arena.

Sweat poured in streams down her back, her neck, her chest. Her hands turned clammy. So clammy she could hardly get a grip on her staff. She swallowed, suddenly wanting to run and hide in the library.

"You didn't tell me this many people would be watching!" she whispered to Zedong. "I'm about to be so embarrassed!"

"Half the people here today lose. It's alright." He reached out and squeezed her shoulder, offering a smile.

She was waiting for him to assure her that she was going to win despite all the odds, but instead he just consoled her that losing wouldn't be that bad.

As she walked to her arena, she watched as a student slammed another down into the ground and pinned him with ice bolts through his robes. When the second student couldn't get up, the first was proclaimed the victor. The surrounding crowd burst into cheers.

It was going to be alright. Even if she lost, this would be a learning experience, right? She could improve. Learn more. It would be fine.

So why wouldn't her heart slow down? It pounded all the way to her assigned arena.

A master was there, garbed in black, to referee the match. "Song Liena?" he called.

She could still run. If only her magic was invisibility! She could slip away until this was all over. Maybe she could even remain invisible for the rest of her time here, slipping into the classes that she wanted to learn from, but no one would know. No one could make her fight.

"Nonsense," she muttered to herself as she stepped forward.

"Wei Ling?" he called.

A short, slight girl stepped out of the crowd. Her staff might have been taller than her by nearly a foot, but there was no mistaking the determination in her round, heart-shaped face.

"Take your places," said the master.

Places? Zedong hadn't told her where to stand! She cast about frantically but followed the girl into the enclosed arena. She stole a glance at the neighboring arena, at how the others were standing opposite one another. She scuffled to the side opposite where Ling stood.

She could do this. Ling had only been here longer than her. The girl had no other advantage, right? After all, Liena had worked hard on a farm her whole life. She was strong. She was taller, bigger.

She let out a big gust of air through her clenched teeth.

She could do this. She could *do* this.

Yes.

The master brought his fingers to his mouth and whistled.

The girl came flying across the arena. Liena squawked, flashing back to Shu's "training" from last night. She threw up her staff, dodging to the side as she did so. Her bare feet slid around in the sand and hampered her speed. Stupid sand! She needed to run *away* and she needed to do it *fast!*

There were boos from the watching crowd. Someone shouted, "Coward!"

No, she wasn't a coward. She was just practical. A practical person didn't engage in a fight that she couldn't win.

The girl charged again, swinging her staff out in front of her. Liena made another squeak, and when she held up her staff to defend herself, the girl knocked it out of her hands. It went flying over the rim of the arena. The crowd dodged.

Weaponless, Liena stared back at the girl.

She lifted her weapon, let out a yell, and charged.

Liena shrieked. She ran, hating the confines of the arena.

The crowd was shouting. Telling her to use something, to try some type of attack she didn't know, telling her to roll under Ling's guard. What was a guard?

One sound blow to her shin ripped a cry from her throat. And then she was on the ground, staring up at the victor. Ling didn't look satisfied, her brow pinched. She almost looked irritated.

The crowd was booing.

Did that mean they were rooting for Liena to win?

Then she heard what they were saying.

"What a horrible fight."

"Worst arena battle I've seen."

Her leg stung. She wasn't sure what was more humiliating: being knocked to the ground by someone two thirds her size or being offered a hand up by the same girl. She swallowed her pride and accepted the boost.

"Medics are that way," said the master without looking up as he scribbled on a scroll.

Liena swallowed, trying not to limp as pain radiated up her leg with each step, and nodded at the master.

Zedong was at her side the next instant. "That'll have a nasty bruise."

"Fang Zedong, the encourager."

He slid his arm under her shoulder blades. "Here, grab on to me. I'll help you to the medic."

"Yin Tai and Fang Zedong!"

Liena and Zedong froze, looking at each other as her hand gripped his neck.

"Your battle!" she said.

"Dragons," he cursed. "Here, lean against this pillar. I'll help you when I'm done."

"I'm not an invalid." Farm life had taught her much about working even in pain. If she wasn't feeling well while she harvested, it was just too bad. After all, if they didn't get the harvest in, they'd starve during the winter.

And then she would be feeling *worse*.

Zedong left her, hurrying toward his arena nearby. She leaned against the pillar, refusing to lean down and roll up her trousers to see if a welt had appeared. At least it wasn't broken. Liena had a sneaking suspicion that the girl could have easily broken her leg, or even worse, aimed the blow at her knee instead.

Zedong took his place opposite the burly boy, and even though he was tall, he suddenly looked small. It took her a second to realize it was because of his body language—he folded in on himself. As though braced for a beating.

She ground her teeth. Was that what she'd looked like? She and Zedong had much to learn and improve on.

The shrill whistle pierced the air.

Zedong and his opponent circled each other; the latter almost snarling. Like he was already part animal even though he hadn't shifted yet.

That was when she noticed one of the tall spectators at the neighboring match.

The prince.

Her stomach clenched. She immediately looked away. She would focus on Zedong's match.

She was just in time to watch the boy pounce. The opponent was human when he leapt, but slavering dog when he landed. He knocked Zedong backward, so hard that his back hit the arena and his neck snapped backward.

Liena gasped, covering her mouth with both hands.

The crowd didn't seem alarmed. They cheered. Cheered as Zedong tried to defend himself with his wooden sword. They shouted advice to both. The boy shifted again, this time a viper.

And Liena thought her heart might stop in her chest. One bite . . .

But the master only kept watching and making notes. He didn't intervene. Her heart raced, her lungs so tight she could barely breathe.

Come on, Zedong. Come on.

The boy shifted again, becoming an enormous, muscular tiger. Liena thought her heart would stop right then, watching as the tiger growled as Zedong scooted desperately to the back of the arena, his face wild with fear.

Should she intervene? Was there anything she could do? The boy shifted back into a viper and struck at Zedong. Zedong hopped out of the way and yelled at it in a rage. Finally, Tai shifted back into his human form, knocked Zedong to the ground, and pinned him there.

When the master proclaimed the winner, the boy leaned down to offer a hand to Zedong. Zedong, however, smacked it away with a snarl. "That was not fair!" he shouted, scrambling up and facing his opponent. "You can't just turn into a viper like that!"

"Yes, he can," said the master with lowered brows.

"And if he'd bitten me? Would you have just labeled it an accident?" Zedong shouted at the master. "You would have let him! You would have let him kill me!"

"Enough!" snapped the master. "Fang Zedong, you are dismissed for detention. Go immediately."

Zedong's face whitened, but he held his ground. "You would have been glad to be rid of me, wouldn't you? If I'd died? Then you wouldn't have to figure out what to do with the failing student!"

By that time, Liena had already hobbled over, and she reached into the arena and grabbed Zedong's arm. He reacted sharply, nearly throwing off her grip. But when he turned and saw her, his eyes widened.

She gave a wince. "The medics?"

Zedong turned to the master, but Liena tugged his attention back to her.

"It's alright, just leave them," she said.

"Detention," snapped the master. "Not the medics."

Zedong's face was a murderous shade of crimson. "*After I*—"

"It's alright!" said Liena, pulling on him. "I'll go with you."

"You can't walk!"

"Yes I *can*," she snapped, gesturing for him to follow her. He growled, vaulted over the edge of the arena, and landed next to her. He made to storm ahead. If she hadn't grabbed onto his arm—for support, she hoped he thought—that he slowed down enough for her.

"That dragon-blasted, phoenix-scorched, qilin-cursed idiot of a shifter! And that master is a rotten, cracked dragon egg!" Zedong snarled.

She winced at all the cursing. "It's alright. It's just a battle. They weren't going to let anything happen to you. Here, where is detention? I'll come with you."

"You are *not* going to detention with me."

She blinked. "Why not?"

His jaw clenched, his face still pale. He shook his head. "Don't. And don't do anything that will get you in detention. Ever."

She frowned, her heart suddenly quickening. "Why? What is it? What's wrong? Are you going to be alright? Zedong—?"

"The medics are that way," he pointed, prying her hands off him. He stormed in the opposite direction, down a corridor darker than the rest.

CHAPTER
8

A FTER SHE VISITED the medics—who had almost nothing to give her except a poultice to apply at night for the bruising—Liena went to find detention and Zedong.

It took some while of wandering student-strewn hallways before she stumbled her way back to the corridor Zedong had vanished down for detention. There were no students here, only monster statues glittering in the patterned light cast from sun through decorative screens. It was eerily quiet, and as she walked deeper into these twisty hallways, it felt rather like her first day. Like she was small and stupid, like she didn't belong here and never would.

Voices. Footsteps. Coming from a hallway she was about to intersect.

Liena froze. Her first instinct was to duck behind one of the pillars, or a lattice screen nearby. She forced herself to stay where she was and keep walking.

She wasn't doing anything wrong. There was no reason to hide.

"This is a bad idea," said the first voice.

"Absolutely not. He's the perfect student for it. Always in detention."

Liena's heart quickened. Were they talking about Zedong? And that second voice—she recognized it. From somewhere. It rubbed at the back of her mind, buzzing near her ears like an annoying fly.

"Why don't you use that new girl instead? There's even less to lose with her."

"I don't like her."

Master Gu. That was who the voice belonged to. Now Liena had to fight to keep her steps from faltering.

"Pfft. Why?" asked the second voice.

"She's just not as good of an option as him. Trust me on this."

They rounded the corner. Straight into Liena. She blinked, halting and tilting her head back to look up at the two masters. Master Gu's good eye narrowed to a slit, and the effect was garish on the empty socket. Garish, and terrifying.

The other master was taller even than Master Gu, with a long, pointed nose and cleft chin. He lifted that chin at the sight of her, his sharp brow casting a shadow over his eyelids.

Liena felt like a mouse caught in a trap, even though she couldn't fully articulate why.

"What are you doing, girl?" asked Master Gu.

"I'm—I'm looking for Fang Zedong. Is he here somewhere?"

"He's in detention."

She bobbed her head in an acquiescing bow. "Yes, Master. I would like to visit him."

"What? Do you think detention is the infirmary? There are no visitors. Go back to your studies, girl. You don't have time to dawdle about the Academy. You ought to work and catch up."

Liena pursed her lips. It was on the tip of her tongue—a question of what detention *was*. Instead, she ducked her head in another bow-nod and scurried on to the library.

She didn't see Zedong until the next morning when it was time to train in the pits. He staggered to her side, looking pale and slightly gaunt. His eyes were hollowed out, and at first, she didn't even recognize him.

At breakfast, he scarfed down two bowls of congee in hardly a second.

He never said a word to her.

Zedong's moods were like weather: fair one minute, stormy the next. She tried to be patient with him, but it was always a relief when he sat down across from her in the mess hall or the library and he wore an easy expression on his face.

"What are you writing?" he asked as he spread out his study materials.

"Practicing my characters, writing down what I remember from history class," Liena said, smiling and folding up the parchments she'd been working on.

"Practicing more characters?" he said with a smirk. "You'd spend your time better practicing combat."

She glared at him. "I *know*. But speaking of combat, I think I'm going to go to bed now. What do you say about getting up extra early to practice?"

He groaned.

"Shh!" she said, stifling a giggle. "Not too loud!"

Around them, scattered throughout the library, other students were hard at work studying. Zedong gave her a withering look then shrugged. "Fine. If you say so. You're making me rue the day you came and sat next to me in the mess hall."

She rolled her eyes, packed up her studies, and took her candle. "Goodnight."

The hallway was dark. The sparse moonlight on the *mó guǐ* statues cast strange and terrifying shadows on the wall. Liena paused, glancing at the shadow of fangs protruding not even a full pace away on the wall from a slavering dragon mouth, a long tongue curling in the air. She looked the other way and found the statue that cast the shadow.

Funny how the original object seemed so much smaller than its shadow.

As dark and scary as everything looked at night, she was half tempted to curl up on the floor and fall asleep. She was so exhausted that the thought of trudging the entire way to her dormitory was daunting.

Another dot of candlelight appeared around a bend ahead, and as she kept walking, the outline of the dark form beyond the pinprick became clearer.

Shu grinned, stopping once they intersected. "Hi Liena! Going to bed already?"

It wasn't an *already*. It was a *finally*. Liena forced a smile anyway.

"Hey, I've noticed that you've been spending so much time with Zedong," said Shu casually.

Liena said nothing, fighting to keep her face neutral.

Shu prattled on. "It's really kind of you to notice someone like him and spend time with him. I mean, sometimes it's just really exhausting for me to spend time with someone like him. People that I should be helping, but it's just so *draining*. I admire you for it."

Someone like him.

Liena bristled. "He's not a charity case. He's my friend."

Shu blinked, then laughed a little. "Of course, he is. I only meant that sometimes we have friends, and sometimes we have *friends*." She gave a little wink, as if that was supposed to explain everything. "But you might consider expanding your friendship horizons. You realize he's failing at everything, right? You don't want it to rub off, you know. Especially with your situation."

Her situation? Was she *"someone like him"*?

"Anyway, I'd better run along. Our group is studying together tonight for our Nuances of Battle Strategy exam tomorrow. See you around!"

Our group—she was going to study with the prince.

Jealousy had no place in the heart of someone like Liena. She growled, clutching her candle closer, and hurried on to her room.

But then she turned around and was just in time to see a tall form enter the hallway and follow after the direction Shu had gone. Crown Prince Nianzu was heading toward the library, and she kicked herself for abandoning it so soon in favor of early morning combat.

CHAPTER
9

E VERY DAY, LIENA dreaded the third afternoon bell.

No matter how the months trickled by in a steady stream of unrelenting days and exhausted nights, her stomach did not fail to drop to her toes when that bell rang.

It signaled that it was time for her combat class. After practicing early that morning, her legs felt like mush. It didn't seem to matter how hard she pushed herself or if she slacked off for a few days—she was constantly aching. The last thing she needed was to keep exercising.

But when she entered class that afternoon, her heart immediately lurched.

Normally, the room was empty save for the three masters who taught this class. Instead, there was a row of students on the opposite side of the room, facing the new set of students. They were all *really* large students. Tall, broad, strong students. Not all of them were male, either. There were some very scary and intimidating female students in the lineup as well.

What made her heart lurch was realizing that Prince Nianzu was one of them.

What was *he* doing here, in her combat class?

Was he going to watch her fail over and over again? Oh fathers, please no! Of *all* the classes he had to attend . . .

But what was he even doing here?

Two of the masters had tiny smug grins on their faces. The third was solemn and stern as usual.

"Stop dawdling by the door, students. Take your places."

Liena had her assigned spot. It was at the far end, near the stern master. And across from her spot . . . Her heart raced, her blood pounding like she'd just finished this difficult class, rather than only started it.

The prince was across from her.

It was a small mercy that he wasn't looking at her. Instead, he watched the stern master, Master Yijun. The prince's legs were planted wide, his hands clasped behind him, and his shoulders set back. Fathers, he seemed even bigger up close! Though the room was full of intimidating students, he was definitely the largest.

She wasn't typically a fainter, but she considered faking it. After all, if she passed out, they would have to take her to the medics, right? Then the prince wouldn't see her fail so terribly.

Would it be any less embarrassing for him to watch her swoon?

She clenched her jaw and twisted her sash in her clammy hands.

"Students," said Master Yijun, striding down between the two rows of students with his hands behind his back. "We've spent the last few weeks covering the basics of grappling techniques. You've been practicing on each other thus far. But in the real world, you will not be paired with someone your same skill level and size. You must learn to fight someone larger than you. You must learn to come to a fight disadvantaged and win. Or at least make it out alive." He gave them each a weighty, narrow-eyed look.

Now Liena might truly faint.

The master had reached the end of the line and turned around, walking back purposefully. "Remember what we've taught you so far. When encountering an opponent while disadvantaged, it is especially important to keep your mind under your control. No panicking. No fear."

Of course, the master had to look directly at her when he said *no fear*. And of *course,* the prince had to glance her way when he did so.

She kept her features neutral by grinding her teeth with enough force to break them.

"You breathe," continued the master. "You assess the situation. You look for weak spots. You think creatively. And remember, sometimes the best option is to avoid engaging."

Liena glanced at the mountain of a prince before her.

"I opt to avoid engaging," said a student a few down from her.

There were a few scattered chuckles.

"I second," muttered Liena under her breath.

The master reached the end of his pace and turned half-lidded eyes on the speaker. He smiled and snapped his fingers. "Begin."

Liena's eyes went wide, and she darted back a few steps as many of the larger students burst forward and tackled their opponents. The prince met her eyes for one split second before he moved. His brow was slightly furrowed.

He lunged.

She squeaked, jumping backward, and turned to run.

"No running!" snapped one of the other masters, whacking her arm with a long stick.

She gasped at the sudden burn but didn't have time to do anything else. Her wrist was snatched, her legs clipped out from beneath her, and she hit the ground.

She didn't impact with the force to knock all the air out of her lungs. Instead, she was almost *gently* flattened. She realized belatedly that the prince had caught her ankle in his other hand and lowered her to the ground so she wasn't hurt. It was still swift, still effective, still discombobulating, but far less jarring.

"Don't go so easy on her, Highness," said one of the masters.

The prince released her ankle, glancing up at the master. Was that a glare? She wasn't sure. She didn't have time to consider it either, because then he had straddled her waist, caught both of her wrists, and pinned them to the ground above her head.

She blinked, staring open mouthed up at his face as he held her pinned beneath him. His very, *very* handsome face. A face that was extremely close to hers.

"Oof," she said when his weight pressed on her stomach.

He shifted his weight to his knees.

Half of her mind was devoted to trying to wriggle free of his iron grip, and the other half was screaming, *"The prince is on my stomach! The Crown Prince!"*

Again, he wasn't even looking at her though. He was watching the master, gaze flicking back to her every so often.

"He's got you pinned, Liena," said the youngest master.

Obviously.

"How are you going to get out of it?" he challenged. "With one move he can kill you."

Demonstrating, the prince leaned forward, shifted his grip so he pinned both her wrists with one hand instead of two, freeing his second to pantomime holding a knife to her throat.

She exhaled a large, irritated breath through her nose. "I am aware of my peril," she gritted out. "I do not know how to free myself from it."

But the master had moved on to the next student, saying nearly the same thing to him.

Liena peered up at the prince and chewed on her lip, her heart nearly roaring out of her chest. She found herself gazing over his shoulder at the wooden rafters, trying to collect her composure.

She had to keep a clear head.

If only she had an uglier opponent. That would make focusing easier.

"I'm not pinning your legs," said the prince, letting his free hand fall to his side. It was so infuriating how he was just sitting there, looking so casual while she struggled with all her might. "Try to dislodge me with them."

"I'm not sure they will help much against you," she said honestly.

He grinned then, and her thundering heart came to a screeching halt. It was a beautiful smile, and the hard angles of his face melted into something entirely different. He even had *dimples*.

"At least bring them up," he said, still smiling.

She bent her knees, tilting her face away from him in hopes that he wouldn't see her blush. He switched his grip, so he was holding one wrist in each hand, pinning them beside her head again.

She gave a few half-hearted wriggles, embarrassment taking over her other emotions. "I don't know how," she finally said, gasping.

"Use your hips to throw me forward," he said. "It's all about balance. See how I'm balanced well on my hands and knees? You need to throw me off. That's when you can get out."

She grunted, trying to shove up, but he felt like a giant boulder on her midsection.

"Use your legs to push up."

"You're too heavy!" Then, a second later, "Um . . . Your Highness."

He smirked at that, then shifted more of his weight to his knees, making it easier for her to push up on her legs. This time, it actually worked. He fell forward and caught himself with his grip on her wrists.

"Better!" he said, shifting back again to her stomach. "When you do that, sweep your arms down to the side. It forces me to let go of your wrists to catch myself. Then you can free yourself."

"Like this?" She tried again.

"Faster. You have to catch me by surprise."

It was rude to glare at the future emperor, right? She remembered that too late. He only raised an eyebrow and told her to try again. That time didn't work either, and she wasn't sure if it was because she was doing it wrong, or he was simply too big to dislodge.

Finally, he sat back on his heels and said, "Would you like me to show you?"

She hadn't answered before he was climbing off her and sitting down next to her.

"Let's trade positions," he said. "I'll show you how the motion is supposed to work, then we'll go back again."

She pushed herself up to her knees. "I'm supposed to . . ." Curse this blush on her face! Was the prince the sort who noticed these things? Or was he more oblivious? She prayed he was oblivious.

"Highness? What are you doing?" came the youngest master's voice right as Liena straddled the prince's waist, face as hot an as oven. It blazed even hotter with those words.

"I know what I'm doing," snapped the prince, not even glancing at the master. "He's new," he muttered to her. "Drives me insane."

She blinked.

"Now pin my arms," said the prince.

But that meant getting even *closer*.

Timidly, she leaned forward and gripped his wrists, settling as much of her weight as possible into that grip.

"Be sure to catch yourself."

"Catch mys—"

He moved so quickly she wasn't sure what was happening. One second, she was astride him, and the next she barely managed to catch herself before she fell face first into the floor. She rolled to the side so her stomach wasn't in his face.

"See? That's what you need to do to me."

"I didn't . . ."

"We'll do it again, but slower."

This time, he did things one by one, slowly, with a break in between, so she could understand. He pushed up on his legs, throwing her off balance, and swept his hands down to his side so she was forced to break her hold to catch herself from face-planting.

When they switched places and she finally did it right, he said, "There you go!"

He was smiling again. She grinned back.

"Now," he said as he shifted back to his knees again, "you have to get out of this position. If you're not fast enough, I can catch my balance, pull back, and land a punch to your face." He pantomimed the blow. "So, you need to grab hold of me around the waist—to prevent me from regaining my balance—and then you have to—"

"Switch!" cried a master.

The prince pulled himself up before offering her a hand. She hesitated for a split second. Then she placed her hand in his and he hoisted her up. They bowed to each other, and she watched as the large students shuffled. Shu was across her now.

And Shu didn't soften the first blow when she knocked Liena off her feet.

CHAPTER
10

T HE NEXT MORNING in the pits, Liena tried to practice with Zedong the things she'd learned in yesterday's combat class, but they kept fighting through it all.

"No, Zedong, I'm trying to practice this maneuver, not the one where you pin my legs! I need to master this before I can do that."

"Why *not* do this one? Just try it!"

"Because I don't *want* to do that one!"

Back and forth they bickered until Shu approached, grinning. Behind her, her two sidekicks trailed.

"If you practice just with each other, neither of you will improve," she said. "You'll never know what your blind spots are unless you fight with more people."

Zedong's eyes flashed. Apparently this morning, he was the contrarian. He stood, disentangling himself from Liena, and faced Shu with wide-planted legs.

"A duel, then," he snapped.

Shu's eyebrows shot up. "Why, it would be my pleasure."

Before she had a chance to brace herself, Zedong was plunging toward her with one of the wooden swords.

Liena sucked in a gasp, scooting out of the way. Warning bells blared in her mind, but there wasn't anything she could do, was there?

Shu clamped her hands together swiftly. There was a loud popping sound, and the air glimmered around her. Zedong smashed into a glittering forcefield.

Just as quickly as it appeared, it vanished. Shu's fist shot forward where the forcefield had just been and landed a blow straight to his mouth. His head knocked backward sharply, and bloody spit flew from his lips.

Liena was a hair's breadth from shouting for it to stop.

But Zedong snarled, plunging his sword back toward her again. The forcefield flew back up, blocking every blow. Each moment that he was unbalanced because of his own blows, she struck.

"Enough!" Liena cried, scrambling to her feet, and preparing to intervene.

"Stay back!" growled Zedong, wiping blood from his face. "Or I'll hit you too!"

Liena drew back sharply as Shu laughed.

"But you wouldn't hurt her, right?" said Shu. "She's your *friend*. And if you hurt her, you wouldn't have anyone to help you study."

Those words sent a fire blazing down Liena's spine. Apparently it was the same for Zedong, because he let out a cry and barreled toward Shu in another fruitless effort.

Shu hit him so hard with her forcefields that he was flung backward to the ground.

She stood over him, picking up his fallen sword and shoving it against his throat. "I win," she said with a smile. "Good practice though!"

Zedong looked like he might murder her. Liena ran to his side.

"Don't worry about her," she said with false joviality. "I've never seen someone with forcefields before! We should watch how other people fight her to get an idea of—"

Zedong jerked his arm away from her. "Stop trying to make me feel better!" he snapped.

She let go, lips parting as she stared at him.

"I think I'll just . . . go . . ." said Shu, cringing. Her ever-near friends giggled, Lei almost bursting out in full on laughter.

"You're bleeding," said Liena, turning her sleeve inside out and dabbing at his split lip. "Let me—"

"I'll do it myself!" he said, shoving away her hand and pressing his own sleeve to his mouth. His breath came fast, his scowl turning his features downward.

"I'm sorry," she said, swallowing hard. It made no sense that she suddenly wanted to cry, but she did. It almost seemed like Zedong was angry with her, not Shu.

He glared at her.

Maybe he *was* angry with her. Maybe he wasn't just taking his anger out on her.

But if she was only a friend to Zedong when he was helping her, or things were easy between them, then what kind of friend was she?

A fair-weather feather, as they called them back home.

Perhaps he needed a moment to himself though.

"I'll go fetch some water for you," she said quietly.

He didn't stop her.

She got up and hurried away, the urge to cry stronger than before. She dashed her unbloodied sleeve across her eyes and swallowed. This wasn't about her. She shouldn't make it about her. That started with not feeling sorry for herself.

On her way back with a waterskin, she rounded a corner near the lotus pond and very nearly froze in her footsteps.

The prince was ahead, striding down the covered walkway, sweat dripping off his nose and sticking his garments to his torso.

To her surprise, he glanced her way, just happening to meet her gaze. Was that—did he just do a double-take on her? It was too late to know for sure since his gaze quickly fixed ahead. She shook her head, blinking, and finished hurrying toward Zedong. She knelt next to him, not quite looking at him as she handed him the water.

"It's not very cold, but I hope—"

"Do you like the prince?" Zedong asked.

Now she did meet his eyes, hers wide and rounded. His were narrowed. "N-no!"

"Then why were you staring?"

It was a valid question. How had he noticed that? She'd paused for hardly a second. And if Zedong had noticed, who else might have noticed too? Her cheeks heated.

"I suppose I'm curious," she said, lowering her head.

Zedong snorted. "You and every other girl here."

"No!" she cried, a little too insistent. To be lumped in with every other girl? It turned her own mouth sour. Zedong's mood was getting to her.

"Well, if things don't go well with the Crown Prince Nianzu," said Zedong with a dark lift of his lips, "there are at least a dozen other princes running around here. And princesses too. Hey, they might be in some of your classes. Even if they're years younger, you might graduate at the same time."

Did he mean that to sting? She actually thought he might have. She chewed on her lips.

"Do you feel any better?" she asked.

"I'm fine," he said, clambering to his feet. Sometimes she forgot how tall he was until they were standing close together, and she had to tilt her head back to look into his eyes. Not as tall as Nianzu, and far lankier, but he was still much larger than her. Large enough to easily best her in a fight, even unskilled as he was.

But Zedong wouldn't hurt her. No matter how angry he was. Not physically, that is.

Liena turned away, hands twisting in her sash. "I suppose we should go to breakfast."

CHAPTER
11

L IENA WAS ON extra alert during her first Poisons and Foreign Substances class. It didn't matter how much her body ached, or how exhausted she was. She refused to let her mind drift for even an instant.

She wouldn't be one of the students that became a warning to the next generation of students.

"In a month," said the master, "once we have covered all our material, we will have an exam where you must identify different poisons by smell and appearance."

One of the students nearby let out a relieved sigh. He turned to his neighbor and whispered loud enough for Liena to hear, "I'm so glad we have this master instead of Master Linjou, because I heard he made his students arrange the poisons in order of most lethal to least, and then made the students drink what they thought was the least lethal."

"Did they have the antidotes on hand?"

"For the poisons they have antidotes for," replied the first student.

"Silence!" snapped the master at front. "Whispering in class—detention!"

Both the students' faces went white. Everyone else turned stiff as statues. No one made a sound, but the atmosphere in the room was palpable. *Detention? Just for this?*

Dread welled up in Liena's chest, but she didn't move. Neither did the offending students.

"Detention!" cried the master. "Off with you!"

The two students looked like they'd seen a *mó guǐ*. But slowly, they rose from their mats and, with bowed faces, turned and exited the room.

It appeared everyone else but her knew what detention was. She wasn't sure she wanted to find out.

She glanced toward the doorway where the students disappeared. To her surprise, there was Master Gu, staring with her one good eye straight at Liena. Her heart leapt to her throat, though not from excitement. The master turned, escorting the two students toward detention.

That night when it was *finally* time for supper, Liena tried to find Zedong, weaving her way through the tables toward their typical spot, when a voice cut through the din of the mess hall.

"Hey, do you know if barbarians are allowed at the Academy?"

Liena might have had knives shoved through her feet, nailing her to the floor, for how quickly she froze. She glanced toward the speaker, finally recognizing her as one of Shu's followers.

It was Shu who replied, "What kind of a question is that? Barbarians can't wield magic!"

And then, in a flash, Zedong was at her side, his face an alarming shade of scarlet.

"Don't talk about her like that!" he snarled at Shu and the other girl.

Liena wanted to melt into the floor and vanish. She could only hope the prince was not here yet.

Oh, he was. He was a few tables down. Looking straight at Liena with a frown.

Just kill me now, she thought with mortification.

Shu's eyebrow arched innocently, her eyes sliding to Liena. "Talk about who? Liena? Wait, is she a barbarian? I guess that explains the accent!"

Her accent was that obvious?

Zedong was about to throw a punch at Shu, his swollen lip and bruised face not a deterrent at all. And Liena couldn't watch that happen again.

If he hadn't shown up, Liena wouldn't have been singled out. It didn't matter that she was only *part* barbarian; the nuance apparently didn't count. Now Zedong had shouted it to the world.

"It's alright, let's just go," said Liena, grabbing his elbow and pulling him away.

This time, she succeeded. Her shoulders nearly sagged in relief.

But as they made their way through the now much quieter mess hall toward their spot, she realized he was trembling. Shaking like a leaf caught up in an autumn gale.

Had he ever stood up for someone else before? Someone besides himself?

"It is alright," she whispered again, sitting across from him like usual. The mat beneath her felt extra thin and threadbare now, and she kept readjusting to get comfortable. "It's not a big deal. Let's just eat."

His shaking had grown worse, and now it was so bad he could hardly lift a pair of chopsticks.

"Zedong—"

"My magic worked," he snarled. "I heard them speaking to each other. Trying to make fun of you. It was intentional."

"Song Liena."

Liena and Zedong both jumped at the sound of her name boomed across the mess hall. She didn't want to look up, didn't want to see the visage she knew that voice belonged to.

But she couldn't delay. Not with the scene they were making in front of the entire Academy.

Her face burning, she got to her feet.

"Liena!" Zedong hissed.

She cast a helpless look at him, then bowed her head and shuffled back through the tables to where Master Gu stood waiting for her.

"Come with me," said the master, turning on her heel and marching out of the mess hall.

Liena wound her hand into her sash and followed, ducking her head even lower. If she was going to detention for doing nothing—

They went to a darker corner of the Academy, an echoey place where no other students or masters were. Then Master Gu grabbed both of Liena's arms and dragged her close. Close enough to smell sour mint and crushed ginger on her breath.

"You've been nothing but a problem since you arrived," snarled the master. "I'd send you to detention for the scene you caused in there—"

But I didn't cause the scene! she wanted to protest.

"Instead, no supper. You need to learn to not drag others down with your problems. You are behind, and you need to focus on catching up. You don't have time to get involved with friends and enemies, girl. Now off with you."

That didn't seem reasonable. Nevertheless, Liena drew in a deep breath through her nose as she made her way toward the library. The moment she was safely out of view from Master Gu, she clenched her hands into fists.

CHAPTER
12

Z EDONG STILL HADN'T shown up in the library that evening. Liena tried not to worry, tried not to let it bother her. She bent over her work, careful not to accidentally lean too far and catch her hair on fire from the candle she kept close.

The characters swam before her eyes, but she tried to focus. Tried not to think about earlier that day, staring up into the prince's face. Tried not to worry about where Zedong was and why he wasn't here.

Was he still angry with her?

That hardly seemed fair.

She sat back. These days, instead of sitting cross-legged like normal, she had been sitting in various stretch positions and rotating as she studied. She was woefully behind in her flexibility, but she hoped these little things would pay off eventually.

Around her, the library was mostly quiet. There were rows of desks toward the back of the library where most of the students studied, past the expanse of scroll shelving. This desk, however, along with a few others, was tucked into a little nook near the far wall and papered windows. She was almost completely hidden from view, except the shelves ended so she had a clear line of sight to the library door. Sconces provided minimal light, not even enough to read the characters sewn into the tapestries that lined the wall.

It had a very distinct paper-and-ink smell. Paper and ink, plus a substantial amount of dust thrown in for good measure. That scent was the first thing that always greeted her when she entered.

There was shuffling in the shelves nearby, and Liena tried to ignore the sounds. Some annoying student not being quiet. She chewed on her lip, silently rehearsing the things she'd learned in her Poisons and Foreign Substances class. She *wanted* to be studying history, but she didn't *need* to be studying history, because that was the class she was doing the best in.

Movement made her look up.

There was a head, poking out of the bookshelves.

She gasped, startling at first. Then she immediately colored, and her eyes widened.

It was the prince. And he was looking straight at her.

She nearly turned around to see if there was anyone behind her. But no, he was looking at her.

"Sorry about earlier," the prince said with a wince and one squinty eye. "About the grappling. I always feel bad for new students. The masters like to stack the odds and make you feel like you know nothing. I guess for some people it's very motivating? I never thought it was."

She pursed her lips into a smile, trying not to let her jaw gape open. Inside, she was screaming. The *prince* was talking to *her*? When he didn't even have to?

What was she supposed to say in response to that?

"Um . . ." she started. Her mouth dried up, her tongue feeling like a dead whale in her mouth, and she ended up giving a shrug and another smile.

"You'll get there," he said. "It just takes time, patience, and diligence. Seems you've already got the diligence."

She blinked once, twice, rapidly. He thought she was diligent? And what was he basing that information on? Seeing her this once, or had he perhaps noticed her here before?

She blushed deeper. "Oh! I . . . uh . . ."

"Any chance I could study with you? I think I would get more done than with them." He waved his hand in a vague gesture toward the back of the library. Did he mean the crew he normally spent time with? "They talk too much."

She might have gaped at him for a moment, but she managed to mumble, "You are welcome to join, Your Highness."

"Nianzu," he said, sitting down across from her and flashing a dimpled smile her way. Right in Zedong's seat.

It didn't seem like something she should point out. After all, if Zedong wasn't here . . .?

He set down his bundle of scrolls, uncorked one of the ink wells on the table, trimmed a quill, and let out a big sigh, facing his studies. A furrow appeared between his eyebrows.

She peeked a glance at him, hoping the table was large enough that he couldn't hear her heart hammering in her chest. Then she sucked in a breath, wrenched her eyes downward, and tried to focus her brain on her studies before her.

Not on the very handsome and very royal young man across from her.

She wasn't going to get anything done.

At least it shouldn't be too hard to pretend she was busy.

"What are you studying?" he said suddenly, interrupting her thoughts and making her head jerk upward.

"Oh!" she said, and immediately hated herself for sounding like such an idiot. "I'm studying the list of poisons we learned about today."

"Poisons?" he asked, frowning. "Isn't that a third-year class? And aren't you a first year?"

Was he impressed? He seemed impressed. "I . . . they accelerated a few of my studies."

He raised both eyebrows. "Well done."

His praise came as a shock of lightning to her gut, making her toes tingle. She barely had the presence of mind to ask in return, "What are you studying?"

"It's Advanced Magic Theory. This stuff makes my head spin."

"Magic Theory?"

"If you keep accelerating this fast, you'll probably start taking your first Magic Theory class soon. They're hard, and in my opinion, very tedious. But all good stuff to know. It helps you understand how magic works, gives you a detailed profile of the different types of magic. Everything we know about magic. Well, of course, except—"

He broke off suddenly, then ducked his head toward his studies.

Except what?

She stared at him a moment longer than she should have, but this time for a totally different reason. Finally, she looked back down at her work and tried not to let her mind spin out of control.

The next morning, Zedong didn't show up to practice with her.

"*Mó guǐ* is a term used to designate the various types of magical monsters that stalk our lands," said Master Gengxin in class.

She wouldn't worry about Zedong. Or blush about the prince. She would pay attention.

"We are still discovering new species, though the most common ones are well known. Dragons, for example, are creatures we're all familiar with. All of you should have seen at least a dragon skin." This was said with a bit of a sniff, as if the master couldn't get away with an eyeroll.

But Liena noticed the sniff.

"They're not large creatures, but they can be fearsome when provoked. Your job as a magic-wielder is to destroy all *mó guǐ* you come across. They are dangerous and are a threat to the people of our empire."

Liena glanced around the classroom, at the students sitting before their short desks with their writing utensils set out. None of them seemed to be struggling to pay attention as much as she was.

"A fox spirit is one of the most cunning of the *mó guǐ*," said the master. "Their magic is illusions. Are there any illusionists in this classroom?"

One student raised her hand. When the master called on her, she said, "I am not an illusionist. But my older sister is one."

The master nodded. "Very well. Then you must be familiar with how illusions work. In the case of a fox spirit, or a nine-tailed fox as they are sometimes called, they can search your mind from at least a distance of one li, but it is suspected that they can do so further than that. They hunt out your weaknesses, preferences, and then they shift their appearance to become that which is most alluring to you. In olden days, they simply manifested as very attractive men or women. These days, their cunning is sharper, and they tend toward manifesting as someone close to you. Someone that you already trust.

"They *will* take advantage of your weaknesses. Thus, the first rule to dealing with fox spirits is to always know your own weaknesses. If you think that you would never fall to one, then you probably will. The next rule is to always have a healthy skepticism. Do not leave your mind behind when something emotional happens. Fox spirits prey on the emotional especially because they are easier to deceive.

"Whenever you are in the field, especially if you are in the wilderness, you must always be on high alert. Being too trusting of your companions, for example, can lead to danger. You must look for inconsistencies, improbabilities. A surefire method to test for fox spirits is to ask a suspect to transfer their blood to you, since illusions cannot bleed—"

The bell rang, startling Liena.

"We will continue our study of the *mó guǐ* tomorrow. After that, we will learn about the importance of interpersonal dynamics on a mission, how to keep personal relationships personal and professional relationships professional, how to keep them from overlapping. That lesson can be summed up in the words: *don't court your comrades.* But for the next several days, *mó guǐ*. Class dismissed!"

CHAPTER
13

D READ KNOTTED IN Liena's stomach as she made her way through the crowded mess hall. She sat down where she normally did, but the space across from her was empty. Where was Zedong? Why wouldn't he—

"Liena!"

She turned, already relieved at the sound of that familiar voice.

Zedong was muscling his way toward her, and his face was . . . Well, she'd never seen him like this. He practically glowed, almost as if he had a mini sun trapped inside his chest that spilled out through his eyes, his smiles.

This certainly wasn't what she was expecting.

"What?" she demanded, leaning forward as he sat down across from her with a wide grin on his face. "Tell me what is wrong with you!"

"Wrong?" he asked, unable to stop grinning. "Everything is *right!*"

"Then tell me!"

"Nope."

Liena's chopsticks froze on their way to the bowl of marinated bamboo shoots. She snapped them in his face. "What is this nonsense? Tell me!"

He only whistled happily, piling his bowl high, then higher. She glared at him, folding her arms on the table and staring at him. He glanced up from beneath his lashes, though not at all in a girlish way, and grinned at her.

In fact, it was surprisingly cute.

"Zedong," she growled.

"Master Gu has offered to tutor me privately!" he practically exploded.

Liena's chopsticks froze yet again. But this time, it wasn't from irritation, but shock. "What?" she said, then shook her head. "Master Gu? The one with the dragon skin and missing eye?"

"The same!"

"I thought . . ." She didn't want to burst his happy bubble—she'd never seen him so happy!—but what was she supposed to do? Cautiously, she said, "I thought you didn't like her."

"Didn't like her? Well, it wasn't like she was the most cheerful master around this place. But now I realize that she's much kinder than I originally thought. Liena, don't you know what this means? This means I might actually start to do well in my studies! And if so, I can improve and get a good appointment. Even with my terrible magic!"

"Your magic isn't terrible," she said immediately. "And you're already improving and doing so much better in your studies."

"Yeah, but not like *this*. Do you know how often this happens, that a master offers to tutor a student? It happens *never*, Liena."

Memories flashed in her mind about Master Gu and whoever she was with the other day. Hadn't she said something about Zedong then? Liena's hackles raised. Slowly, she said, "Do you think . . . Aren't you concerned at all about Master Gu though? Do you think she truly intends to help you?"

Zedong's eyes narrowed, and this time when the smile vanished, it didn't return. "You're envious of me, aren't you? I thought you'd be happy for me! Of all the people that I thought—"

"Zedong!" she cried, reaching across the table toward him. She instinctively gripped his hand in hers, giving it a little squeeze. "I don't mean to be this way. I *am* happy for you. I just. . ."

She trailed off, because he was staring at her hand in his. Immediately, she pulled it away, stuffing it into her lap as she flushed.

When Zedong lifted his eyes to hers, those dark orbs glowed with an intensity so foreign to his face.

She looked back down at her food and began shoveling bites into her mouth.

They didn't say anything more during the meal.

If getting a vision in the middle of preparing for the matchmaker had been bad enough, getting one in the middle of class was ten times more embarrassing.

"Magic is something you are born with, not something you develop," said the master on the first day of her entry-level Magic Theory class. The prince had been right—it hadn't been long before she'd been enrolled in one.

"Its use can be honed by each individual user. You can become more skilled in how you wield your magic, you can explore its limits, but you cannot make yourself have magic that you don't, and you cannot break down limits of your magic.

"It stays dormant until it expresses itself, usually around six or seven years old in a child. It is only in rare cases that magic develops after adolescence." The master glanced her way, then continued. "Magic is genetic, though how magic is transferred from one generation to another is not fully understood. You will learn about that more as you advance. The specific theory on the genetic aspect of magic is called Dadong Theory."

Suddenly, the master's lecture seemed much further away. She was hot—*so hot*—and the world began growing dark around the edges. The ground pulled at her, hard. So determined to drag her down. She knew what was happening.

She fought it.

Around her, as her awareness of the classroom slipped away, she could see the fragments of students turning to look at her, at the master saying something to her. She might have been screaming, felt the loss of control of her limbs.

She was powerless to stop the vision. And it just *had* to come in the middle of class.

Lavender light erupted around her, and the darkness melted into an image. It was a girl, one that was about her age. And . . . she looked shockingly similar to Liena. She tried not to let her mind jump to conclusions as she watched the girl walk out onto some unfamiliar portico during the heat of the day. Her robes were fine silk, dark blue and embroidered with stars and moons.

She walked with grace, but with meekness. Her shoulders bowed forward, just slightly. The glance up that she cast was soft and timid. She was looking at . . .

Oh.

Liena's heart about stopped beating in her chest.

The girl was approaching a huge, tall form. *Nianzu.* He stood proud in golden robes emblazoned with tongues of fire and suns. He was much older, though still strikingly handsome. There was also a heaviness, a weightiness to his presence that she hadn't felt around him.

He wore a crown.

He was the emperor. Liena was having a vision about Nianzu when he would become emperor. And that girl . . .

His face was stern, a little hard-edged, but it softened into a very small smile at the girl. His eyes warmed, and there was affection in his dark gaze. When the girl stood next to him, he placed his hand on her shoulder and gave a gentle squeeze.

The lavender grew brighter, sharper, cutting off the vision. She could hear distant screams that she knew must belong to her. The lavender dissipated, leaving her in darkness.

The world didn't clear for several minutes. She stared at blackness, wishing it away, feeling blind and helpless. Her limbs were flailing—completely out of her control. Then, like the clouds parting after a storm, daylight broke through the dark.

Filling her vision was a concerned visage, and a rather close one at that.

Zedong.

Relief washed through her, and her straining muscles collapsed on themselves. Slowly, she began to feel her fingers, her toes, her tongue back under her control.

"Drink this," said a brisk, unfamiliar voice.

Liena was hoisted up enough, and she coughed and sputtered her way through a glass of water mixed with something that tasted very dry. Zedong stared with pursed lips, his eyes wide.

"Are you alright?" he asked softly.

She swallowed, nodded.

"Was that . . . a vision?"

Another nod.

"Seven valleys," he muttered. "I thought you were . . ." He stopped himself and didn't finish.

She became aware of the fact that she lay in a bed, covered by a blanket in the infirmary, and that Zedong's hand was gripping hers. She started to remove it, feeling suddenly self-conscious and awkward, but then she forced herself to leave it. If it comforted him, she didn't need to yank it away.

"If that was a vision," said the brisk voice, "then you are required to report it."

Liena chewed on the inside of her cheek but nodded. When Zedong asked what her vision was, she merely shook her head and closed her eyes. She felt drained to the utter dregs, and she didn't *want* to tell him what she'd seen.

Somehow, she thought he would be angry if he knew.

They didn't let Liena stay very long in the infirmary. It didn't matter how exhausted or weak she felt; she was not injured and therefore should return to her classes. On her way, however, Master Gu stopped her.

"Come with me, girl," she snapped.

Liena could barely find enough voice to squeak, "Where are we going?"

"To the headmaster's office."

"Oh."

Was she in trouble for having a vision during class? Was she to be punished for not having better control over her magic? She hadn't thought she was supposed to control it, considering that they branded her magic as uncontrollable. But now that she thought about it, no one had said what the consequences would be for disrupting class with explosions of magic.

And the Academy was known for being strict and harsh.

With palms sweating buckets, she followed Master Gu.

The entry to the headmaster's office was almost taller than the main entry to the Academy complex. The arch was either painted gold or solid gold, rimmed with intricate patterns of ruby red mosaics. The long beams of the afternoon sun caught the glittering entrance, and the flashing was almost blinding. Liena forced her hands to unwind from her sash and fall to her side, forced them to be still. She lowered her head as she passed under the entrance.

Wait, why was she holding herself so meekly? As far as she knew, she'd done nothing wrong.

She lifted her chin to find herself the focus of three masters in black robes. They sat in their own alcoves, behind a low desk with a cup of tea next to the scrolls and parchments covering the surfaces. She noticed that the master at the forefront of the room had a completely clear desk besides his tea. It was easy to recognize the headmaster's bald head, the gray eyebrows and beard. Yet up close, she was surprised to find all his facial features drooped. His eyes angled downward, following the tilt of his mouth. Somehow even his moustache drooped.

A pair of serving girls, one holding a pot of tea and the other holding nothing, were dismissed by a sweep of the headmaster's hand. Then, to Liena's surprise, he flicked his hand in Master Gu's direction.

Master Gu met the disinterested gaze of the headmaster's with a potent glare of her own. There almost seemed to be a slight power struggle, except it was all on Master Gu's side, as if she didn't want to obey the headmaster's bidding, and the headmaster simply didn't care.

Master Gu bowed and strode out of the room. Leaving Liena facing the three imposing figures in black.

"Song Liena," said the master to her left. "Do you know why we have summoned you?"

No. But she had a strong suspicion. Ought she to voice her suspicion? Or pretend she was utterly ignorant? In the end, she opted for a small head shake.

"Words," snapped the master on her right.

"No," said Liena.

"No *what?*"

"No, Master," she said, unable to keep from lowering her head slightly.

All was silent, and when Liena peeked up again, she found them all watching her carefully. She stiffened.

"We have summoned you here because of the matter of Fang Zedong," said the headmaster.

Liena's spine snapped straight as her eyes widened. She tilted her head to one side. Zedong? What did he have to do with any of this?

She suddenly remembered Master Gu pulling her aside. Was this about that? Had she unwittingly broken some Academy code? There went her hands again—reaching up to grip her beads. She shoved them down by her side.

"You have befriended Fang Zedong, have you not?"

Liena started to nod, then said, "Yes, Master."

"You have been helping him in his studies?"

She hesitated at first. "We . . . have been helping each other, Master."

The headmaster eyed her, still managing to look bored as he did so. He stood, stepping down from his alcove, and strode past her with hands clasped behind him. They were swallowed up in the depths of his black robes.

He began pacing the length of the room. "Do you know what sort of marks the Fang boy was receiving at the beginning of this term?"

She had an idea, certainly, but he'd never given her specifics. "No, Master." She resisted the urge to turn around and watch him pace.

"He was failing so disastrously that we were considering expelling him," said the master to her left.

"Indeed," echoed the headmaster. "Do you know how often we expel students?"

"No, Master."

"Almost never. Most of our students are hard-working, willing to devote themselves to the success of their careers, their families, and their descendants. But there are always a select few who do not even try. Fang was one of them. Do you know what happens to expelled students?"

"No, Master."

"They are magic-wielders, and by law all magic must be wielded in service to the emperor—may his face shine like the sun to all generations!—which means that if they do not graduate from the Academy, they are illegal magic-wielders."

Liena had no idea where this was going. She stayed silent, racking her mind for what he intended for her to understand.

"We cannot release them back into society," continued the headmaster. "Do you know where we send them instead?"

"No, Master."

The master to her right interjected, "They are sent on *mó guǐ* exterminations."

A stone dropped into her gut.

"It is rare that they survive even their first encounter with a *mó guǐ*," said the master on her left.

The room started to go black again, but this time, it wasn't because of her visions. She shifted her weight, breathing fast in and out through her nose.

"We had been weeks away from sending Fang Zedong on a *mó guǐ* extermination," said the headmaster. "But then you came, and he began improving immensely."

Liena swallowed, feeling faint as she thought of the hand that had covered hers not even a full hour ago.

"Your intervention in his life saved him from a gruesome fate," said the master on the left.

"You are officially commended by the Academy," said the master on the right.

The headmaster paced his way to the front of the room, where Liena faced. He studied her for one long minute.

He flicked his hand in a dismissive gesture. "You may leave now."

Liena kept her spine tall, kept her hands firmly at her side, and kept her chin from drooping as she walked out of the room.

The moment she was on the other side of the door, she gasped in relief.

But then Master Gu stood before her, one eye narrowed to a slit as the dying sun caught the lines of her scars and empty socket. "Back to class, girl," she snapped.

She expected Master Gu to march back with her, but instead the woman stormed off in another direction. Liena wondered how soundproof the headmaster's office was. And if Master Gu *had* overheard, then why wasn't she happier? After all, she seemed to have taken an interest—for good or for bad—in Zedong.

As Liena walked the other way, she couldn't help but turn and glance over her shoulder.

She met the gaze of Master Gu across the hall, who was doing the same thing.

CHAPTER
14

ONE OF THE things Liena had been dreading for weeks was the Night Games.

It didn't matter how many months she had been here at the Academy; she still felt woefully unprepared. All day in class, she was jittery. It didn't help that she was perpetually sore from the combat class she was still failing and the morning hours in the pits.

The teams were announced a fortnight ago, and she had been glad that she and Zedong were on the same team. However, they had missed most of the team preparation meetings because no one cared to invite them.

"I am very anxious about the Night Games," she told Zedong as they practiced their wax wood staffs in the pits that morning.

"Why?" he asked, shrugging and landing a blow she barely managed to block. "It's just a game. You can even hide during the game if you want."

"I don't want to be *useless*!" she cried. "But I barely understand the rules, and I certainly don't know any strategy!"

"Pfft, the rules are easy," said Zedong. "All you do is try to find their dragon egg—don't worry, it's not a real dragon egg—and not get snatched by the other teams. And don't let the other teams steal your dragon egg."

"But—"

"Besides, the team captains will tell us what to do."

"What happens if you get caught?"

"You get taken to their team's incarceration unit. Usually, it's just a tree they're guarding, and they tie you up so you can't escape. It's not bad."

"Can you get away once they snatch you?"

"Of course. We call them *raids* where a few team members assault the incarceration unit and free the captives. It's risky business, but sometimes if you've had a lot of your team be snatched, it's your only option for trying to win."

"Where do people hide their dragon eggs?"

"All sorts of places. The smart teams also set up decoys, sometimes even multiple decoys."

"This is all so overwhelming!"

"You'll be *fine*."

That was the end of the conversation, and all that Liena had to stew about throughout her classes that day. She thought of a million more questions to ask, but Zedong didn't share most of her classes, so she wasn't able to ask him.

How long do the games go?

She was *very* tired, after all. She was perpetually sleep-deprived these days.

If I am "snatched," can I fight my captor? Or do the rules demand that I go with them?

Her nerves frayed to little ribbons during supper. Many of the older participating students—apparently there was an age-requirement on this game, though Liena would have preferred a skill-requirement—were already wearing their team's colored sashes and headbands. The chatter in the mess hall was especially loud.

Zedong was late for supper, so she didn't get to ask him any questions. He was training with Master Gu more in his free time, always leaving their training in the pits early and coming late to dinner. Occasionally he even missed their evening study sessions in the library. Nianzu hadn't studied with her again, and even though she told herself *not* to overthink things, she was beginning to wonder if she'd scared him off or something. Perhaps he realized more how desperately far behind she was and didn't want it to "rub off" on him, like Shu had said.

But tonight, Liena couldn't be worried about Zedong, or what Nianzu thought of her. She was too worried about the Game. As she was leaving to dress for it, Zedong finally entered the mess hall. He grinned and waved at her across the distance, and she gave him a wince in return.

The sun was setting, and usually Liena loved the sight of it. But now, it only served to make her jittery. Her stomach felt like a mess of exploding butterflies.

She didn't want to be that one worthless person on the team.

"Here's how this is going to go," said their team captain with all the authority of an Academy master. He was Zuan Wan, the plant-wielding student she'd watched battle Nianzu. Even though the prince had won that fight, Wan was a fierce, top-ranking student. She was happy to be on his team. Though she would have been happier to be on Nianzu's team.

They were the white team, representing the North. It didn't matter that half their team wasn't from the north.

"Where did these names come from?" she whispered to Zedong.

He shrugged. "No clue. They've always been this way though."

North, East, South, and West. East was blue, because that direction faced the ocean. North was white—because of the snow? West was green, and South was red.

Liena had originally thought the Night Games would be played in the Academy gardens. There was plenty of space, lots of places to hide. But the masters guided them right out of the west gate protecting the palace, out of the city limits of Suguan, and into the mountainous wilderness.

The hike to their team's designated "encampment" was brutal. She was huffing by the time they reached the copse of trees denoted with a white flag in the front. A master was waiting with writing utensils and a tablet.

"You," said Wan, pointing at one girl. "Since you have feral senses, you'll be our primary scout. And you, since you have augmented speed, you'll be my runner. Those two of you, you'll come with me to hide the dragon egg and set up the decoys."

He went through, assigning special roles to everyone on the team. There were easily fifty people on the team, and surprisingly, Wan knew each one. Probably because he was the captain and studied the team roster.

When he got to Liena and Zedong, he scrunched up his face, pretending to ignore the whispered, *"How did we end up with both of them?"* from a nearby student, and then said, "You two . . . You can be dragon egg hunters."

Which meant that they had no special skills to offer the team, so they were added to the force of offense.

"He thinks we'll probably just get caught," said Zedong.

The adrenaline was kicking in, almost overcoming Liena's worry. She couldn't stand still and wished the sun would fully *set* so they could start the Game. She needed to run off these jitters! She wasn't going to be a useless team member. She wasn't going to just get caught. Or at least, she wasn't giving up so easily.

She wanted to prove Wan and Zedong and everyone else wrong.

"As always," said Wan, "make sure you're wary of *mó guǐ*. We're probably good, but we are in the wilderness, so be careful."

Wait, there were *mó guǐ* in this area?

The anxiety was back.

"Relax," said Zedong, bumping her with his shoulder. "There are so many people on this mountainside that it's unlikely any monsters will come out for a snack."

"You always know *just* what to say to ease my nerves," said Liena dryly. "Snack? Really?"

Suddenly, Zedong leaned down and whispered in her ear, "When this is done, I want to tell you about what I've been learning from Master Gu!"

"Sure," she said, unable to keep her brow from wrinkling at the way her skin prickled under his breath. It wasn't exactly unpleasant, though it definitely wasn't *pleasant*. It set her on edge—as if she wasn't already on edge—and added another worry to her slough of them.

Was Zedong starting to . . .?

She mentally shook herself. He was just a friend, and he knew that, right?

A piercing whistle shrieked through the air just as the sun dipped below the mountain, and their world was plunged into night.

The Night Games had begun.

CHAPTER
15

W HITE HEADBANDS FLAPPED in the darkness as the North Team dispersed into the wilderness. Liena stayed near Zedong as they began creeping through the dark.

"The other teams have their own encampments that are in their directions, relative to us," whispered Zedong. "They each have their own advantages and disadvantages. Ours, for example, requires some serious hiking and we have the sand dunes for cover. It's also great for hiding the dragon egg. The South is the most forested, and it's known for having more *mó guǐ*. The East is lit up by the city lights, so it's harder to be sneaky. And the West is basically on the side of a cliff, so it's very hard to breach, but there's almost no place to hide a dragon egg there that isn't out in the open."

"Makes sense," said Liena. "How about we try East? I'm not interested in *mó guǐ* and the west sounds like something I'm ill-equipped for."

"Sure. But we'll have to split up as we hunt for the dragon egg."

"How big is the dragon egg?"

"Uh . . . it's basically life-sized."

"How big is that?"

He made a fist and held it up. "About this big."

Liena wrinkled her brow. "How does anyone find them?"

"The Night Games can last a long time."

She tried not to groan at the thought of being awake all night. Instead, she nodded at Zedong as he split off from her and tried to ignore how her blood roared with adrenaline. The air suddenly seemed colder, and she wished she had a cloak to ward off the late autumn chill.

East.

Find the dragon egg.

Don't get caught.

She could do this.

Crouching to minimize her form and her shadows, she moved quickly from tree to tree, trying not to trip over rocks or snap twigs. She still managed to be easily the loudest thing in this wilderness. The world was so quiet, she would never have guessed that hundreds of trained students slinked through its shadows.

She spotted another student. She froze.

The student glanced her way, then motioned her forward and kept moving. Someone on her team? It was hard to tell, but she thought her headband was white. Well, she wasn't trying to snatch Liena, so Liena decided not to worry about her.

For the next twenty minutes, she kept heading toward the light of the city above the trees. It was eerily silent.

Then the shouting began.

She immediately ducked behind a boulder, folding herself into a tiny ball so the footsteps would keep running past her. There was suddenly a ruckus, and surprisingly near. At the same time, more shouts and strange sounds—sounds of magic clashing—echoed across the mountainside.

Liena half considered the idea of staying put behind her boulder, but after waiting several long minutes, she forced herself to come out of its safety. She was *not* going to be a useless team member. Plus, if there was fighting nearby, perhaps she could use that distraction as cover to hunt for the dragon egg.

It didn't take her long to reach the East. The area was much less forested, much more illuminated, and a beacon seemed to shine on each of her movements. An idea popped in her head to remove her headband, but she immediately dismissed it as cheating. If it was something students could do, everyone would have done it already.

Sentries—that was what Wan had called the students he tasked with guarding their encampment—marched through the trees. The East's sentries stood in the light, but she was fairly certain she could make out other hidden ones, their shapes mostly concealed in the few hiding spots near the encampment.

Didn't Zedong say something about how some teams buried their eggs?

She eased into a crouch in the sparse shelter of a tall wintersweet shrub, surveying the landscape before her. Where would they have hidden the egg? Where would *she* have hidden the egg?

Liena mulled over that question as she watched the movement of the sentries. The obvious place to hide an egg was in the darkest, most secretive place in the encampment. But with the illuminated East sector, those would be all the places that enemy players would be trying to hide as they scouted the area. That meant their chances of discovering the egg would be higher.

Where did Liena least want to go? She least wanted to dart right into the brightest, most open places. Because there, she was most vulnerable and open to attack. So, if Liena had hidden the egg, she would have put it . . .

There.

In that clearing. With the five sentries wandering nearby, and possibly more hidden within easy range.

Liena chewed on her lip, fingers fiddling with her beads. If her intuition was right, and they'd buried the egg in the center there, then identifying the spot shouldn't be too difficult. The problem was having enough time to dig up the egg before she was snatched.

She couldn't do this part alone. She had to find some teammates.

A hand clamped over her mouth.

Liena squeaked against it, her body jolting in shock. That was followed by a bitter, heavy pang of disappointment. The game had only just started, and if she was caught now—

She turned to find a grin and a pair of sparkling dark eyes. Her own eyes widened, eyebrows shooting up. Oh fathers, she hoped he couldn't feel the heat of her cheeks.

It was Nianzu.

He put a finger to his lips, still grinning, then let go of her mouth and crouched next to her. So close, his shoulder almost brushed hers. She fought to regain her composure, trying to recover from the horrid startle, and tried to not think about how close the Crown Prince of Zheninghai was to her, with all his dimples and . . . and . . .

"Where is it?" he whispered.

She glanced sidelong at him, at the green headband on his forehead. *West.*

"Aren't you a team captain?" she whispered instead. "Why are you here?"

"Why am I here? As in, why am I not lounging back at the encampment? Do you think that because I'm a team captain, I won't fight? Or because I'm a prince, I won't go to war?"

Her face must have betrayed her sudden horror, because he gave a quiet snicker and bumped her shoulder with his. *Bumped her shoulder.* Her face flamed.

"I'm only teasing," he said with a smile. "Now, where did you find the egg? You had a look in your eye."

She glanced at him, at the green headband, and raised one eyebrow.

He raised an eyebrow back. "Oh. I see. Shall we make a deal?"

"What sort of deal?"

His grin widened. "You tell me where you think East's dragon egg is, and I won't snatch you."

Her jaw dropped. She stared at him for a long second. Then she was scrambling to her feet to run.

He sprang after her.

She only got a few feet before he caught her and spun her back around toward him. He gripped both of her wrists in each hand, holding them up in the air between them. He gave one glance over his shoulder, presumably to ensure they hadn't been spotted by the East team.

He looked far too pleased to have her captive.

"Tell me where you think the egg is," he said. "And I'll let you go."

"I'm not betraying my team."

He winced, squinting one of his eyes. "Last chance."

She glared at him.

He shrugged. "Then you're coming back with me to West."

"Can I fight you?" she asked, bracing herself.

"Fight me?" he said and canted his head to one side.

"Is it against the rules for me to resist snatching?"

A lopsided grin burst across his face. "No, it is not. By all means, resist."

She shot him a sour look. Swiftly, just like she'd done in her combat class, she slammed her knee upward. He let go of one of her wrists, caught her leg, and yanked on her other wrist. She stumbled and fell forward against his chest.

Oh fathers, have mercy on her. She had to get out of here, or her team would never know where the dragon egg *probably* was. But she was suddenly so discombobulated, caught off-guard by the smell of his robes and his quick maneuver to pin her arms behind her back. She mentally ran through the tricks they'd learned in class recently, trying to find some evasion to break his hold.

Nothing came to mind, and wriggling was to no avail.

"I'll give you one more chance to tell me where the egg is."

When she tilted her head up at him, hoping against reason that he wouldn't see the color on her cheeks, she found him trying to suppress a grin. Clearly he found it *endlessly* amusing that he was so much bigger, stronger, and more skilled than her.

A ridiculous thought cut across her sanity. Ma would have fainted if she'd seen her like this, caught in the arms of the Crown Prince of Zheninghai. Ma probably wouldn't have noticed that he was restraining her.

Movement around his arm caught attention, and, at risk of being too obvious, she peeked a glance.

Zedong was waving his arms at her. Subtly, of course, to not catch the attention of the sentries. But Liena shook her head slightly, to communicate to him that he didn't have to rescue her. That was when an idea hit her.

"Ow!" she cried, seizing up in Nianzu's grasp. "Ah!"

"What?" came Nianzu's immediate, concerned answer. He dropped his grip on her leg, loosened her wrists. "Did I step on your—"

"My foot!"

He shuffled back a step—just barely, probably because he was wary—but it was enough for Liena to drop to the ground as though to clasp her foot.

"Liena, are you alright? Did I hurt you?"

If she wasn't so preoccupied, she would have found his concern almost as adorable as his dimples. Instead, she focused on scooping up a rock and, leaping to her feet, she hurled it directly at the clearing where the sentries were, and the egg probably was.

Zedong's brow wrinkled before he turned and followed the trajectory. The sentries whirled, and half a dozen pairs of eyes landed on Nianzu and Liena, though Zedong remained hidden.

Suddenly, Zedong's eyes widened with realization.

Nianzu growled low in his throat. "Serves me right for underestimating you," he said, and in one swift, smooth motion, hoisted Liena up over his shoulder. She squeaked, eyes flying wide. "At least I'll get the marks for snatching you. Hang on," he called as he pinned her kicking legs. "It's going to be a bumpy ride!"

He broke into a run, and it was all Liena could do to not vomit down his backside.

She managed to get a grip on his robes and push herself up enough to see their pursuit. Half the sentries chased after them, and she could hear their shouts, "Team captain! Get the team captain for the bonus marks!"

Nianzu spun around and even after he stopped, her brain kept rattling around in her skull. Heat and light burst around them, and then he was running away from their pursuit again.

Liena looked up in time to see the sentries halt before a huge wall of fire. Her eyes widened. Nianzu's hand clamped back down to pin her legs, and she yelped at the heat.

"Sorry," he panted. The heat dissipated.

"Get him!" came more yells from the East. "He's got the egg!"

Nianzu let out a growl as Zedong burst in a full sprint from the trees, carrying in his hands a small round object. Liena nearly shrieked with joy, but then Nianzu was running even faster, up a steep slope.

"North has East's egg," he shouted to someone—or multiple someones—as he ran. "Intercept it! Fang has it!"

"Why don't you put me down so you can go after it?" Liena asked after making sure she had a firm hold on the contents of her stomach. The world looked so much worse, so much steeper from where she dangled over his shoulder.

"If I get you back to the incarceration unit," wheezed Nianzu as his grip tightened on the back of her knees, "before Fang gets the egg back to your encampment, we get marks for your capture."

"But. . ." She shook her head, clenching her teeth and fighting another stomach convulsion. These rules made no sense. "But I thought the egg was more valuable than one captive."

"It is. Didn't they explain the rules of the game to you?"

"Well, I think so, but I'm confused about—"

"There are four eggs—wait, hold on—Hey! You there! Find out what happened to East's egg! Any news of the others?"

"Yes, Your Highness! And no, Your Highness!"

"Send my runner!"

"She was snatched, Highness."

A growl reverberated through Nianzu's shoulders and into her midsection. She smelled smoke. "I'll go rescue her in a minute," he snapped. "Let me guess, South?"

"They were waiting for her, Highness."

"Well, then find Shi Mu and make him the temporary runner until I get her back."

"Yes, Highness. Um, did you just carry that captive all the way up the slope?"

She had no way of knowing, but somehow she could just *feel* that Nianzu grinned in response to that question. The world swam, and she went flying through the air. She landed on wobbly feet, but a hand pushed down on her shoulder, forcing her to sit. She couldn't scramble away because she was so busy making her head stop spinning and her stomach stop churning.

Nianzu was barking orders to someone else, and in return he was handed several lengths of rope. She scooted backward, finally able to think again, and bumped into someone who said, "Ouch!"

Another captive. Liena didn't have time to see how many captives were already there before Nianzu caught her by her ankle and dragged her back, quickly binding her feet with the rope. Sweat dripped off his nose, his brow, his chin, and his teeth were clenched. As he worked, he kept glancing up at the master, as though he raced against time.

"Four eggs," he panted as he moved to bind her wrists behind her. Her struggles didn't seem to slow him down as he worked. "Three must be found before the game can end. The team with the egg that isn't found gets the most marks. But each time an egg is successfully stolen, the horn blares and it marks the end of an age."

"An age?"

"Three ages during the game," he kept going. For as gentle as he'd been in her combat class, he apparently didn't have any qualms with tightening the bonds on her wrists until she was sure her fingers went purple. "The longer someone is held captive, the more marks you earn. A mark for one age, two for two ages, and six if they're captive for all three ages."

He finished the bonds, backed away and held up both hands.

That very instant, a horn blared.

Nianzu glanced at the master standing at attention, with a tablet in his hands that he was writing on. The master gave one nod, apparently indicating that Nianzu had completed the task in time.

The prince let out a relieved sigh, then said with one last glance her way, "Finding dragon eggs isn't the only way to win this game." He turned, barked a few orders to the sentries—including a very stern one about not letting the captives escape—and hoisted himself down from the ledge.

It was at that moment that Shu climbed up with another snatched captive. "Nianzu!" she called to him. "I'm so furious I missed the horn! What are you—"

"Ren Ru was snatched," he called back, his voice carrying above the ledge as his head disappeared. "I'm going to free the South captives. Might see if I can get North too."

With that, the prince was gone.

And no one came to rescue Liena.

CHAPTER
16

NORTH GOT EAST'S dragon egg, but West won the game.

By the time West's snatched prisoners were released, Liena's hands and feet had lost all feeling. Her body was heavy with exhaustion, and she wanted to do nothing but sleep. Or die. She was done with the Night Games.

At least, she was done for a few months. Then they would happen again, and again, and again, for the rest of her time at the Academy.

The next day, Liena almost never saw Nianzu, but she always knew where he was. Everyone crowded around him, random students coming up and congratulating him on winning. Even the students who were too little to play in the game!

It slowly dawned on her what an enormous deal the Night Games were to the students here, how much it shaped their world. She had thought it was just a little game, but when people wouldn't stop talking about the Games for an entire *week*, recounting all the triumphs and defeats and discussing future strategies, she realized how important this was.

The next night, she only caught a glimpse of the prince's grin when he entered the mess hall before he was enveloped in people. Zedong was also congratulated much more than she expected. There was a grudging sort of respect in those congratulations, and Shu even stopped by to say, "That was incredible! I never would have guessed you capable of that!"

It took Liena's gentle but firm grip on his arm to make him not lash out at her.

Shu glanced at her following friends, a half-pitying glance as if to say, *"He can't even take a compliment."* They snickered.

Liena dug her nails into Zedong's arm. A sharp warning. Only when they retreated into the library to study after supper did she finally feel like she could think or talk about something other than the Game.

Zedong was busy cutting his quills, his movements brisk and chipper—so unlike him. She watched him carefully, setting down her own quill and leaning forward to say, "You had something to tell me."

His eyes snapped up to hers, and recognition hit. "Oh! Yes! Liena, you would never believe what I've been learning in my lessons with Master Gu. You should come with me. Tomorrow, instead of practicing in the pits. This stuff is absolutely crazy, and it's changing everything for me!"

"What is crazy?" she asked, instantly wary. "Isn't she just helping you on your hardest subjects?"

"Oh no, she's teaching me something completely new. Something none of the masters here talk about, but Liena, it is unbelievable."

She couldn't keep the alarm out of her voice when she said, "What? What is unbelievable?"

"Aww, don't look so scared! I told you it's nothing to be concerned about. It's just . . . Liena—"

Stop saying my name, she wanted to snap. Instead, she held her tongue, and reached for the necklace of wooden beads at her throat. Her finger traced the smooth lines of the biggest bead, the one with the lotus on it. A smidge of her anxiety eased.

"What?" she prodded, much gentler.

He stared at her, glanced around to make sure no one was listening, and then leaned forward. She expected him to finally say what he had been avoiding, but instead, his face darkened, and a snarl of words spewed from his lips in a hushed whisper.

"Magic is so unfair."

She jolted back, taken by surprise. "Unfair?" she echoed.

"What? Don't tell me you don't think so! It's ridiculous. The whole lot of it! Birth determines everything. It determines your magic, your family, and your magic determines your place in this society. So, if you're a magic-wielder like you and me, then you will never amount to anything. You cannot improve and grow. Instead, you're stuck with whatever measly powers the fathers saw fit to bestow." This last sentence was spat out with utter vehemence.

"What?" Liena said. "You don't mean—"

"I can't become Prince Nianzu," said Zedong, his voice so much harsher and darker than she'd ever heard it.

"What?" she said again, sounding stupid in her own ears. "What does Prince Nianzu have to do with any of this?"

"He's strong, he's powerful; no one can beat him in the Night Games, or in the arena battles, or even in practice. And he's holding back! He literally cannot battle other students at full strength because he will kill them. Liena, how is that fair for the rest of us?"

"I don't think fairness has anything to do with it. He is going to be the emperor. He comes from a line of mighty fire wielders. Of course, he's strong and powerful."

Life wasn't fair. Her job was to make do with what unfairness she had been dealt. Her job was to rise above the unfairness, to succeed even when no one thought she would. Even though she had so far to go, she'd already advanced through several classes in just a few months. Sure, she was still failing her combat class and sure, she'd lost all her arena battles, but she was no longer in class with all the six-year-olds. She even had a class with twelve-year-olds.

"This isn't about fairness," Liena said. "This is about hard work."

"But it *isn't* about hard work, is it?" Zedong said, his eyes taking on a shine that was almost . . . almost wild. It unnerved her. "You've been working so hard—harder than almost anyone else here—and yet look at you. You're smart, diligent, but you're years behind. *Years,* Liena."

"Thank you," she replied dryly. "If I ever need a morale boost, I'll be sure to come to—"

"What if magic didn't work like this?" he interrupted. "What if everyone started at the same place, and the effort that you put in directly correlated to the level of success that you saw?"

She drew away from him sharply. A frantic look over her shoulder revealed no visible eavesdroppers, but she couldn't quell the rising alarm in her heart. "What are you saying?" she demanded, voice barely audible. "Zedong, you aren't talking about . . . about . . ." She didn't want to voice it. Didn't want to say the words.

Black magic.

"What if talent wasn't a thing in magic?" Zedong pressed. "What if it was all skill, effort? What if—"

"Good evening!" chimed a new voice.

Liena and Zedong both whirled to see—oh fathers! *Him.* She tried not to look desperately frantic and desperately hopeful at once.

The prince stood there, his study materials tucked under one arm and a smile on his face. "Mind if I study with you both? Or am I interrupting something?"

"You *are* int—" Zedong started to snarl.

"Not at all!" cried Liena quickly, hoping her voice didn't come out too high and squeaky as she tried to cover Zedong's idiocy. When Nianzu grinned and began to take a seat, she shot a look at Zedong, telling him to stop saying things that could land him in the headmaster's office. He glared back at her. Then he looked at where Nianzu had chosen to sit: next to Liena. He ducked his head and began writing furiously on his tablet.

Nianzu glanced at Zedong, tilting his head, then glanced at Liena. She gave a small smile and shake of her head, hoping he understood her telling him to leave Zedong alone.

He didn't.

"I don't believe we've met," said Nianzu pleasantly to Zedong. "Not officially, that is, though I've seen you around. Fang, isn't it?"

Zedong grunted in response. Liena twisted her hands in her sash.

Nianzu merely cast one questioning look at Liena, said a quick, "Nice to meet you," and arranged his study materials on the table. He was quiet, unlike the last time he'd come to study with her. No *What are you studying?* questions.

Liena wished he would ask. Wished she dared ask him. She peeked at him while she pretended to keep studying, growing curious at his pile of scrolls. What subject was making his brow furrow like that?

It didn't matter. She was being stupid.

She dipped her quill and bent over her work, forcing her mind to focus. Magic Theory truly was no child's play, and it was the first subject she'd encountered here at the Academy that sent her mind spinning.

Tonight, however, she couldn't get her brain to stop stewing. She was more concerned than ever about Zedong. What in the seven valleys had he been talking about? What sort of idealistic nonsense had gotten into his mind? Would it affect his studies? His ability to get an appointment? What if the masters found out? Could he be punished? What if he was expelled after all?

Surely it wasn't . . . *Surely* black magic wasn't involved.

Combat class was a constant source of anxiety. She was improving by leaps and bounds in her opinion, but the problem was that everyone else was too. Improving was one thing, catching up to her peers was an entirely different thing.

Was she doomed to lose every one of her arena battles?

It didn't help that Nianzu was right next to her—he'd sat next to *her*—and that maybe if she leaned a little closer she might bump an elbow or knee against him. Which seemed like the worst thing to be thinking about now, with so many other more important things to be worried about.

She wasn't going to get anything done tonight. But she wasn't leaving until she finished. She needed to whip her wayward mind and heart into shape.

Nianzu was the first to leave. He bid them goodnight, kindly acknowledging Zedong even though Zedong only grunted in response. Liena gave him an extra warm smile. She hoped it would make up for all of Zedong's rudeness.

He smiled back, giving a small nod, and turned to leave.

She went back to her studies, but as his footsteps faded, she snuck one more glance before he disappeared through the doorway.

And found he was looking back at her too.

Her face went hot, so hot that she immediately ripped her eyes away—so quickly that she didn't see what he did. Mortification and elation twisted in her gut like an exquisite blend of deep oceanwater and expansive midnight sky.

That was it. She was finished studying. There was no more hope that she would get anything done.

"I'm tired," she said.

"I hate him," said Zedong.

"Zedong!"

"Look at you!" he snapped, slamming shut his scroll. "You're so . . . red-faced!"

Deeper mortification rippled down her spine, sending her face into a dark shade of scarlet. She didn't have anything to say. How could she even begin to defend herself? And why should she? *Zedong* was the one being a pigeon-headed mongoose!

"He is going to be the emperor," she said sternly. "You must be careful what you say about him."

"He's going to be the emperor, so what? Not all of us want to be in love with him, *Liena*."

His words were like a slap. So sharp, she recoiled from him. But then she fixed him with her fiercest glare, unwilling to be struck down by him. Unwilling to let him get away with this.

"You aren't angry at me," she said. "You're angry about your magic, and you're taking it out on me, which is no way to treat a friend."

That got his attention. His scowl shifted into surprise, his dark eyes refusing to leave her face. "What do you mean?" he asked, his voice suddenly much quieter.

"What do I mean? I mean that you keep doing this, where you are angry at something, and then you are cruel to me. You'll drive people away by doing that, Zedong. You'll drive *me* away! I know it's hard to cope with our circumstances. I know it hurts you to be around powerful magic-wielders all day. But that doesn't mean you should be unkind to me!"

He stared at her, as though in shock. As though he'd never made that connection before.

"I'm tired," Liena said again, feeling a lump forming in her throat. "I'll see you in the pits tomorrow."

She left him gaping after her.

CHAPTER
17

S HE WASN'T EXPECTING to find Nianzu in the hallway outside the library.

She'd been just about to let a few tears slide free, relieved to be swallowed by the darkness of the Academy at this late hour. Her dormmate never stirred when she came in this late, so no one would be awake to ask about her puffy eyes.

But when she slipped into the darkness, she saw a tall shadow further down the corridor, leaning against a carved pillar. He was playing with a tongue of fire in his hands, letting it dance over his knuckles, from one hand to the other, almost like it was a crawling bug. He rotated his hand to keep the fire from falling, catching it in his palm and letting it slide to his fingertip. He held it up, staring at his finger like it was a candle. It illuminated his face, sharpening the chiseled angles. He wore no smile, his resting face looking almost severe in its repose.

Liena never would have guessed him a final year student in that moment. She would have thought herself gazing upon a hardened warrior. The soon-to-be crowned emperor.

She paused in the doorway, fairly certain he hadn't seen her yet. Was he . . .? No, absolutely not. He definitely wasn't waiting for her.

She stared a moment longer, watching him play with the fire. Watched how casual he was with it, as if it were like folding paper cranes or butterflies during a boring class. It made her lips part in awe. There was a twinge inside of her, as if someone had plucked on the strings of Zedong's bitterness. It surprised her to realize that perhaps the smallest seed had taken root in her heart.

What *was* it like to have such magic? What *was* it like to be a star pupil of the Academy? A team captain of the Night Game, one that everyone adored, who couldn't be beaten in the arena battles? One who had to hold back to keep from obliterating his opposition?

She silenced the traitorous thoughts and straightened her spine. There was no use in entertaining such notions. She was a low-magic seer. No one of note. And that was perfectly *fine*. She would take what she had, and she would be grateful and diligent with that. She would not squander what meager magic she had, wouldn't squander this opportunity at an education, at a future besides farming and fear of starving.

Just because she couldn't be fully part of it, just because she couldn't fully belong to it didn't mean she couldn't make the best of it. For herself. For her family back home.

"Liena."

She startled, swallowing hard as Nianzu snuffed his fire out with a flick of his fingers and tilted his head toward her. It seemed extra dark when his fire was gone, but she could still see his smile. One that hadn't been there a moment ago.

"Have you been standing there long?" he asked, pushing off the pillar and coming toward her.

"Um . . . no," she lied. Her mind scrambled for some excuse, and she found herself pointing at his hands as he approached. "I was simply fascinated with what you were doing. How do you do that?"

"This?" he asked, holding out his hand to her. A spark flared to light in his palm, then danced into a hearty flame.

She stared at it, feeling its heat on her face. When she glanced up at him, he had a small, amused smile on his face.

"Has no one shown you their magic up close?" he murmured.

She shook her head, eyes drawing back to the mesmerizing fire. "How do you create it?"

He shrugged, snuffing it out. "It's instinct. Like breathing. I just"—He opened his palm, and a new tongue sprang to life—"and it's there."

"It's incredible," she breathed. "And it doesn't burn you?"

"No," he said, calling more fire and holding it up to his chin. The light made him look ghoulish. "Fire cannot hurt me. Though it *can* singe my hair. Which is a tad inconvenient at times."

She let out a little laugh.

"And you?" he asked, closing his fist around the blaze. Smoke curled through his fingers. "You are a seer?"

He knew? She hadn't told him, had she? She nodded, almost wanting to lower her head. It seemed so paltry next to his power.

"What sort of visions do you have?" he asked, as if he were genuinely interested.

An image flashed in her mind. One of him, with glittering sunbeam robes and the gravitas of an emperor. She quickly looked away from his eyes and shook her head. "I cannot make sense of them. They're too confusing. Too fuzzy."

She hoped that would be enough for him.

He shrugged. "That's what I've usually heard from seers. Have you met any of the other seer students? I've never seen you spending much time with them."

He'd noticed that? She assumed he was too princely for such things, but perhaps he was a particularly observant individual, one who remembered many things about many people. It was the only way to explain why he'd noticed anything about her at all.

"I've met a few," she said. "I just . . ."

He twisted his fingers and his little tongue of fire reappeared. He went back to playing with it, balancing it so it didn't fall to the ground and snuff out. "Let me guess: it's hard to make friends here."

Her gaze darted upward, finding the firelight reflected in his. He was watching her with a surprising amount of interest that sent Liena's rationale scurrying to understand *why* he would be paying her any attention.

Why he would be trying to understand her.

"It is difficult at times," she admitted.

"I don't really like the culture here at the Academy," said Nianzu easily. Being the Crown Prince gave him much more liberty with his tongue. "They turn out good warriors certainly, but I don't agree with all their methodology. I dislike how uneven the playing field is between different students."

Apparently she was emboldened by his attention, for she immediately challenged him. "But how will disadvantaged students learn to succeed as well as advantaged students if special accommodations are made for them everywhere they turn? Will the difficult obstacles only be for the advantaged students, the ones who are strong enough to handle them? How shall those of us who are disadvantaged learn to be strong on our own?"

Nianzu's hand stopped moving, his fire landing in his palm and flickering. His smile wasn't as sunny as she'd seen some of his others— it was more . . . *intrigued*.

"But I'm sure you've thought of that," Liena hastily added. "Your Highness."

She clamped her mouth shut, hoping she hadn't said too much.

He snuffed his fire out and then gestured with his hand down the darkened hallway. He was smiling. "I was waiting for you because I want to introduce you to some friends of mine. I agree with you that it is difficult to make friends here. Mine are alright—you'll like some better than others. I'd like to introduce you all the same."

The prince started walking, clearly expecting her to follow. But she stood rooted to the ground, staring bug-eyed at him. She wrapped her arms tighter around her studies, blinking up at him.

He turned, saw where she stopped, and flashed a dimpled grin. She almost couldn't see the dimple because of the darkness, but knowing it was there somehow made it more visible.

"They won't eat you," he said dryly. "And if they try, I'll beat them up."

He winked. He *winked*.

At *her*.

It was a wink, wasn't it? Not just a trick of the lacking light?

She lowered her head to stare at the floor, gripping her studies tighter, and followed after him. He slowed until she walked beside him, and all she could think was that Nianzu must have a doppelganger, because there was no way in all the seven valleys the Crown Prince would defend the likes of her.

Her footsteps slackened when they stepped outside, and laughter rang out from further down the portico. She recognized that laugh. She braced herself when Shu's unmistakable tall frame came into view. But she forced her footsteps to match Nianzu's, even though she desperately wanted to delay this.

Shu only had power over her if Liena gave it to her.

She wasn't about to turn into a snarling dog like Zedong did when she came around. She would remain composed.

"Evening," said Nianzu to the group. "Sorry I'm late. I got caught up studying with Liena and Fang."

"With Liena and Fang?" repeated Shu, looking surprised. "So *that* was where you were! Were you helping them with their studies?"

Liena refused to let the subtle barb affect her.

"Oh, no," said Nianzu easily. "We were all studying our own things. They focus so well I find I can get twice as much done when I study with them."

Wan tilted his head to one side. "Liena . . ." He swiveled his attention to Nianzu. "Is she the girl you were telling me about?"

The prince coughed.

"You truly can study better with them?" said Shu, raising her eyebrows. Her gaze fell to Liena, and Liena did not mistake the slight narrowing of her eyes. "I've heard you're doing really well for coming so late, that you've skipped ahead nearly three years, which is faster than anyone else that I know of. But you're also older, which I guess goes to show how stupid we are when we're young!"

There was a bit of laughter, but Liena only smiled.

"Well," said Nianzu, "it appears some of you already know each other. But this is Liena. She's a seer, and is new this year. Like Shu said, she has been accelerating very quickly through her studies. I thought you all would like to meet her."

There wasn't a hint of a backhanded compliment in his words. Like he didn't begrudge her for coming late at all.

"Liena, this is Shu," he continued. "She has forcefield magic. This is Wan, and he can control vegetation. Shi Mu here is an evanescer, and Jadaala Peng is a river-bender."

"Fang said he found the East egg because of you," said Wan.

"It was very vexing," said Nianzu with a dramatic sigh. "But we still beat you anyway."

Wan flung his hands wide. "That's because you blew through all the other team's incarceration units and made it impossible to keep anyone captive for all three ages!"

Shu smirked, crossing her arms over her chest. "It sure was nice being on the same team as him."

"Quit your gloating," growled Wan. "We still got in second place, and you can be sure I'll be adjusting our strategy for future games."

"*If* you stay team captain," said Shu.

Wan shot her a look, flinging up his hands again.

"He'll stay team captain until we graduate," said Nianzu. "The only team captain who's got any risk of losing his place is Lin because of Hanying always breathing down his neck."

Liena stood by the prince's side, listening quietly as they bickered about the Night Games and talked strategy for the next round. It wasn't that she wasn't interested, but rather that she didn't have anything to add, and she was very exhausted. She listened, said nothing, and looked for a way to slip out of the conversation.

She didn't belong here anyway.

After the conversation dragged on and switched topics to their combat classes, their recent frustrating Magic Theory exam, and other random Academy doings, Liena glanced around. She didn't want to interrupt, but somehow turning around and walking away didn't seem very polite nor appropriate, especially when the prince had specifically invited her into this conversation.

Thinking of nothing else to do, she gently touched Nianzu's arm. She could almost feel Shu's hawk-eyed gaze burning into her movements, her fingers on his sleeve.

He glanced down at her. "Yes?"

"I'll see you later?" she said. It came out as a question, and the moment she said it, she realized that while she intended it as permission to leave, it certainly sounded a lot more like a request to spend more time with him. She flushed and quickly added, "I think I'm going to turn in for the night."

"Yeah, I'll see you later," he said with a smile.

"Hey, before you go—" It was Shi Mu.

Liena stopped, peeling her hand away from Nianzu's arm and avoiding watching Shu's eyes as they followed her hand's descent all the way to her sash. "Yes?"

He cocked his head to one side and pointed to his mouth. "Your accent. Where are you from?"

They all looked to her, and Nianzu's attention seemed to sharpen, as if he'd wondered the same thing. She bit her tongue, debating how to best respond. If she hesitated too long, she would look ashamed of her heritage. But she didn't want to throw out the words that had elicited scowls from other masters.

"I'm from the north," she said with what she hoped was a simple smile and not a grimace.

"Near Butagin?"

She nodded.

"Can you speak their language?" asked Shu. Somehow, the question seemed guarded. Almost like a sort of test.

She had to fight to keep her hands from drifting up to her necklace. "I can speak a little, but not well."

The atmosphere had clearly shifted in the group, and Liena wasn't quite sure why. But she refused to let herself be troubled by it. Instead, she ducked her head in a polite bow and excused herself.

Her heart pulsed in a confusing rhythm the entire way back to her dormitory.

CHAPTER
18

YOU ARE SO bad at this," said Zedong.

She lay flat on her back, her arms landed painfully on the ground above her where they still gripped her wax wood staff. "You're not a very good teacher," she retorted, scowling at him.

"I've showed you a million times."

"At breakneck speed!" she whined.

"Need help?"

A figure towered in Liena's view. One with a grin. She scrambled upright, holding her staff in front of her like a shield. Zedong scowled at Nianzu, who was leaning on his own staff as sweat dripped down his face and body, making his tan training clothes stick to his skin.

"You two need to mix things up," Nianzu was saying as Liena brushed dirt off her robes and face.

"We're doing fine," grumbled Zedong.

"The more people you fight with, the more you'll improve," said the prince. He braced his legs, holding his staff in both hands. "Fang, you first."

That meant she was second. She swayed on her feet, scooting out of the way of Zedong's furious scowl.

"I don't—" he started.

"It's just practice!" said Nianzu. "Come on. Arena battles are in a couple of days. Pick up your staff!"

She did *not* want to think about fighting another arena battle. Her hip was still sore from the last one.

"Yes, Highness," said Zedong sourly.

Nianzu made the first swing, arcing down the staff at Zedong. Zedong reacted, bringing up his staff in both hands to block the blow. The prince swung the back end of his staff upward, and Zedong grunted as he yanked his down to block. Their weapons clashed between them, and Liena gasped and jolted when Nianzu straightened his and shoved the tip straight for Zedong's face.

Zedong's eyes flew wide. He dodged, but the movement wasn't smooth. He stumbled, and Nianzu took the opportunity to smack his already unstable feet, then land a blow on his shoulder that sent him sprawling. The prince stood with his staff against Zedong's throat, his usual grin replaced by a stern expression.

"You could have blocked that," he said. "Much less disorienting than dodging and far more effective. Let me show you."

He offered Zedong a hand. Zedong stared at it before his eyes trailed up toward Nianzu's. His jaw clenching, he reached up and accepted the aid. Liena nearly melted with relief that he didn't say anything stupid.

"Your right side is very strong," Nianzu said as they continued practicing, demonstrating by landing a few blows that Zedong countered and blocked. "It's here"—He whacked the side of Zedong's waist, though not hard enough to injure—"where you aren't switching to the proper defense. This is where your enemies will take advantage of you."

"Enemies like you?" snapped Zedong.

Liena's eyes went wide as saucers.

Nianzu merely raised an eyebrow, but there was an edge to his voice she hadn't heard before, a sharpness in the gaze he fixed on Zedong. "I should certainly hope not." He set the heel of his staff on the ground and found Liena watching. His jaw was tight, a clear sign of his irritation, but he kept his tone controlled. "Your turn, Seer?"

She clutched her staff, blinked, and gave a short shake of her head.

Nianzu laughed. "Oh, come on. You know I won't hurt you."

It took two deep breaths before she found the courage to take those first steps toward him. He was so huge, like a looming . . . horse? She couldn't think of a proper comparison as she braced herself across from him. There was a strong temptation to squeeze her eyes shut.

"Are you ready?" he asked, smirking.

"I—I just . . ." she started, then met his gaze and knitted her brow, frowning. "Here's the thing: I cannot beat someone who is four years younger than me, so I do not know how fighting you will help when I cannot possibly beat someone of your size."

He relaxed his stance, leaning on his staff. "It's not just about beating. It could be about preventing injuries, minimizing damage, creating an opportunity for escape, or even outsmarting your opponent. Fighting isn't only a strength or size game."

"Strength and size help though."

He grinned mischievously and lifted one eyebrow. "Strength and size *do* help, you're correct, but they're not everything. Now, you've stalled long enough and it's nearly time for breakfast. Get into position."

She bit her lip and gripped her staff in both hands.

Nianzu exhaled, shooting her a look. "You're tense. You can't fight if you're bracing yourself like that. Ease up."

She drew in a deep breath. Tried to relax her muscles. But her heart wouldn't stop pounding, and if she slackened her grip anymore on her staff, it would slide away from the sweat.

In two strides, the prince had crossed the distance between them and, sidling up behind her, reached out and drew her shoulders back. "Don't curl in on yourself," he said. "Ease up. Loosen this grip. You only need to hold it with your thumb and index fingers. The rest are for stability." He reached around her and adjusted her hands, ignoring how slick they were. His chest bumped into her back.

It took everything to keep her focus on his words, to not squeeze her eyes shut to block out the sudden uproar of the blood in her veins. There was no way the students in the pits around them weren't staring, wondering what they were doing, why the prince was helping her.

It was finally finding Shu staring from across the stretch of sand, her face almost stricken, that made Liena focus on what Nianzu was saying instead of his warmth at her back.

"Trust me," he was saying softly. "You don't have to be afraid."

She nodded wordlessly, relieved when he stepped away and took his place across from her. She funneled every ounce of willpower in her bones to meet his gaze steadily, to not flinch away.

Were his cheeks slightly pink?

They were exercising. Of course he was flushed. She shouldn't be so arrogant to think she might be the cause of that color, and instead should be worried about her own cheeks betraying her. If she stayed in this awkward limbo any longer before their fight began, she might drown in her own embarrassment.

She charged. She swung at his shin, hoping to catch him off guard. Unsurprisingly, it didn't work. He blocked, stepping in closer and trapping her staff, swung it in an arc over their heads and into the ground. Before she could even think, he slid his staff straight up to her face, stopping just below her jaw. She flinched.

They stared at each other, and she couldn't begin to interpret the expression on his face.

MAIDEN OF CANDLELIGHT AND LOTUSES

The bell rang. It was the most welcome sound she'd ever heard.

Nianzu dropped his staff, letting out an exhale and turning half away from her to run a hand through his hair. She released her own pent-up air and went to grab Zedong and escape.

When she looked for him, however, he was already gone.

"There are an assortment of magic traps that you could potentially run across in your career," said Master Qing during her Magic Theory class. "Does anyone know any of the types?"

"Illusions."

"Indeed, illusions are one of the biggest. Others?"

"Zuan Wan has made some plant traps!"

"Very good."

Jia, who was sitting at the front of this class, raised her hand and said, "Siren lures."

"Very good," said Master Qing. "Siren lures are another example of very powerful magical traps that you might encounter. They are the subject of today's lesson. Kang Lei, please enter."

The girl who sauntered in was none other than the beautiful girl who hung around with Shu and laughed hysterically at all her jokes. Her movements were liquid confidence, her lashes fluttering and thick. Exactly the type of person who would be a siren.

Liena refused to make eye contact with her.

"This is Kang Lei, one of our final year sirens. She will be helping in class today as we all learn how siren lures work, and how to avoid them."

Lei held up a black stone. "This is the anchor for siren spells. It is a stone made from obsidian. Naturally occurring from volcanos. A siren's magic has several facets, but the important thing for you to know is that a siren can anchor spells into these stones and plant them. If you come across a brigand—an illegal magic-wielder not employed in the service of the emperor—you could risk being caught

141

in these traps. They are called *lures* because they will lure you in. Some lures will only trap you, while others will kill you.

"The secret to getting out of these spells is to dislodge the anchor. For very, very strong lures, you might even have to dispose of the stone before you are safe."

"Rise, class," said the master. "We will demonstrate."

Liena got to her feet nervously, her heartrate already kicking up a few notches. They were led into the main hallways of the Academy. Since class was in session, everything was empty and quiet.

"I have planted a lure somewhere in these halls," said Lei. "It is your job to find it and disable it without being ensnared."

Liena glanced up, alarmed. Were they not to receive more instructions on how to find it and not get caught? How to resist the pull of the lure?

Apparently not.

Lei and Master Qing stepped off to one side, folding their arms across their chests and surveying the group of students. A few of the students hesitated, glancing around. Others immediately began searching.

"Usually," called Lei, "lures ensnare one of the senses. You won't know which one, however, until you've already been caught."

Liena wanted to mumble something under her breath about helpful instruction, but instead she gritted her teeth and faced the corridor before her. The easy solution to not get caught in the lure was to not hunt very hard. But what was the point in that? This was an opportunity to learn, so she didn't want to squander it. Even if she *was* terrified about being caught in the lure.

Where ought she to start?

Other students were poking their heads around decorative screens or reaching around pillars with their hands. Liena saw her dormmate far ahead, keeping her eyes closed as she crawled along the wall, feeling with her hands.

Surely there was a way to do this that made sense.

She mulled over what little she knew about the lures. They ensnared one of the senses. The senses were sight, touch, sound, taste, and smell. Those were also the things that Liena would rely most on to find the anchor. Which meant that she had to rely on other things. Things like logic and educated guesses.

If she were a siren, where would she hide a lure?

She supposed it depended greatly on what type of lure would be set. Which sense would be used as a teaching opportunity for the rest of the class? Would it be sight because it seemed like it would be common? Or something like taste because it was strange and unexpected?

Did lures even ensnare by taste?

Or would the lure be set up to trap via sound, because it was a strange sort of "middle ground," between the other senses?

Protecting against sound made sense. She wouldn't be relying on it to find an anchor anyway. Swiftly, she tore off little strips from her sash and stuffed them in her ears. To protect her other senses . . . She could plug her nose, which should protect her against a lure that ensnared by smell. But if she closed her eyes too, then she wouldn't be able to navigate.

She nearly let a growl escape her throat. There *had* to be a proper, systematic approach to this. Their masters simply didn't seem obliged to enlighten them.

At some point, regardless of poor instruction, she had to start searching.

She plugged her nose and left her eyes open. It was a calculated risk she had to take. And if she did get caught in the lure, it would be embarrassing, but they would discuss it as a class and that would be the end of it. She could stomach a little more humiliation. After all, she was about to be clobbered tomorrow in another arena battle.

Where would a siren hide a lure?

She studied the student-hallway before her. Pillars lined the length of the hallway, painted a brilliant red that contrasted with the ornamental and intricate sapphire and turquoise paint of the ceiling and support beams. On the pillars were drawn characters that read various things like "Discipline," "Integrity," and "Loyalty." The paper windows were covered by gold edged screens with geometric embellishments on their frames.

At each interval down the hallway, there was a *mó guǐ* statue. These were, apparently, not all life-sized. She had been told qilins were much larger than dragons, yet all the monsters were roughly the same size. There was a qilin, with its cloven hooves, antlers, and fiery beard. It was painted amethyst, striking with its nearly liquid black eyes. Further down the hallway, a jade dragon spread its wings, gold glittering in the pattern of scales along the length of its body. A golden phoenix was next, its wings tipped with curling fire.

Once upon a time, fire had made her more uncomfortable than it did now.

Kang Lei seemed the type of person who wouldn't hide the lure anchor just *anywhere*. She seemed the sort of person who would want to hide it in a clever place.

And no one had found it yet.

Liena carefully made her way toward the statues. At first, it seemed like there would be no place to hide a black stone on them. When she stopped at the dragon, there was no spot to lodge a smooth stone. When she inspected under the phoenix wings, she found nothing.

It wasn't until she began investigating the qilin, carefully looking around its antlers, its hooves, and behind the beard, that realization hit her. She glanced at the eyes.

Two orbs of smooth, almost watery black.

She felt no pull, no enchantment clamping down on her limbs or her mind. She frowned. Clearly it didn't enchant by sight, then. Perhaps smell or sound? Which was why it wasn't affecting her?

If one of these stones was the lure, she had to dislodge it to deactivate it. How was she supposed to pry the eye out of a carving?

She didn't want to touch it. But how else was she to find out if it could be moved without touching it?

She pulled her sleeve lower, long enough to cover her hand. With uncertain movements, she reached up toward the right eye, positioned high above her. She poked the edge, but it didn't move. Brow knit tightly, she angled her nail to wedge it into the molded socket.

Nothing was happening.

She could almost feel Lei and Master Qing snickering behind her. Moving to the left eye, she stood on her tip toes and began poking and prodding it.

It gave almost immediately.

Liena gasped as it loosened, revealing a stone almost identical to the one Lei had shown in class. But it loosened too much, and instinctively, she reached up to keep it from falling.

Her skin stuck to the stone. She let out a yelp, trying to pull back. But it caught her fast, dragging in her other hand until both were suctioned to the head of the qilin. No amount of yanking could free herself.

"Ah!" cried the master. "It appears someone has found the lure. Gotten caught in it, too."

There were scattered chuckles. Her face heated, but she reminded herself that it didn't matter if she got caught. She'd found the lure and had almost dislodged it properly. None of the other students had done that.

But it certainly didn't feel like a positive thing when the students, Master Qing, and Kang Lei all gathered in a circle behind where she was nearly hanging from the *mó guǐ* statue.

Her arms were already getting tired.

"Observe, students," said the master, his voice muffled through the plugs she had in her ears and couldn't remove, "how this one was activated by touch. As soon as the victim touched its surface, it ensnared her."

Astute observation.

The master and Lei continued to lecture the students, but Liena couldn't pay attention. Not like this! Not while standing on her toes with her arms stretched above her head. She gritted her teeth, waiting any minute for someone to release her.

It was half an hour before the bell rang, signaling the end of classes for the day and supper time. Her arms felt like they were going to fall off, but she sagged at the sound of that bell. *Finally*. Lei would break the hold the enchantment had on her, and then she could go eat. She was starving.

"Class dismissed," said the master.

Liena craned her neck to see the students disappear down the corridor toward the mess hall. Her heart pounded in anticipation of relief.

But none came.

She twisted around to see Lei and Master Qing walking the other way.

"Master!" she called, suddenly frantic. "Master!"

They both turned, looking confused as to why she ought to be calling out to them.

"Will you not free me?" she asked, unable to keep the whimper out of her words. "Class is over—"

He said something back, but she couldn't make it out.

"My ears are plugged!" she said. "I cannot understand you!"

Master Qing let out a sigh, as though vexed, but she couldn't begin to guess why. He dismissed Lei with a wave of his hand, and Liena nearly panicked. He approached her, pulled the fabric out of one ear, and said with a furrowed brow, "Were you not paying attention during class? Must I repeat what I said then?"

"I couldn't hear clearly!" she exclaimed, gasping as she tried to pull harder on her hands. "Won't you free me?"

"The trap was set to release tomorrow morning," he said.

Her heart stopped in her chest, the blood draining from her face. "Tomorrow? But, but I—"

"Lei made sure it wouldn't overlap with any arena battles," he said, as though this was some significant consolation. "She also made it escapable."

"You're not going to free me?" she gasped.

His brows narrowed. "Of course not. We learn by doing here at the Academy. Do you think that if you happen upon a lure in the real world, you will be able to beg your way out of it? Of course not. You must learn to break out of lures."

"But *how*?"

Desperation tightened her chest until she could hardly breathe, could hardly think. She tried to calm her breathing, like she was learning in her other classes, but the anxiety was nearly overwhelming.

All night. She could be here all night.

"I explained the theory of it just now with Lei, but apparently you weren't listening."

Liena barely kept her tears at bay.

He tapped one of her aching arms comfortingly. "Don't worry. You're a clever student. You found the lure in the first place. I'll wager you can find your way out again."

With that, he left her.

CHAPTER
19

THE ANSWER TO her distress was not to panic. She had to keep a clear mind, assess the situation, and make a rational decision. It hadn't taken her long to find the lure, had it? Surely she could figure out how to escape it within a reasonable time frame, right?

She drew in a deep breath—

—and nearly burst into tears.

Her arms hurt so much, and she couldn't even stand with her feet flat on the ground. How was she to figure out how to escape her predicament all stretched out like this?

"Think, Liena, *think*!" she whispered to herself. "No tears. Tears serve no purpose except to express frustration. Tears will not get you out of this."

But all she could think about was that if she had just stood back and watched, she would never have been in this position in the first place.

"Stop it," she growled to herself, still only able to hear out of one ear. "At least things can't get worse."

Why did she even say that? She knew they could.

As if on cue, they did.

Students began filing into the hallway, heading to supper. At first it was just one class, then several classes, until the hallway was almost crowded.

That was when the jeers started.

She doubted many of the students intended to be cruel, but the laughter—even the quiet snickers—cut to her heart like daggers. A few students openly mocked her, making jokes about not paying attention in Master Qing's class. The cruelest was a group of boys near her age. They dared each other to steal a kiss while she couldn't rebuff them, which was humiliating enough, but then someone called out, "Who would want to kiss a barbarian?"

Raucous laughter. Just when she was relieved that they were moving past her to supper, the last one smacked her across the backside, eliciting more laughter.

Tears burned, but she swallowed them with all her might. Tried to tune out the world around her. If only she could shut her ears like she could shut her eyes! She focused on her breathing, on centering herself.

She imagined standing in a freshly planted field, the warm dirt sliding between her toes, the sun on her face. Pa's figure ahead of her. Ma's constant fussing.

Strangely, what helped her begin to regroup her emotions was remembering Lao Lao's cane coming in a swift arc for her unsuspecting hands. She remembered that last day at the market, when Lao Lao had brought her the beaded necklace that was now tied around her throat.

She breathed out through her nose. Deep breaths.

It was only her pride that was wounded. Sure, her body hurt, but there was no physical injury to her. Once the rest of the students cleared out of the corridor into the mess hall, she would think about escaping the lure.

"Liena!"

That voice wrenched her out of her carefully crafted composure. She whirled—as much as she could—and saw Nianzu storming toward her, fists clenched and smoke swirling from between his knuckles. Mortification sent her curling closer to the statue, as if that could keep him from witnessing her humiliation.

"I'm reporting those boys to the office," he said once he reached her side.

Her eyes widened. He'd seen that? Oh *fathers*. Shame colored her cheeks.

"Kang Lei," he growled. "Her and her nonsense! Why the masters tolerate these lures she sets up is beyond me. I've told her before not to set her lure duration past class time! But she doesn't listen to anyone, and apparently she's got the masters on her side. We'll get you out."

This was a regular occurrence? What other students had found themselves in similar situations as her?

She chewed on her bottom lip, chewed it so hard it bled into her mouth. *Don't cry. Don't cry.* Now memory of Lao Lao's cane could do nothing to help her regain her composure.

"Hey," Nianzu said, much gentler.

She turned to look at him and found his face blurry in her vision. Her mouth and throat ached with her effort to not cry, but they didn't ache nearly as much as her arms and calves.

He rested a large, unusually warm hand on her back, leaning down so he was eye to eye with her. "This isn't your fault, understand?"

She nodded as a tear slid free. He brushed it away with his thumb. Then he straightened and surveyed the lure.

"Let's see what options we have," he began, his brow creased, and his voice roughened with irritation. "There's one technique we could perform that is a general approach to breaking compulsions, curses, and the like. It's called the Yanzhao Technique."

"How do we do that?"

He glanced down at her, and she could have sworn his ears turned red. He swallowed and focused his attention back on her hands stuck to the qilin's eye. "Well, the Yanzhao Technique is . . . I mean, I'd do it if you wanted."

"I haven't gotten that far in my classes. I don't know what that technique is."

Now his ears were definitely red. And he was definitely not looking at her. "You know, I think there might be another option or two. I think we can dislodge it, but it'll be hard if you're so . . . far away from it. Here, I can lift you up on my shoulders to make it easier."

She wasn't prepared for his warmth at her back, or his hands around her waist. She flinched involuntarily at first, then forced herself to not think about it as he bent forward and lifted her up so she sat on his left shoulder.

"Are you steady?" he asked, his arms bracing her legs.

A tear of relief escaped her as her arms lowered. She let out a small gasp and nearly sagged against the statue. Instead, she managed to croak, "I'm steady."

The eye of the statue was level with her stomach now. She was so high that she could see all the way to both ends of the corridors, see the disbanding students, and the few that stopped to watch the spectacle.

"Go on to supper," Nianzu growled at them. "Your prince commands it."

"Will you dismiss me too?" came Shu's familiar voice.

Nianzu twisted slightly to look at her and lowered both brows. "Tell Kang Lei she'd better be glad she's not fighting me in the arena tomorrow."

Shu laughed. To Liena, she drawled, "You're quite a lucky girl, having this tiger on your side."

Liena spared her a look and found the dark eyes that stared back at her were none too friendly. She hoped her voice didn't shake too much when she replied, "I am very grateful for his assistance."

Nianzu's grip tightened on her leg. "Off with you, Shu."

Shu's smile went tight, but she attempted to disguise it with a roll of her eyes and a bow. "As you wish, Highness."

"Don't need an audience if it comes to the Yanzhao Technique," muttered Nianzu.

From where she was walking away, Shu froze. She cast one alarmed look over her shoulder that the prince didn't catch.

"What is the Yanzhao Technique?" Liena asked yet again.

"Let's try my knife," said the prince briskly, balancing her on his shoulder with one hand and reaching down with his other to pull a knife from his belt. "Maybe we can use it to dislodge the stone."

"I don't want you to get caught too!"

"Don't worry; as long as I don't touch it with my skin, I should be fine. The tricky part will be to not cut you while I dig it out."

"It's alright if you do," said Liena.

He looked up at her then and smiled. She wasn't sure why he did, but she couldn't deny how good it felt to have that smile fixed on her. She swallowed as he looked away and fixed his attention on the qilin eye.

It was the careful work of a minute before his knife successfully slid into the monster's socket, dislodging the stone so that it clattered to the floor. Liena gasped, her hands falling free.

"There we go!" said the prince. "I'm glad this was a simple one."

She was glad too, but also nervous about what that meant for more powerful lures. Before she could prepare herself, Nianzu was squatting to help her down, and she was gripping his head with both hands to steady herself.

"Easy there," said the prince with a chuckle. "I like having eyes."

She slid off his shoulder, and the feeling of being back on her own two feet, with full government over her limbs, was the most glorious feeling all day. "Thank you," she gasped, rubbing her arms. "I don't know what I would have done."

Her gratitude swelled to the point she was afraid her lungs would burst, or the tears she'd swallowed would stream down her cheeks. But she couldn't properly express it, couldn't properly thank him.

He scooped up the black stone and slid it into his sleeve. He was quiet for a moment, one that was long enough that she considered mumbling another thank you and scampering off. Instead, she waited.

When he finally looked up and met her eyes, his jaw was clenched. "I'm sorry no one else stopped to help," he said.

She blinked. Tried to keep her lower eyelid from quivering.

"You should go eat," he said before she could come up with a response. "I imagine you're very hungry. *I,* on the other hand, need to have a little chat with Kang Lei."

CHAPTER
20

L IENA COULDN'T FIND Zedong at supper. She wanted nothing more than to melt into nothing rather than be alone as she faced the throng of people who laughed at her only a few minutes ago.

But Zedong wasn't anywhere to be seen in the mess hall.

The growling in her throat matched the growling in her stomach. Clenching her fists, she spun to leave. He was probably going to meet with Master Gu, which meant he wouldn't be here at supper. She should just go to the library and take advantage of the extra study time.

Wait—there was Zedong!

He was just slipping out of the doors, his back to her. There was no doubt now that he was going to his lesson.

She should leave him alone.

Instead, she followed him. The only thing that kept her from calling out his name was fear of drawing attention to herself. It

155

probably wouldn't be the smartest thing to tell him what happened to her; it would probably make him angry to the point of being volatile. Yet somehow that was what she wanted. Someone to validate the hurt, rage, and humiliation burning in her chest.

Perhaps what she wanted most was a simple, comforting hug. And she wasn't exactly going to ask for that from Nianzu.

Why was Zedong moving so quickly? She escaped the mess hall after him, but once she did, she stared at the outside world, the crisscrossing of paths that led to the other parts of the complex, the garden, and the palace.

Which way had he gone?

Gritting her teeth, she turned toward the garden. That seemed like a good place for extra lessons. Halfway there, she paused as she passed some of the masters' quarters and offices. This would be more private, wouldn't it? She changed direction, entering through the arched doorway and hurrying down the open hall.

She caught sight of Zedong's white robes before he vanished around a corner.

Gasping in relief, she hurried after him, even faster. If she could only catch him before his lesson started—

But he didn't stop at the offices, or the personal chamber of Master Gu. The latter made her more relieved than she wanted to admit, not that she thought . . . Well, it was somehow better that they weren't meeting there.

"Zedong!" she whispered.

He didn't hear her. His long legs were moving swiftly, and she couldn't quite catch up to him. He turned down a corridor darker than the rest, and the further he walked and she chased, the more she had an inkling of what this area was. She just couldn't remember *exactly*.

The hallways of the complex seemed almost as much a maze to her as when she'd first come. The only ones she'd learned to manage were the ones she frequented. This was part of the Academy she never came to.

Finally, she realized why it was familiar. This was the direction Zedong had gone for detention. So why was he going that way now? Why would they be meeting here? Why not by the gardens, which were so open and beautiful?

Zedong turned a corner. She quickened her pace and rounded the corner after him. Then she stopped.

He was nowhere.

More hallways split off, and there were plenty of closed doors. However, there were no windows, so the only light here came from the lanterns hanging from their sconces. Unease prickled down Liena's spine.

She could pick one of the hallways to explore.

That thought only sharpened the urge to flee. This wasn't important; she could catch him after his class. But now that she was here, the strongest concern she had wasn't for her own self-preservation. It was for Zedong.

Hadn't she been nervous about him meeting with Master Gu? Why hadn't she gone with him before? Why did she give up so easily on this battle until she was certain it was safe for him?

Because she wasn't his keeper. She wasn't his protector. That was why she'd given up.

Well, she wasn't giving up anymore. She might not be his protector or his keeper, but she was his friend. It didn't matter that she felt like a claw raked down her spine, trailing ice in its wake. Now that she had finally made it here . . .

Before she had chosen a hallway to search for him, she heard deep breathing.

Her awareness quickened. Was her mind playing tricks on her? If she didn't know better, she would have thought that sound came from something large. Something very *un-human*.

ANASTASIS BLYTHE

That, however, was impossible.

Her instinct was to pick the hallway farthest from that breathing, to assume Zedong was somewhere else. But her rational mind and her concern for him won out. She set her face toward the darkest hallway, where she believed that heavy breathing was coming from.

The first step into that hallway was the hardest.

After all, the paving on the floor turned different than all the rest. Instead of being white pavement, it was made of large, gray blocks of stone. The sort of filthy and ugly thing she would imagine on a dungeon floor.

The moment her shoe touched the cold stone, she heard the whispers.

They were unintelligible. Quiet, *almost* inaudible, as if they were more tricks of her mind invented by her subconscious. With them came a gust of wind from seemingly nowhere. Just a draft from a half-opened door probably. A steady, distant drip was the only sound punctuating the whispers.

There was a growing stench of . . . manure?

The whispers grew louder until they weren't whispers at all, but whimpers. If that wasn't enough to make Liena pause, the realization that those whimpers were from a male voice sent unease prickling the nape of her neck.

"Something's not right here," she said under her breath. She should turn and run, should flee this place and never look back. But if Zedong was here, and if he was in trouble, she couldn't leave him. She had to figure out what was happening.

Besides, what was the worst thing she could find?

That question was far less comforting than it should have been.

The scent of manure grew stronger. It mingled with the smell of smoke, of acrid decay, and . . . something else.

"Liena!"

Her heart leapt to her throat in sudden fright. A second later, her mind recovered. That was a whimpered cry. And that was Zedong's voice.

She hurried forward, into the darker reaches of the hallway, saying aloud, "Zedong! Zedong! Where are you?"

"Over here!" came the weepy response.

Alarm blared in her senses, and she ran faster until she found a door with a small flip window covered by an iron grate. "Zedong?" she cried. "Are you in there? What are you doing here? I thought your lessons—?"

"It's been a trick all this time," was the muffled admission. "She lured me with lessons, but then she locked me up here."

"Where is this?" Liena demanded, standing on her toes to peek through the tiny window. "I don't understand any—"

"This is detention," said Zedong. There were more sniffles. "She said they're going to expel me after all."

"*What*? No, no, no, this has all been a mistake. Wait here, I'll go get one of the masters. I'll get the prince. He'll understand that this was a mistake and he'll help you get out of this!"

"Don't go!"

"Zedong, I don't want to leave you either, but if I don't—"

"There are keys! You can free me! I can't stay in here any longer, Liena!" At this, he melted into tears, and the piteousness of it sent a knife through her chest.

Her hands gripped the iron grate, her pulse pounding furiously in her ears, her heart aching. "Where are the keys?"

"They are at the entrance to detention, hanging from a hook. Grab them and bring them here. Oh, and be careful of the other doors."

"What's in them?"

"You don't want to know."

"Zedong, what aren't you telling me? I don't understand—"

"Just get the keys, Liena! I'll explain once you let me out."

She was still holding onto the iron, and his face came into view on the other side of the window. His cheeks were streaked with tears, his eyes red and puffy. It cut her to the heart so thoroughly that she gritted her teeth and turned away to retrieve the keys. Indignation nearly suffocated her.

But she couldn't help the glances she took at the doors she passed. These doors were different than the one that led to Zedong's prison. These were all iron, with no peep holes at all. A chill raced up her spine.

That deep breathing was loudest outside one door in particular, a door that Liena paused outside of. This close, she could feel the weight of that sound. She knew without a doubt that whatever was caged inside was not human.

A strange sound suddenly pierced the air, coming from inside the chamber.

It was like a screech, but not like a bird's call. It was like a fingernail on slate, and Liena flung up her hands to cover her ears. She broke into a run, looking frantically for the keys as she ran.

But wait, was this the way she'd come? Or had she only come deeper into the hallway?

She stopped.

The sound grew louder, more insistent, more frantic, and it finally registered in Liena's brain. It was the sound of claws scraping stone.

"Liena?"

She whirled.

There, in front of her, standing in the middle of the hallway, was Zedong. Already outside of his prison. Looking . . . very perplexed and alarmed.

CHAPTER
21

L IENA BLINKED, STARING with a gaping jaw at Zedong.

More footsteps came swiftly down the hall, and Master Gu's scowling face came into view. Liena stared at both of them, uncomprehending.

"Liena?" Zedong was shaking his head. "What are you doing here? Come away from those cells!"

When she didn't move, he moved instead. He approached her, darting wary eyes toward the cells, and, coming up behind her, set both his hands on her shoulders and guided her forward to Master Gu.

"What are you *doing* down here, girl?" snapped Master Gu.

"I-I—" What could she say? She twisted around to look at Zedong, but he didn't look at all like he had been crying recently. "I wanted to tell Zedong something."

"Then why in all the seven valleys did you come *here*?" asked Zedong as he propelled her out of the hallway, past the keys on the wall.

"I was following you and I lost you." She was too baffled to articulate the questions filling her mind.

"Students are not allowed in these quarters!" said Master Gu. "Trespassing is a detention offense."

Zedong stiffened behind Liena, his fingers driving into her shoulders. Did he step closer to her? "She didn't know," he said.

"I didn't see any signs!"

Master Gu fixed that one eye on Liena, as if trying to pry open her brain and read all her thoughts. "Did you see other students in these areas? No, you didn't."

Yes, she did. She saw Zedong, who was presumably going to the meeting place he had with Master Gu.

"You didn't open any cells did you, girl?"

Liena's eyes widened, and she had to force herself to not suspiciously delay shaking her head. "No. What is . . .?"

Master Gu sniffed, turning on her heel. "It is none of your business. Lessons are over for today, boy. Take her away from here. And see that she stays in her proper place, else disciplinary action must be taken."

She couldn't see Zedong nod, but he didn't say anything, so she assumed that was what he did. He guided her out of that hallway, into the place where she'd lost track of him, and then he slipped to her side.

"That hallway is very dangerous," he whispered.

He was walking too quickly again. She wound up gripping his arm and tugging on it to get him to slow down. His head jerked down at the contact, eyes settling on her hands. She pulled them away and said, "I can't keep up with your pace! Why is that hallway so dangerous?"

"Because it's a *mó guǐ* prison. You're lucky nothing bad happened." She stopped.

Zedong craned his neck to look back at her, eyebrows furrowed. "What? Why are you making that strange face?"

Her voice came out in a croak. "*Mó guǐ?* What . . . which . . .?"

"I'm not sure, but I know they have all the main ones. A qilin, dragon, phoenix, and a fox spirit."

A fox spirit.

Liena swayed on her feet. Zedong's arms immediately shot out to catch her, but she steadied herself. "You . . . were never in one of those cells yourself?"

He looked taken aback. "What? *Me*? Why would I be in them?"

Her footsteps became brisker, faster, until she was all but running back down the corridor. Her head was light, so light that she feared it would fall off. The Zedong she'd encountered in the prison wasn't Zedong at all, but a fox spirit wearing him as an illusion. And to think, she'd almost gotten the keys . . .

She might have passed out if she wasn't so furious at herself for being duped so easily.

"What did you need to tell me?" said Zedong.

She blinked a few times and glanced up at him. "What? Tell you—oh!" After a second's hesitation, she shrugged and mumbled, "It was nothing. How was your class?"

His lips were pressed into a thin line, but he shrugged and nodded. "It was fine. I'm just mad at Master Gu."

"Why? Whatever for?"

"Because she told me I couldn't bring you with me to future lessons."

"What . . ." This was her chance. She *had* to find out what he was doing, what Master Gu was teaching him. Because that niggling voice in her head wouldn't give up its premonition. "What is she teaching you?"

"Just helping with my studies."

It was a lie. A complete lie. She could tell even before he spoke the words, when he glanced away from her, and his jaw ticked.

But she was too shaken to press him.

"Want to practice in the pits for our arena battles tomorrow?" Zedong asked just a tad too casually. "One of us might even win."

She glanced sidelong at him. Zedong—being optimistic? She frowned, unable to shake the feeling that something was very, very wrong, even if this change was for the better. "I'm sure the next hour of training will make all the difference," she said dryly.

"You never know," he said, and his lips were turned up in the very faintest smile.

Unease curled in her stomach.

Liena waited with sweaty palms and a raging heartbeat the next morning for the announcer to call her name. At first, she was only nervous for her arena battle.

Then she caught sight of Master Gu hunkering around the edge of the crowd, her hawk-like focus drilled into the clueless Zedong beside her. Her apprehension tripled.

He was already sweaty with shoulders stooped from getting defeated yet again. She wanted to tell him that he did so much better than his last arena battle, that he put up a very good fight, but she suspected he didn't want to hear those things at the moment. He was in a testy mood, as typical after losing an arena battle.

They watched Wan fight Shu. It was a fascinating fight, with Wan shooting out vines at her back while attacking her front, and her evading his attacks with her forcefields. At one point, she even wheeled back and slammed a forcefield into his chest.

The crowd gave a pained, "Oof," at the same time. Shu took a heartbeat to grin.

That heartbeat was enough for Wan to shoot vines out from behind her, grab hold of her ankles, and throw her off balance. She tried to fling up a shield, but apparently she couldn't do so fully because Wan crashed on top of her, pinning her down.

MAIDEN OF CANDLELIGHT AND LOTUSES

"Zuan Wan—winner!" cried the master refereeing this fight.

Liena gave a half-hearted cheer, her eyes darting between Wan wiping sweat from his brow and the ever-prowling Master Gu.

Why was Master Gu here?

Zedong kept scowling. Liena suspected he would have preferred it if neither won. Nianzu was on the opposite side of this arena, and he also broke out into cheers. If she was being honest, he was the reason she had gravitated to watching this fight. And now, when they all cheered for Wan, she stole a glance across the arena at him.

He clapped and brought his fingers to his mouth to let out a loud whistle. He grinned, and, to her shock, his eyes darted up toward hers and held her gaze, his lips still twisted in mirth.

Flustered, she looked away.

And found Master Gu staring at her and Zedong.

She elbowed Zedong's ribs lightly, enough to get his attention. "Why is Master Gu looking at us like that?" she whispered to him.

Zedong's scowl turned down to her, then up until he found his tutor. He shrugged, half-rolling his eyes. "I don't know."

Apparently he wasn't concerned either. Liena bit her lip, forcing herself to not stare.

To their left, another fight was happening. It was her dormmate, pitted against an opponent twice her size. He was a fire-wielder, but his fire was clearly of a different brand than Nianzu's. He was so busy throwing apple-sized fireballs that Jia couldn't get on her feet to attack. It was all the girl could do to defend herself, giving her no chance for an offensive move.

Liena scooted over to watch, her heart immediately clenching in her chest. For a second, she forgot about Master Gu. She knew exactly how Jia felt. Knew that feeling that, no matter how hard she fought, she had been doomed to lose from the very beginning.

The tall opponent knocked Jia to the ground, but before he could pin her, she arched her back and shouted with all her might, "*Champion!*"

"Stand back," cried the master to her opponent. "She has requested a champion. Does anyone volunteer to be Jia's champion?"

Immediately, students surged forward. The master randomly picked one—another girl—and she swung herself over the edge of the pit and landed next to Jia. Jia was panting and leaning on the wall, but she gave a wan smile to the newcomer and bumped her fist with her.

"Reset," said the master. "You may begin!"

The fight started again, but this time with three fighters instead of two.

"I don't understand," said Liena to Zedong.

At first, she thought he might not answer her, but he overcame his grumpiness enough to explain. "If a student is losing, they can request a champion. If they end up winning, they get a zero on their scorecard instead of a single mark if they win, or a negative mark if they lose. The winning point goes to their champion instead. If they lose, the champion gets nothing, and the student still gets their negative point. That's why so many people volunteer to be champion. Low risk, potentially high reward."

"What? You're saying that all this time, I could have requested a champion during my fights and I could have a zero on my report card instead of a negative eight?"

He scrunched his face up. "Technically, yes, but it's not very common to ask for a champion. It's generally frowned upon. Some students make a big deal about never asking for a champion. Usually, the only place it's considered *acceptable*, if you will, is if the fight is especially disadvantaged. Like in this one. He's got to be four years older than her and twice her size. All your fights, you've been disadvantaged because of lack of skill, but you haven't been disadvantaged in size or age. Often you've had the advantage in that regard."

Now it was she who wanted to grumble.

"Song Liena versus Yu Ting!"

"No," Liena whimpered under her breath.

Zedong reached out, and to her surprise, clasped his hand around hers and squeezed. "Don't worry," he said.

She glanced up on him, expecting perhaps a rueful smile but instead finding a darkness in his eyes she didn't typically see there. As if the scowl on his face was rooted in something deeper than losing his battle, as if he was angry she was fighting hers. She squeezed his hand back and quickly let go, trudging to the pit.

On her way, she stole a glance toward the edge of the crowds.

Master Gu was still there. But now, instead of staring at Zedong, she was staring at Liena.

Her opponent was a broad-boned fourteen-year-old girl with invisibility magic. They were to fight without weapons today—no broadswords, no wax wood staffs. Only bare hands. Honestly, Liena couldn't believe she wasn't considered woefully disadvantaged in this fight. But she straightened her shoulders, told herself not to count herself a failure too soon, and climbed over the wall.

They clasped hands first, then backed away to opposite sides of the arena.

She didn't want to look at the crowd surrounding them. Acknowledging them would make her more embarrassed that so many people were here to witness her humiliation. But when a familiar tall figure moved into her periphery, her heart skipped half a dozen beats and her stomach pitched.

She twisted to see Prince Nianzu standing to her right, just outside the arena, large hands splayed on the wall. He gave her an encouraging smile.

As if her adrenaline hadn't already been roaring in her ears! Couldn't he have taken his handsome, dimpled smile somewhere else just this particular moment? He hadn't come to watch her other battles, so why should he start now? Why did he have to watch her humiliation? Hadn't he seen enough of it to date?

Gritting her teeth, she faced her opponent. She wouldn't let him distract her.

167

The master's shrill whistle pierced the air. Immediately, her opponent vanished. Liena groaned.

Instinct told her that her opponent would charge toward her, so if she didn't move, she'd be bowled over in a breath. To dodge left or right?

She wasn't counting on the sandy ground giving away her opponent's footsteps.

Her opponent came flying toward her left. Liena dodged out of the way, darting into the center of the arena and backing into the opposite wall. She watched those footsteps like a hawk, watching as they slowed to a stop.

Perhaps her opponent realized this, because she reappeared fully. Liena stared her down, feeling her spine prickling with Nianzu's eyes. But she wouldn't let herself be distracted.

"Attack!" came Nianzu's somewhat hushed voice.

Attack? She hesitated barely too long. The girl vanished the moment Liena's muscles jerked. Those footsteps came running so fast, she could hardly prepare herself.

It was time to attempt a thing or two she learned in her combat class. Her heart roaring in her chest, she charged toward her opponent, ducked under her guard, and dove for Ting's legs.

Something sharp hit her chin. Liena's head snapped back, and the crowd let out an "Ooh!" at the hard blow.

She saw stars.

That was a knee she had just taken to the face, she was pretty sure. But her adrenaline coursed hot, and once her muscles were in motion, she couldn't stop. Her hands closed around a slender ankle. Ting let out a cry as Liena caught hold of her, and her forward momentum sent her sprawling.

Liena, still hardly able to think from the pain in her face, did all she could to keep her grip on that kicking leg. She shifted her weight blindly, trying to pin the girl's knee to the ground.

The leg she held twisted, like the girl was shifting her weight from being belly-down to belly-up. Liena didn't know what to do now except hang on to that ankle.

"Qilin spawn!" shrieked the girl.

In her vigor to keep track of her opponent's feet, she forgot the girl had arms and fists too.

An unseen force landed a blow to her face.

Liena let out a little cry as it connected with her nose and cheek. She was sent reeling back and lost control of the girl's ankle. Her elbow hit the wall of the arena, but that pain was nothing compared to her smarting nose.

Her bleeding nose, she realized when she pulled her hand away from her face.

She cast about frantically for sign of her invisible opponent and caught sight of Nianzu's face twisted into a grimace.

She was knocked down from behind. Before she knew quite what was happening, Ting had wrestled Liena's arms behind her and trapped her in a hold she couldn't break.

At this point, Liena really didn't care. She just wanted her nose to stop hurting and bleeding so much. She wanted to stop eating sand and wanted to lift her face out of the pool of her own blood.

But she had to lay there until the master declared Ting the winner.

Then Ting let go, climbed off her, and gave her a hand up. Liena blinked sand out of her eyes and pressed her sleeve to her nose and mouth. She barely could get her balance enough to climb out of the arena.

Zedong was there at her side immediately, pressing a towel to her face. "Let's get to the medics," he said with a sigh.

She didn't want to look back and find Nianzu watching.

When she lifted her head, however, it wasn't the prince she saw. It was Master Gu turning on her heel and slipping away into the shadows.

CHAPTER
22

S EVERAL DAYS LATER, during her Magic Theory class, Liena perked up at the mention of the Yanzhao Technique. Finally—*someone* would explain to her what it was! Maybe she could understand why the prince had been so strange about it.

"The Yanzhao Technique is one of our oldest and most effective techniques for breaking spells, curses, and the like," said the master. "Depending on the spell or curse at hand, it may not always work. In many cases, however, it is worth an attempt if you or a comrade ends up in a compromising situation.

"Performing the technique is very simple. It only requires a kiss on the mouth. A common misconception is that this kiss must come from a true love, but that is simply a tale invented by bards and propagated through entertainment. In reality, any kiss on the mouth will work. It is not wholly uncommon to find yourself in situations needing to perform or receive the Yanzhou Technique."

Liena turned her scarlet face down to her notes.

It was that night, when Zedong was skipping their library study session yet again, that her studies were interrupted by a soft rap on her table. She jolted, whipping her head up from her parchments.

It was Nianzu, wearing a kind but surprisingly tentative, smile. He gestured to the mat next to her and said, "May I?"

She nodded, pretending to go back to studying and ignoring him, even though the tail of her eye was glued to his every movement.

It wasn't that she was mad at him—fathers, no! But she hadn't quite recovered enough pride to face him fully after he witnessed her horrendous arena battle. In the irrational part of her brain, it didn't matter that that fight was possibly her best so far, and that for a few heartbeats, she'd had an advantage. It was the worst of them all because Prince Nianzu had watched it.

"How's your face?" he asked.

She opened her mouth to say it was fine but opted just to look at him so he could see the bruises. To her surprise, he reached out and caught her jaw, tilting her face to one side. He let out a little hiss, grimacing.

Nothing like a handsome young man wincing at one's face.

"Ting has an arm," he said.

"And a knee," she replied.

His lips curled slightly in amusement, but his face was grimmer than she expected. He didn't release his grip; instead, his thumb gently tapped near the bruise on her nose and cheek, and the other on her chin.

"You're not going to improve at the rate you need to," he said eventually, his gaze moving up to her eyes.

She swallowed and twisted her face out of his grasp, settling her unfocused gaze on the parchments in front of her. "I know."

"Can I help you?"

She startled. A peek at him revealed he wasn't kidding, that he was serious. She let out a deep sigh and put down her quill. "I don't know how you can help."

"I'm good at combat, aren't I?"

She lifted a brow at him, and he flashed a grin. At the sight of that dimple, she was hit with a sudden wave of boldness. With a saucy smile, she replied, "You certainly are, Highness."

He narrowed his eyes at her. Playfully. She chewed her lip and glanced away.

"And I teach many of the younger students. I'm quite the qualified help if I do say so myself."

"But . . ." How could she phrase her question? *Why would you help someone like me?* She finally landed on: "When would you have time?"

His eyebrow lifted, and he leaned his elbow on the table, propping up his head with his hand and giving her a roguish smile. "What about . . . now?"

"Now?"

"Of course! Why not now?"

"Wherever would we practice? It's too late to practice in the pits, and we can't practice in the gardens—"

He flashed his dimple and cocked his head to one side. "I've got *just* the place. What do you say? Are you in?"

She hesitated, glancing back at her studies. But who was she fooling? It wasn't like her language arts class needed her attention nearly as much as her combat. With a deep breath, she peeked up at the prince and nodded.

"Splendid!" he said. "Follow me."

"We're going to get in trouble!" squeaked Liena.

"We'll be fine," said Nianzu. "Where's your cloak?"

"I don't have one."

"They didn't give you one when you came? Want to use mine?"

"Oh no—I'm not cold."

He reached out and his large hand closed over hers. She nearly leapt out of her skin at the contact and his startling warmth.

"You're not cold, my elbow!" he cried in a hushed voice. "Miss Ice Fingers."

She bit her lip as he swept his cloak around her shoulders. It was so large it pooled on the ground by her feet. He clasped it at her throat and then pulled the folds around her as though wrapping her up in a snug blanket. The garment nearly swallowed her whole.

"You'll warm up when we practice," he said with a grin.

"You're sure we won't get caught?"

"Absolutely positive."

"How are you positive?"

"Because I'm the prince."

Not even the shadows from the overhanging roof of the stables could hide how the moonlight caught on his mischievous smile. Not even her uncertainty could stop her own little smile from responding to his.

"Just follow my lead," he said.

She expected him to bend forward, perhaps reduce his tremendous size to sneak into the stable doors. Instead, he strode right out into the open, right into full view of the guards standing at attention.

They saluted the prince, standing straighter. Nianzu nodded at them and said, "I'll be back in a couple of hours. If students come looking for me, send them on their way. If masters come looking for me, just tell them that I'll be back in a couple of hours, no worry."

The guards nodded. One pointed at Liena creeping out of her hiding spot and said, "What about her?"

She stopped.

Nianzu glanced back at her and shrugged. "Eh, preferably don't tell about her. Not unless they specifically ask about her." To Liena, he said, "Is Fang going to come looking for you?"

She shook her head. Hoped the sudden pang she felt at his question wasn't evident on her face.

He returned to the guards again. "Should be no problem. Which of these horses are on their rest days?"

Liena waited, twisting her hands deep into the folds of Nianzu's enormous cloak as he talked to a stable boy and started to select two horses. He shot a quick glance at Liena. "Have you ridden before?"

She shook her head.

"Just one horse then," he said to the stable boy.

Her stomach immediately wound itself into an even tighter knot.

When the horse was saddled and ready, the prince turned and gestured her to come forward.

"I suppose we had different ideas of what breaking into the stables and stealing a horse looked like," she said dryly.

He grinned and mounted in one swift motion. It snorted in response, flicking its tail impatiently. He leaned down and offered a hand to her, and she hesitated at first.

"That is a very big horse," she said.

"Quit stalling."

With a deep breath, she placed her hand in his. "Now what?" she managed, glad suddenly for the darkness.

He shifted their grip so they held each other's forearms. "Foot in the stirrup—try not to trip on that cloak—and swing your leg over the saddle to mount up behind me. I'll give you a lift."

Liena was very surprised when they managed it on the first try. But her thoughts eddied from her brain when he said, "Wrap your arms around my waist to hold on. I'd rather you didn't fall off. I have no intention of adding to the collection of bruises on your face."

As if being pressed up to his back wasn't close enough!

But if she delayed, it would betray her fluster. So, squeezing her eyes shut tightly, she slid her arms around his midsection and braced herself. At first, she held on because His Highness commanded it. When they left the stables, however, she held on for dear life.

"Do you have to go so fast?" she said into his shoulder.

She felt rather than heard his chuckle rumbling through his back and into her chest.

"We aren't even cantering, Liena."

"Oh." She wasn't sure what a canter was, but apparently it wasn't very fast.

She held on tighter as they rode out of the Academy complex, terrified that masters would come chasing after them at any moment and demand they return to their dormitories. They didn't, and soon thrill swallowed up her fear as they were enveloped in the winding darkness of the Suguan streets. Her first time free of the Academy since she'd come here!

The city was so much larger than she realized, and quiet at this time of night. They came across a few patrolling wardens that Nianzu pointed out.

"Many graduates become wardens," he said. "Protectors of our cities and villages."

She knew what a warden was. They had them back even in her home village. But she didn't say anything, content to listen to his low voice carried along in the cold breeze. Lanterns hung outside empty market stalls, bright against the night. Everything was deep blackness and warm yellow. She twisted around to see the mountain rising behind them, casting the Academy into deeper shadow.

Clearly, the prince was very familiar with this route. He didn't stop to agonize over which street to take. He simply knew, and around them, the fine homes near the palace corridor drifted into humbler abodes. Further, and the scent of the ocean grew stronger. She smelled salt and brine strung on the wind.

It was beautiful.

She gasped when she realized where they were going. "Is that the beach?"

"Sure is. What do you think about a nice oceanside training session?"

She hadn't meant to squeal. Perhaps it was the wind, or the wild bit of rule-breaking rebellion burning in her blood, or the heat of his cloak around her shoulders and the warmth radiating from his back. But squeal she did, and the moment Nianzu helped her dismount, she was racing toward the waterfront. She kicked off her shoes, letting them go flying behind her, and unclasped the cloak too.

She shrieked the moment the icy waters washed up on her bare toes. "Cold! Cold!"

Nianzu laughed. When she glanced back, he was tethering their horse to a tree on the edge of the beach. He kept grinning as he removed his own shoes and picked up his cloak from the sand and slung it over the saddle.

"Oops! Sorry! I hope I didn't—" she started to say, robes hiked up around her calves.

"You'd better get ready," said Nianzu with a playfully stern expression on his face. He cracked his knuckles, widened his stance, and lifted up both hands toward her. "We're not wasting time."

Her eyes went wide and she skittered away from the waterfront. "Wait, but I'm not ready!"

He'd already charged. And then she was staring up at a starry sky, lying in a bed of sand.

"Your enemies won't wait until you're ready," Nianzu was saying, standing over her. "You have to be ready, even when you're not ready."

She glared at him.

"Up!" he said. "The longer you delay, the more advantage you give me. I could have killed you so many times by now."

She stared up at him, and something snapped inside her. So much pent-up frustration from these last few months, from all her failures, from being so behind, from being humiliated so many times—it all came bursting for release.

Did it matter that she was behind? That she had failed so often before now?

No, it didn't.

Failure wasn't going to be her story.

She wasn't giving up on arena battles. She wasn't going to become like Zedong, who went into his battles believing he'd already lost. No, she hadn't lost until she *lost*. Until that moment, she could win.

She rolled up, got her feet under her, and faced the prince.

"Neutralize your stance," Nianzu ordered. "I can tell from how your feet are positioned that you will dodge right if I come for you."

What had he said about enemies not waiting until she was ready? She darted forward.

Nianzu yelped, dodged, and flipped her onto her back in a flash. But as she lay in the dirt, she saw his raised eyebrows, his parted lips. She was up before his face split into a grin.

"Good! Excellent use of surprise! Now you need to learn how to leverage that surprise on someone of my size. Do you know what one of your biggest weapons is against me?"

"Um . . . my brain?"

He snorted. "Well, I suppose yes, if you can outsmart me. What I *meant*, however, was your leg. My arms are longer than yours, so I can land a punch on you at a distance that you can't even come close to me. You can use your leg to bridge that distance, to land a kick at me that will keep me further away from punching you in the face. Your goal is to keep your distance and keep moving."

Back and forth, he charged and showed her how to better block, duck, and stay out of his range. Instructed her on offensive techniques that required speed and surprise, that would give her leverage over a stronger opponent.

"Your enemies will force you into a defensive position, and will back you into a hard spot," he said, charging at her so she stumbled backward into the frigid ocean.

She gasped at the cold, and before she knew it, she was tripping over her own feet. She flailed her arms, desperately trying to regain her balance before she plunged into the icy waves.

"Careful!" the prince said, catching her around the waist.

Her fall stopped, the tips of her hair touching the water. And suddenly, she was staring up at Nianzu's face framed by starlight, held suspended over the water by his arms. Her feet froze in the water, but she hardly noticed.

He was staring at her too, his mouth open and all trace of stern instruction gone. His brow pinched slightly as his eyes roved over her face. They came to lock on her eyes, their dark depths seeming to swallow her whole.

"You are . . ." he started to breathe.

Her mouth went dry, her own eyes trailing down to his lips. She thought . . . No, she couldn't think. She could only wait and shiver, wrapped in his arms and staring up at him, for what the Prince of Zheninghai might do or say next.

He closed his eyes, breaking their contact, and gave his head a little shake. "You are . . . *so dead*. I could have stabbed you here"—He shoved a pretend knife into her ribs, all the way until his fist bumped her side—"or here." This next slice was across her neck. "I could have stabbed you straight in the chest. Or, if I'd held a knife in my other hand—"

She pushed out of his arms and stumbled to shore on numb feet. She flashed him her driest smile. "Thank you, Highness, for not butchering me."

When he met her eyes, his brow was knit and his eyes seemed made of glass, too reflective in the night. He trudged out of the water, ignoring the wet trail of his robes as he came and sat on the sand. He gestured to the spot next to him. "Will you sit with me?"

Why did he ask that? He could simply order her, and she would do it.

She sat by way of answer.

He was quiet, staring out at the expanse of the ocean. Liena tried to find the point the water blended with the night sky in the distance, but it all melted into darkness. She drew her knees up to her chest and wrapped her arms around them, glad for the exertion, otherwise her entire body would be as frozen as her toes.

"Liena . . ." he started to say, then trailed off, as if he wasn't sure where he intended to go.

"Yes?"

He turned to look at her, and what she saw in his face wasn't the bright and cheery prince who strode around the Academy like he owned the place. He looked older, more worn, and . . . *heavier*. He glanced away and sighed. "Sometimes I just don't think I can do it."

She waited. And waited.

Finally, she whispered, "Do what?"

"Be emperor."

"Oh."

She couldn't fault him for feeling that way. Not one bit. At the same time, when she looked at him, she saw the glimpse in her last vision. Of him—tall, mighty, firm, with the magnitude of an emperor. And from what she'd heard and seen, his magic was like none other.

A magic that could single-handedly destroy armies.

"Why?" she asked softly. "Why don't you think you can do it?"

He was silent for a few moments, before chuckling ruefully. "I just . . . I see my father. I see who he is, how he is so . . ." He shook his head again. "And here I am, stealing a stable horse for a jaunt down to the beach with a girl."

Why did that make her flush? She stole a glance at him, and didn't think these feelings of inadequacy came from this particular jaunt to the beach.

"When I first arrived," she said, "you were called out of class to visit the Glorious Emperor."

It was a question, even though it was a statement.

"You saw that?"

She nodded.

He gave another rueful chuckle and sighed, before evading her question. "I think I noticed you, was drawn to you at first because when I saw you . . . In some ways, I felt like I was looking at myself. Watching you work so hard, even though you were almost predetermined to fail. Like that combat class when I had you pinned. Sometimes, that's how I feel about being emperor. Like none of this will truly prepare me for it, and that nothing *could* prepare me for it. I suppose I feel like I'm being set up to fall on my face. Not unlike what I just did to you tonight. I knew you weren't going to beat me, but that didn't stop you from trying, now did it?"

He was looking at her now. She could only chew on her lip and tighten her arms around her knees.

When the silence persisted, Liena said, "One might call me delusional."

"Or perhaps just the sort of thing I needed to see in my life."

She couldn't look at him. Didn't dare look at him.

"I don't think you need to worry too much about being a good emperor," she said quietly. "Not that it matters at all what I see—"

"What do you see, Liena?"

She started to twist toward him, to glare at him for fishing for compliments. But when she met his gaze, she saw a vulnerability shining there. As if he truly didn't know what she thought of him. She frowned.

She couldn't very well tell him *exactly* what she saw, now could she? At least handsomeness was no indication about the sort of ruler one might be. She wasn't obligated to share that little tidbit.

"You aren't arrogant," she started.

He snorted.

"I mean it! The fact that you would choose to associate with someone like me speaks to your humility, which is an often-overlooked trait in a leader." Not that she had any idea what she was talking about, but Pa had said something like that before, and it made sense to her.

"Someone like you?" He looked genuinely puzzled.

Did he expect her to spell out for him that she was a lowborn, half-barbarian millet farmer with weak, unpredictable magic? Instead of answering, she continued. "You have a good and kind heart, but you keep your standards high. For people, for me, for the Academy. You don't leave the work to everyone else—"

She stopped because he had scooted closer. And he was grinning.

"What?" she snapped, arching away from him.

"I wasn't expecting you to patch up my ego so thoroughly."

"Patch up? I was only answering—"

He interrupted her. "I don't think I've ever told you this, but I like listening to your voice. Your accent is very . . . I like it."

Her face flushed crimson, and it was so hot she could have believed the prince held his dancing fire up to her cheeks. No, he certainly had never told her that. She ducked her head.

"What is that necklace you always wear?" he asked, a smile still in his voice.

Her fingers instinctively went to grasp the beads. "My necklace?"

"You touch it when you're nervous. Makes me think it's important to you."

"Oh," she said lamely. "I didn't realize it was so obvious."

"Don't blush so; it's nothing to be embarrassed about. May I see it?"

She unclasped it and handed it over without protest. Anything to get his eyes off her red cheeks. How could he tell that they were flushed? It was so dark! This was absolutely unfair.

Nianzu took the necklace, and it looked so tiny in his large hands. He fingered the beads, then squinted and brought it closer to his face. "Is this a lotus? For your name?"

She nodded.

"Who gave it to you?"

"My family." Technically Lao Lao, but it was Pa's money that she'd spent, and it was Ma's fault they all went to the market together, so Liena figured it was fair enough to call it a family effort.

He handed it back. "Do you miss them?"

"Every day."

"When will you see them again?"

She shrugged, hoping that movement disguised the sudden emotion clogging her throat and filling her eyes.

The prince sat back, staring at the ocean. "You don't have enough tangus for the return journey?"

She shook her head, ducking her head once more.

He sniffed. "At least that is easily remedied. Would you like to go during the Academy's off-season? In a few months?"

She blinked through tear-studded lashes at him. "What?"

His eyebrow lifted and he sighed as he leaned back until he was laying on the sand, hands clasped under his head and one knee bent. "One of the advantages to being the future emperor is that I have a rather significant coffer to my name. And it's not like I have much to spend it on."

She turned toward him so sharply he half-flinched. "No, you cannot! I couldn't ask it of you. My parents always taught me to not be in debt to anyone, and I know they would certainly panic if I'd indebted myself to the Crown Prince!"

"What? You think I would ask for repayment from you? Truly, Liena, you wound me." He pressed a hand over his heart, and she rolled her eyes before she could remember that he was *the prince*.

"I won't ask for something I cannot pay for," she replied.

"You're not asking. I'm giving. Shall you not receive my generosity?"

How could she explain the sort of pride of poor people? That they took pride in having little—or having nothing—because that little was provided by themselves? That they took pride in knowing that they depended on no one?

There was little dignity as it was in being poor. But becoming a charity case meant humbling oneself, admitting they needed another's help. It didn't make complete sense, but for someone with no dignity, one had to hang on to those bare scraps.

She shook her head. "You are kind, Highness, but—"

He rolled into a sitting position, planting a hand on the ground between them and leaning closer. Why did he keep coming close to her? It made no sense.

It was almost as if he *wanted* to be close to her.

"Then I'll make a deal with you," he said, smirking. "I will give you the funds for your journey home *if* you agree to indulge me every night for the next two weeks and train with me here."

"*Every* night?"

His grin went lopsided. "I drive a hard bargain."

"But what about exams? What if I need to study?"

"Then you owe me another night later."

She scowled at him. He lifted a brow.

"And here I was, thinking you liked being around me. Apparently my presence is more offensive than I originally thought."

She tried to glare at him, but couldn't keep a straight face. She twisted away from him, hiding the way her mouth melted into a grin. "I don't understand you, Your Highness."

"Better enjoy my mysteriousness now while it lasts. Soon you'll think me a demented dragon."

She whirled toward him. "I will not! Why would you ever—"

He caught her wrists, grinning. And to her own surprise, she didn't resist him. In fact, she wouldn't resist him if he drew her even closer.

"We ought to head back," he said.

"Wait!" she said, more vehemently than she intended.

He stopped, let go of her wrists. Something gleamed in his eyes, like the stars in the midnight sky above them. "Yes?"

Maybe she shouldn't ask this question. Maybe she should let it go. But it had been plaguing her ever since the first time he'd studied with her, and after trailing Zedong, she wasn't willing to let this opportunity slide. She *needed* to know her friend was safe.

"The look on your face is making me nervous," said Nianzu.

"Tell me about black magic," Liena blurted.

He stared at her, a mix of horror and shock on his face. She'd caught him off guard, enough that when he tried to school his face into neutral bewilderment, she wouldn't accept it.

"When we were talking about Magic Theory classes, you said they teach everything *except* something. You cut yourself off. You were talking about black magic."

"Liena, don't—"

"I know you don't want to tell me. But I need to know."

His eyes nearly burned straight through her. "Why do you need to know?"

She stopped, her tongue catching. If she told Nianzu about her suspicion, what would happen to Zedong? She didn't even know the penalty for wielding black magic. Somehow, she knew it was a price no one would want to pay.

"You mentioned it," she said helplessly. "You said it wasn't covered in our class. I'm just . . . curious."

He didn't buy it. Not for one second. The look he gave her was utter skepticism.

"Do you know someone who is using black magic?" he asked, his tone dark and serious.

She shook her head, staring up at him, silently pleading with him. There was nothing she could say to convince him, so saying nothing was her only hope. She held her breath.

He let out a sigh, jaw working as he shifted his gaze to the ocean. "Serves me right for being an idiot and letting that slip."

She waited, hoping he couldn't hear her thumping heart.

"I will tell you under one condition and one condition only, that you never, *ever* speak of this to anyone. Because it's illegal and I don't want you getting into trouble over it."

She nodded.

"Promise me?" he said sternly.

Why did making promises to Nianzu feel like betraying Zedong? Even though she did it to protect her friend? She did it anyway. "Promise."

185

Another sigh and a moment of hesitation later, Nianzu began. "The real name of black magic is Wungfao, but no one calls it that. It's illegal because it's very dangerous."

"Dangerous?" She tried to keep the panic out of her voice but couldn't tell if the prince was fooled. "How is it dangerous?"

"Well, it's not something you're born with. It's potions and spells and the like. Dark stuff. But the reason it's called black magic is—well, there's darkness in all of us, right? We're none of us all good and noble. What makes black magic so dangerous is that it essentially feeds on our own darkness. It brings it out, magnifies it. It makes our faults tenfold, and it *shows* us those faults. Black magic is volatile, unpredictable, because how it manifests is different person to person, depending on their own sins and evil tendencies. It often drives people mad. After all, isn't life a game of us pretending we're not as bad as we truly are? Once you're faced with the depths of your own depravity, can you even hope to not lose your mind?

"*That,*" finished the prince, "is why it's dangerous and illegal."

"Oh," she said.

Nianzu was watching her carefully, and she desperately hoped none of her sudden, irrational fears showed on her face.

"This isn't taught at the Academy," she said, more of a question than a statement.

"Of course not. It's taught *nowhere.* Nowhere except some dusty old tomes that are hidden away from the students. Now, if your curiosity is sated, may we head back? Or do you have any other empire secrets you would like me to divulge?"

The bite in those words was subtle, but sharp. She flinched slightly, tilting her head away as she mumbled, "Forgive me, Highness, I shouldn't have—"

"That was cruel of me," said Nianzu quickly, shaking his head. He stood up, dusted sand off his robes, and offered her a hand. "It was my own fault for letting it slip, and I shouldn't begrudge you for that. Forgive me?"

By way of answer, she placed her hand in his, letting him draw her to her feet.

"I know many things that could hurt many people," he said as they walked back to the horse. "Your manner puts me at ease, and if I dared, I'd tell you everything that weighs on my mind. Things like black magic, and my father's attempts to keep it contained. But I'd never forgive myself if unburdening myself put you at risk. In time, perhaps I can share more with you."

In time? What was that supposed to mean? In time, he would go on to be emperor, and she would graduate late and be sent off to an appointment in some far corner of the empire. If she was lucky enough to even get an appointment. She scooped her shoes up out of the sand, dumping them upside-down to empty them.

Nianzu mounted the horse, then leaned down and gripped her forearm. "Let's get you back to the Academy. You look like you're going to fall asleep standing up."

CHAPTER
23

"HEY, YOU NEED to wake up."

Someone was poking her hands. The entire world was groggy, like she was trying to work her way through a vat of oil. She groaned. That insistent voice kept plucking at her awareness, but all she could think about was how warm and tired she was.

"Liena."

"Huh?" she tilted her face up, still not opening her eyes.

"We're almost back to the Academy. You need to wake up."

"Academy?"

"Sit up and open your eyes."

She obeyed, albeit very slowly and with another series of groans. It took her a moment to register that she was atop a horse, leaning against Nianzu's back, her arms wrapped around his waist, and his cloak about her shoulders.

"Oh!" she said. "Forgive me, I—"

He craned his neck back to say, "It's late and we've both had a long day."

She nodded, using every last bit of her strength not to lean forward again. They arrived back at the stables within a few minutes, and Nianzu helped her dismount before following and handing off the reins to the stable hands and thanking the guards.

Then he turned toward her and held out his hand. "My cloak, if you don't mind. I'd let you keep it, but . . . it might be conspicuous."

She glanced down at the garment's edges trailing on straw and nodded. But that didn't make her any less regretful to undo the clasp and hand its warmth back to him. She tried not to shiver too obviously.

"Follow me," he whispered, and darted out into the night.

She followed, still slowly waking up. Unlike when he approached the stables, Nianzu kept his back hunched, and his eyes alerted to the stillness of the Academy. She kept close to him, attempting to stay in his shadow.

He slipped onto one of the porticos, made for the nearest door, and beckoned her inside. She immediately recognized the corridor that led to the library. Not too far down was where it branched off toward the girls' dormitories.

Nianzu slid into the shadow of a pillar, taking her elbow and drawing her in close. "This," he said with a mischievous glimmer in his eye, "is what I like to call Operation Phoenix Feather. Get back to the dorms without being caught."

"Do you do Operation Phoenix Feather often?"

A lopsided grin was his only answer. She huffed a silent chuckle. Funny how the world didn't seem quite as cold as it had before.

"Operation *duck!*" Nianzu hissed suddenly, dragging her with him from behind the pillar into an empty classroom. He slid around the back of the door and pulled her into the cramped space after him.

"What?" she demanded.

He was a great big lump of shadow, but she could still see how he lifted a finger to his lips. His mouth quirked. She tried to stifle a giggle.

Her giggle vanished the moment she heard footsteps. Nianzu tensed as those steps came closer. He shifted his stance, planting one forearm on the wall as though to make the two of them take up less space. His attention was fixed on the crack in the door, the very barest hint of light catching on the severe cut of his jaw above her.

The footsteps continued past them.

She sagged, realizing only now how tense she had grown. Nianzu's head swiveled down to her. She caught a flash of teeth in the dark.

"See?" his low voice rumbled. "Operation Phoenix Feather is always loads of fun."

It was dark—too dark to see clearly, but she saw when the light in his eyes shifted as he stared down at her. She was suddenly painfully aware of how close they were, how dark it was, and how he looked at her. They weren't even touching, but her skin flamed with the mere possibility.

He lifted one hand, and for a gloriously terrifying moment, she thought he would touch her face. Trail the rounded edge of his knuckle down the curve of her cheek in a gentle caress. But at the last second, he planted his hand on the wall instead, encasing her in the space between his arms.

If she tilted her chin up, would he kiss her? Was she brave enough to find out?

Then—voices.

She tensed, glancing up at Nianzu with a small smile. He responded by pressing a finger to his lips as he tried not to grin.

Who would have thought the Crown Prince of Zheninghai was so fun-loving? To her dying day, she would be glad she had an opportunity to participate in his games. Nothing would come of this . . . infatuation of hers. That may or may not be one-sided. But for now? Now it sent her heart racing, her blood thrilling, and her mind spinning. And then, one day, when she settled down with some good, nobody young man to build a life, she would remember these moments.

These moments when she came alive, when her whole being sparked with heady excitement.

The voices grew louder, and when Nianzu grinned and cupped his ear to pantomime eavesdropping, she nearly let out an exposing snicker. And when he noticed and immediately covered her mouth with one of his huge hands—giving a pretend rebuking glare—she burst into a blush that swept to her toes.

"What? I wouldn't," said one of the voices. A girl Liena didn't recognize.

"You wouldn't?" the other girl gasped.

"Absolutely not! The Crown Prince is going to have a harem full of women. He may be handsome and smart and powerful and whatever else, but I don't want to be one of the hundreds competing for his attention."

Nianzu's hand over her mouth tensed, then slid away. But the voices continued.

"Even if he was the *emperor*?"

"Even then."

"Oh, I would! I don't care if I'm one in a thousand. If he would give me even a fraction of his attention, I'd die happy."

"And then you get to watch him summon all the other beautiful women the rest of the time?" the first girl scoffed.

"It would be worth it."

"It would be torture."

The voices faded away, disappearing around a bend in the hallway toward the girls' dormitories. They left a gaping chasm in their wake, one that stretched between Liena's suddenly painfully throbbing throat and Nianzu's averted gaze.

The silence was so thick she couldn't swallow, could hear the racing and throbbing of her own pitiful, *stupid* heart. They didn't move, but the space between them widened with every halted breath.

She stared at the crack in the door, willing herself not to cry, not to give in to the emptiness filling her gut and spreading through her limbs. She felt the moment his eyes finally returned to her face.

She didn't have enough courage to meet those eyes.

Nianzu pushed back, turning away from her and letting the cold air wash over the exposed skin and prickling hairs of her arms, hands, face, neck—places that had been so *hot* only a few heartbeats ago.

She stepped out of the corner. Silently, she tried to skitter around the door and make her escape from the deafening stillness between them. His voice made her freeze on the threshold.

"Liena . . . I'm not my father."

Her heart soared with frenzied hope. He wasn't his father; he wouldn't have hundreds of women at his beck and call. He would . . .

He would, what? Devote his life and self wholly to her, a low-magic seer, half-barbarian farm girl? She squashed those stupid, impractical, *idiotic* notions. She summoned every ounce of practicality, of indifference, to say, "Don't you want to be?"

He didn't answer.

Who was she fooling? *Only herself.*

She slipped into the hallway beyond and fled away from the prince.

The next day, when Liena was practicing with Zedong in the pits, a master stopped by and held out a long, heavy garment to her.

"His Highness said you had no cloak."

CHAPTER
24

THINGS WERE DIFFERENT between her and Nianzu the remainder of their beach practice sessions. No sitting by the shore and talking. Everything was much more professional, distant, and transactional.

It was her fault.

She was the one who had allowed herself to be too friendly, too easy around him. She had forgotten her place and was determined to never forget it again. With each practice, he was progressively harder on her, to the point that it became her goal to not break down into tears.

It didn't matter if she fell on her face a dozen times. So long as there were no tears, it was a success.

She hadn't failed. Not in his presence, at least, for the entire duration of their beach practices. That didn't mean she didn't cry later as she was falling asleep.

When the Festival of New Lights happened in the middle of winter, classes were suspended for the week. Liena had never been to a festival like this one, one that involved an entire *city*, filling the streets of Suguan with parades, dragon dances, paper lantern making, and sweet, hardened candy. Hundreds of families came to the Academy to see their children, families from all over Zheninghai. Families apparently wealthy enough to afford the travel.

Liena's family, of course, was not one of them.

She stayed in the library most of the week, trying to get ahead in her classes as much as she could. When homesickness stabbed her heart, she reminded herself that Nianzu promised her a trip home in the off-season. There was no need for tears now. She would see them later.

Besides, everything was vastly quieter in the Academy when all the students were off celebrating. It was far more productive studying.

Zedong eventually dragged her out to watch the lantern ceremony, and Liena begrudgingly admitted that she was very glad he did so. Despite being crammed like sardines in a barrel in the crowd, they managed to get a clear view of the balcony that the royal family released their lantern from, followed by everyone else in the city releasing theirs.

It was magic.

A dark sky full of thousands of flickering candles, illuminating the city and reflecting on the ocean. But what captured her awe the most was not the lantern release, but the royal family.

She'd never seen the Glorious Emperor, and he was even more glorious and resplendent than she'd ever dreamed. He looked rather like Prince Nianzu, and his golden robes reflected the light of the lanterns. He was so stern, so serious. She felt like a tiny grasshopper, standing in that crowd watching.

The prince was there too, standing in front of a dozen other younger siblings. It was the only time she'd seen him all week. He was as tall as his father, wearing white and golden robes that were second only to his father's. Looking at him then, she never would have guessed how often he smiled. He looked almost like he had never smiled in his life, standing up there so solemn. But he looked every inch the Crown Prince, every inch the future mighty Glorious Emperor.

Perhaps that was the moment she realized how different their worlds truly were.

It was easy to forget what it meant that he was the Crown Prince.

"Always scribbling away."

Liena jerked her head up, instinctively smashing a textbook on top of what she'd been writing. More characters. She should be studying Magic Theory instead.

Nianzu's eyes flicked from her face to the textbook, then back up to her face. His smile was kind, but these days it was more tentative. As though he wasn't quite sure she would smile back.

A lump formed in her throat. She looked down and began playing with the end of the quill. She gave him a smile but made sure she wasn't looking at him when she did. "Highness," she said. "You startled me."

"A good warrior—"

"—never startles," she finished for him, catching herself too late.

He grinned at that. "Do you want to meet with me first thing tomorrow to go over tips for the Hunt?"

She did want to. Far more than she wanted to let show. But she shook her head ruefully. "Zedong and I are meeting to practice first thing tomorrow."

Was that disappointment on his face? She wasn't sure. He shrugged.

"Zedong can probably answer most of your questions. He'll know a little bit of the strategy too. If you change your mind, though, I'll be in the pits training. You can always interrupt me."

This time, she couldn't help but smile at him. "Thank you."

"I'd stay to study, but I can't tonight. I guess I'll see you at the Hunt, if not sooner?"

"See you then," she said with another smile.

He looked around, as though trying to leave, but like he had something else to say. She didn't know, didn't want to jump to conclusions.

Finally, he gave a little wave, turned and left.

Liena was walking between classes the next day when she spied the prince's head poking out over the rest of the students. His classes weren't near this wing, were they? She didn't remember seeing him before between these classes. Her pulse quickened, even as she ducked her head. She didn't think he'd seen her, and perhaps she could slip on past him easily enough—

He navigated the crowd, coming straight toward her. But he wasn't looking at her. In fact, he strode right past her. Relief mingled with disappointment in a combination that sent her stomach swooping.

Something caught her hand. Something very, very hot.

It was only for a split second that Nianzu's hand gripped hers.

She was so shocked to her core that she almost stopped moving. It took everything in her to not let her jaw drop open and crane her neck around to watch him vanish into the crowd.

Perhaps the biggest surprise of all was realizing that her hand wasn't empty.

She fisted her hand around what felt like a small rock and hurried to her next class. Only once she was safely seated, with all her study materials set out on her desk, did she open her palm and see what Nianzu had slipped to her.

It was a wooden bead.

Bewilderment, mixed with a gnawing suspicion, hit her. Was this for her necklace? Did he want her to wear it? Brow furrowed, she rolled it over in her palm.

MAIDEN OF CANDLELIGHT AND LOTUSES

There, painted on the bead's front, instead of a lotus like the one she already had, was a tongue of fire.

CHAPTER
25

"THERE ARE DIFFERENT approaches to the Hunts," said Zedong the next morning as they sparred in the pits. "Some people try for glory, and others for survival."

Liena's blow lost its momentum, and Zedong easily evaded her. "Survival?"

"Of course. That's what happened to one of the students two years ago. I don't think he quite knew what his goal was, but let's just say that he got a little too close to a *mó guǐ* he didn't have the capacity to kill. So it ate him. Don't give me that look like you're going to pass out!"

She blinked, forcing her eyes into focus. "Pass out? I'm not going to pass out!"

Her feet wobbled uncertainly. She glanced to the opposite end of the pits where Nianzu was practicing with a master.

Zedong sighed, setting down his wooden sword. He plopped down on the ground, hooking his elbows around his bent knees. "I'm sick of these pits."

She stayed on her feet, practicing the different sword movements Nianzu had taught her. "What does that have to do with the Hunt?" she asked.

"It has to do with the Hunt because I'm sick of *all* of the Academy."

She paused her parry, side-glancing at him. "It does get exhausting. But you're only a few years from graduation."

"Can't you stop studying or practicing for five seconds? You're giving me a headache."

She stopped and fixed a full glare on him. Dropping her weapon, she sat beside him, breathing hard from the exertion. "What's the matter?"

Zedong shook his head, looking away from her. "Nothing's *wrong*. Aren't I allowed to be discontent once in a while? All this study stuff is just grating. All the students who have strong magic get to spend more of their time honing their magic, while we just have to make sure we have memorized our dynasty emperors in the proper order and learn so much stupid fighting stuff."

"Well, if our magic doesn't require honing—"

He snorted. "You say that like it's a good thing."

She drew in a deep breath between her teeth. Apparently Zedong was in one of his moods. She would rather tell him to quit this and get back to practicing, but instead she sat and waited. He had been patient with her when she first arrived, so she would be patient with him.

"How are lessons going with Master Gu?" she asked instead of answering him.

He snorted again. Why did he keep snorting?

"Bad?" she asked, frowning.

"I can't very well explain how they're going, now can I?"

"You can't? Why not?"

"Because you don't know anything."

She glared at him. "You're doing it again. You're angry about something and you're taking it out on me."

"Because you don't *understand* anything!"

"Then help me understand! You've given me no information to understand! You're acting like these masters here, who say to go do this and such, and then they don't tell you how to do it."

"I am *not* like these masters."

She drew back from the vehemence in his tone. "Zedong, listen, you—"

"I *what*?" he snapped, fully facing her. Something flared in his eyes, something that she could have sworn was blue, even though his eyes were dark. But it was gone, and he was staring at her with the passion of a blazing fire. "Liena, of all people, you should understand."

He reached out to her, one hand going to cover hers in the dirt. She jerked back, both surprised and frustrated.

"Understand *what*?" she demanded. Her traitorous eyes glanced toward Nianzu, just in time to catch him averting his eyes from her, a frown on his face. She resisted the urge to scoot further away from Zedong.

He didn't answer, just kept staring at her in a way that made her feel like his soul burned hotter than the prince's fire, and that it was a blaze that would consume all in its path. Where was the awkward friend she'd met on her first day? Who was this Zedong before her?

She wasn't about to give up on him. But until he started talking rationally, there was nothing she could understand and nothing she could do to help besides be here.

"Why don't we do wax wood staffs?" Liena said, standing up and brushing her robes off. She didn't realize she was trembling until she went to the rack and picked one up. Zedong growled behind her, but didn't protest when she handed him a staff.

They practiced in silence until breakfast, and he told her nothing else about the Hunt.

Maybe she would be able to find Nianzu at supper? Or even a little bit before the Hunt? She still had *quite* a long list of questions, and she had no intention of being a snack for a *mó guǐ* tonight.

Nianzu was busy through supper and up until the Hunt.

He'd said that she could interrupt him at any time, and she believed him, but he was always surrounded by people! Was she supposed to elbow her way through them only to ask the Crown Prince—the future emperor—for the basics of how the Hunt was to work, as if there was no one else she could ask?

She resorted to asking Jia.

"Oh, it's basically just where they put you in the middle of the wilderness and tell you to hunt *mó guǐ*," said Jia. "Most people don't *actually* hunt. Instead of treating it like the Hunt, they seem to treat it like the Hide."

She snickered, and Liena's eyebrows raised as she watched the girl fight to keep a straight face through her own joke.

"But do students die very often?"

"Oh no. There aren't very many *mó guǐ* in the area. They don't take you that far out, and there are masters patrolling the area, but usually there's one or two accidents every few years. Though, now that I think of it, we've had a rather dismal streak the last three years."

Wonderful. Absolutely wonderful.

"The students that have been killed, are they usually hiding or hunting?" she asked.

"Usually hunting. But I do remember one who was hiding. Hid in a cave right next to a nest of dragon eggs. The idiot!"

"So the goal is to survive to the end of the night?"

"And kill a *mó guǐ*! The students who kill a *mó guǐ* are usually final year students, and at the end of the year, they get celebrated with everyone during Graduation festival, even if they're not graduating. It's a high honor."

Liena took in a deep breath and forced a smile. "Thank you. I am grateful for your help."

"Any time!" said the girl before bouncing off to the dormitories.

The cart bounced beneath her, rattling her joints and jostling her brain. She gripped the edge, trying to avoid falling over in front of the other students. It seemed like she was the only one struggling; everyone else seemed a balance extraordinaire. Her balance had improved in leaps and bounds since coming to the Academy, but she still couldn't compare to her peers.

It didn't help that she was weighed down with unfamiliar weapons.

Some of the faces in this cart were familiar. She recognized Na, one of the earth-wielders. The evanescer, Shi Mu, whom Zedong had explained was destined to marry the girl he sat next to, Nuan, because she was also an evanescer. To keep the bloodline pure. It was yet another reminder of why it was so ridiculous that Liena had futilely tried to maneuver herself into the same cart as the prince. He wound up in a cart three ahead of theirs, and she couldn't see him.

Of course, Zedong was next to her. Tonight, he was quiet, despite how his eyes sparked in the night.

In the cart behind them, she saw Kang Lei. Her hair blew in the wind, her beautiful face set like some fearsome warrior maiden. Shu was in that cart too, though her beauty couldn't compare to Lei's. Not that beauty mattered a goat sneeze.

"How far out are we going?" she whispered to Zedong.

"Eh, probably just a little farther. Got to go where we'd actually run into *mó guǐ*."

If she didn't know better, she would have thought he was excited.

"You don't seem afraid," she said.

"Pfft! Afraid? Why would I be afraid?"

She wasn't sure why that made her smile, but it did. In response, Zedong flashed her a cocky grin and folded his arms across his chest.

"If you're afraid," he said, leaning a little closer, "you can just stay by me."

"I probably will," she answered as she fixed her gaze forward. "You're just hiding, right?"

"Hiding?" he scoffed. "Of course not! I'm hunting this year."

Her knuckles whitened as her grip on the cart's edge turned frantic. "Wait, you're hunting? But—but you and I are no good at fighting! If we can't beat other students, how can we beat a monster?"

"You forgot that I *did* win my last arena battle."

How could she point out that that was the only arena battle he'd won this year? And it was against someone younger than him? There wasn't a way to point it out without offending him, so she said nothing, only swallowing thickly.

If she didn't have to cling to the railing so tightly, she might have touched the beaded necklace around her throat. Especially the new bead that rested on the cord now, its little painted flame turned inside.

"Off!" cried the master driving the cart.

Liena's heart immediately leapt into her throat, and she froze as the other students climbed out of the cart and dropped to the ground. She scanned the gathering group of students, found Nianzu's tall form bent in conversation with a few others.

Maybe she could ask to stay close to him?

But he would be hunting too, wouldn't he? Besides, she wasn't sure she could forgive herself if she left Zedong alone and something bad happened to him.

"Come on," said Zedong, poking her shoulder. "You don't have to be worried. I'll keep you safe."

She met his gaze and paused as she studied those dark irises. He meant it—and he believed it, that he could protect her. He offered her a hand down from the cart. With one last glance over her shoulder at Nianzu, she accepted and hopped down.

The masters herded the students into one large group, shouted a few last minute, basic instructions about how far they could go, to be especially wary of fox spirits, and so forth.

With a piercing whistle, the Hunt was begun.

Before Liena could think, Zedong grabbed her hand and started pulling her off in one direction, deeper into the wilderness as the other students dispersed around them. She glanced back to see Nianzu heading another way. He seemed to be looking around the group of students as he went.

Was he looking for her? It didn't matter. What *did* matter was—

"Zedong! Where are we going?"

"To the West side! That's where more monsters are!"

"But I don't *want* to find any monsters!"

"Aw stop being so scared. Just keep your eyes open. I'll do all the fighting."

She was starting to feel worse and worse about this situation. This seemed the exact sort of way to become a warning for the next round of students. But she couldn't leave Zedong now, and with each step, he dragged them further into the wilderness until she couldn't tell right from left and up from down.

It was so dark.

It was like the Night Games, but *far* more terrifying.

"I've heard finding a water source is a great way to find *mó guǐ*," whispered Zedong, tugging her closer to his side. "They need to drink, after all. I was looking at some maps earlier today, planning, and there's this stream that runs through this part of the wilderness. If we can just find it—"

"You were *planning* for this?"

"Of course! You think I would run into a situation like this unprepared?"

"Yes, I did think you would!"

He gave a dry snort. "And you're the one always giving me grief about being encouraging."

"I can't help it if you start acting differently! What am I supposed to do? Expect the unexpected?"

"Of course! I'm turning over a new leaf, Liena. No more losing battles. No more hiding during the Hunts. No more of that. I'm winning from now on. I'm going to be a top student before you know it!"

Why was this declaration more disconcerting than assuring? She should be very glad to hear this! Should be glad her mopey, unmotivated friend finally caught a vision. She couldn't be glad, however, that she let herself be dragged deeper into the middle of nowhere.

"Phoenixes should be the easiest to spot," said Zedong in a hushed whisper. "Since they're bright and burning. Dragon scales should catch the moonlight easily—aren't we so fortunate that the moon is full tonight?—and plus they're smaller. Qilins are big enough that even in the dark they should be visible, especially since they usually travel in herds."

"I'm worried about fox spirits."

He waved a hand. "I wouldn't worry too much about one of those. I was reading that they're not very common here."

"You were *reading* this?"

"Stop sounding shocked, Liena. I told you that I'm turning over a new leaf."

"But what if we come across the one or two fox spirits in the vicinity? It would be so hard to tell, since they could show up as anyone and easily deceive us. We might think it was a classmate or—"
A friend.

Liena shuddered, glad for the darkness to conceal the way she reached up to touch her necklace. She wouldn't ever forget the sight of Zedong's tear-streaked cheeks and puffy eyes through the grate of that peep window in the *mó guǐ* dungeon.

208

"Quit fretting! We'll just do what they taught us in class whenever we see a person: we'll look for discrepancies."

It was useless to keep fighting. Liena let the subject drop and prayed desperately that she would survive this night. Tomorrow's classes were going to be utterly miserable.

"You hear that?" Zedong asked, his head perking up.

"No."

"The water! We're close."

"What do we do once we find the water?"

"We lie in wait."

That was actually a much better plan than she expected, one that she wasn't as terrified about. She could find a safe little nook and perhaps even take a nap while Zedong sat up and watched his stream for his monsters.

A part of her twinged with guilt. She touched the sheathed knives in her belt, the strap for the broadsword slung across her back, and the unfamiliar *jiaun* holstered at her hip.

She should probably try to hunt a monster rather than take a nap. But. . .

Surely a girl could pick and choose her battles, right? Next year, or the year after, when she was more confident with these weapons and her own skills, she could consider hunting a *mó guǐ*.

A memory hit her. The words of Master Zhong when she first arrived.

"Sweet girl," he'd said, *"you are one of the most likely candidates for monster fighting. You do not have battle magic and you are a low magic-wielder. You will likely be given a post in a village, and you will be little more than a deputy, fighting crime and monsters alike. When you have visions, you will be required by law to submit them for review. Is it the most practical matching of magic and skill to an appointment? No. But that's the way things are."*

She drew in a deep breath, eyes flitting every which way, and forced back the worries that insisted upon plaguing her.

The night was dark and heavy, yet alive with the gentle coos of nocturnal birds. The chittering sounds of bugs that had been so loud during the Night Games were much quieter now because of the cold. Instead, the wind howled and caught in the leafless trees and knocked their branches together. The ground was uneven, rocky patches interspersed with low shrubbery and rough stretches of grass. She nearly tripped over her own feet half a dozen times.

She didn't want to be easily spooked, but, well. . .

"Here it is!" Zedong announced quietly.

She pulled her hand out of his, coming alongside him as he parted a tall screen of reeds. The water gurgled around mossy stones, reflecting the full moon overhead on its rippling surface.

The last thing she wanted was to get too close to that water and fall in. No doubt it would be frigid.

"Where do we wait?" she asked.

Zedong glanced up and down the bank, moonlight catching on his furrowed brow. "Um . . . Let's find a good spot. You go that way, I'll go this way."

"Shouldn't we stay together?"

He stopped, turned, and gripped both of her shoulders and gave her a little shake. "Quit with the paranoia! Don't you trust me?"

She glared at him, not about to let him guilt her. "I'm staying close to you," she said. "I don't care what you say. I'm not wandering off on my own."

He rolled his eyes but said nothing more.

It took them nearly a half hour to find a perch satisfactory to both Liena and Zedong. He wanted a clear view at as much stretch of water as possible, and she wanted a place where they weren't exposed targets.

They finally found a copse of trees on the opposite side of the bank. One treacherous crossing later, after Zedong almost accidentally made Liena fall into the water, they settled down to wait.

She sat so they were back-to-back.

"Why don't you sit next to me?" asked Zedong.

"Because then anything can sneak up on us from behind," she replied crisply. "If we're going to be in a place that's open, we need to watch all angles. You can keep an eye on your monster trap, but I'm keeping an eye on our safety."

He sniffed but didn't protest.

The quiet darkness of the wilderness around her made her antsy while somehow still managing to lull her to sleep. She was determined to stay awake, because despite whatever Zedong said, she didn't trust him one lick to keep her safe. As the minutes trickled by, however, it became increasingly difficult to keep her eyes open.

"Liena?" he said.

"I thought you told me back there to be quiet, so I didn't scare away the monsters."

"For father's sake, I know you don't want to be out here alright? You don't have to remind me every five seconds."

She flinched. Hoped he hadn't been able to feel it.

Those words cut deeper than she wanted to admit.

After all, she didn't want to be a poor sport, even if this *was* the absolute last place she wanted to be right now.

"Sorry," she mumbled.

He bumped his back into hers. "It's fine."

They sat in quiet for another long while. She chewed her lip, wound her fingers into the folds of her sash, and wrapped her cloak—the one Nianzu had sent for her—tighter around her shoulders.

"Do you think it's weird and unfair that magic is genetic?" said Zedong, breaking the silence.

She didn't want to go down this road again. But the way he asked it wasn't the weird way he'd been saying things recently. He asked it genuinely, like he truly cared what she thought. And honestly, she was rather starved of easy, friendly conversation. She just wanted to go back to how they used to interact, before he started meeting with

Master Gu. Before she was constantly worried about *what* Master Gu was teaching him.

"I suppose it's unfair," she responded. "But unfair doesn't mean bad necessarily."

"What do you mean?"

"Well, it's impossible for life to be completely fair, and if it *were* all fair, then everything would be exactly the same."

"That . . . makes no sense."

"No, it does! Think about it. Here at the Academy, everyone's magic is different. That gives everyone different strengths and weaknesses. But if everything was to be exactly fair, we'd all have to have the exact same magic. Then we would lose all the beauty of the different types of magic, different types of strength."

"It doesn't have to be the same to be equally strong."

"But you're talking about strength as if there's only one version of it. I think there's many different types of strengths, and we can be weak in one area while being strong in another. I'm not physically strong, but I'm—"

"You're smart," he said. "And you're determined."

She smiled, staring up at the twinkling stars in the sky. "And *you*, you welcomed me so quickly. So much quicker than anyone else here has. That's one of your strengths. You are kind. You're loyal."

He was quiet.

"In places like the Academy, it's easy to believe that there's only one kind of strength," she said. "Because the Academy values magical strength and physical strength over other things. That doesn't make those other things any less important. It's about balance. Differences bring balance to the world."

She trailed off, content to listen to the gurgling stream behind her and stare up at the night sky through the trees.

A twig snapped nearby.

CHAPTER
26

Z EDONG STRAIGHTENED BEHIND her. She got to her knees, staying crouched. "What was that?" she whispered. Her blood hummed with a terrified rhythm.

"Not sure," he said, slowly standing. He unholstered his *jiaun* and fumbled to nock two arrows in their slots. "Best to arm yourself," he whispered.

Liena patted her *jiaun*, then her knives, and ran her tongue over her dry lips. Which one should she use? She'd rather that she didn't need to use any of them!

The *jiaun* made the most sense, but she was too unfamiliar with it. The broadsword seemed a little extreme, and it was heavy besides. She opted for what she figured was probably her most useless weapon: one of the three knives in her belt.

It made her feel better than the other options.

Zedong crawled closer to the stream while Liena's eyes frantically searched both sides of the bank for any sign of movement. The reeds waving, the rush of the cold wind around them, and the burble of the stream—all of it, so innocuous—sent her skin crawling.

She smelled smoke long before she saw anything.

"Phoenix," said Zedong eagerly. "Or a dragon."

"Or . . . a fire wielding student?"

"It is *not* a handsome prince, Liena," he snapped. "Wait here. I'm going to investigate."

"No—no! Wait!"

But he had already darted down the riverbank, abandoning her. Liena shivered, her blood pounding. Her eyes strained against the dimness, looking for any sign of anything that might possibly be alive.

It wasn't until the last sounds of Zedong's quick movements faded that the moonlight caught on glimmering scales.

Her heart nearly exploded in her chest then and there, but she forced herself to breathe. She crouched beside a tree trunk, eyes zeroed in on the silver flashing on the opposite side of the bank, downstream from her.

Her eyes widened in their sockets as she watched a creature nuzzle its way through underbrush until it reached the stream's edge. It was still partially hidden, but she could make out a long, silvery snout, a sinuous neck, and talon-tipped front claws. Slitted eyes like a cat's blinked in the night. The smell of smoke grew stronger, and Liena watched as it submerged its mouth into the water, causing it to sizzle and steam into the night air.

It was a dragon.

A dragon come for a drink.

She wouldn't panic. Would *not* panic. After all, it didn't know she was here. It was rather occupied with taking its drink.

Should she try to kill it? It seemed like an idiotic notion, one that could easily get her killed. But then again, when would she ever have a chance like this again? Could this change things for her? Make her less of a nobody?

Was it stupid to think she might be able to make more friends if she'd killed a dragon? Perhaps it would bridge the gap between her and some of the other students.

Whatever the reward, she had no intention of being stupid. If that dragon looked up and saw her, it could blast her into oblivion. The image of an amethyst dragon hide hanging on a hook in Master Gu's office flashed before her mind. And the image of a scarred, eyeless socket.

She had to do this very, very carefully.

Without moving, she ran through the weapons on her person. Despite how unfamiliar she was with it, she opted for the *jiaun*. It was the only thing she had that could shoot. She trusted her knife throwing skills even less than her ability to line up a pair of sights, even though she'd only fired a *jiaun* a handful of times and hadn't yet had a class dedicated to archery.

Her movements were clunky, awkward, and painfully slow. Her first task was to load the weapon without alerting the dragon. She gritted her teeth, trying to even her breathing as her heartrate skyrocketed.

The dragon sank its talons further into the muddy bank, scooting closer to get better access at the water. Now, she saw the tips of its wings over the top of the shrubs it hid in. Half-folded wings that wafted in the breeze and glistened in the night like precious metal melted down to liquid.

Finally, she held up her *jiaun*, trying to remember which contraption on the top was the sights. It was too dark for this sort of thing! What if she accidentally pulled the trigger before she was ready?

Despite her determination to not do anything stupid, this was feeling stupider and stupider by the moment. Yet part of her insisted that this was a *Hunt*, and if she was to be trained in fighting *mó guǐ*, it started with not letting this one go.

After all, if she didn't kill it, it might go off and kill something else.

Soft snorting nearby made her freeze.

The dragon lifted its head out of the water, arching its head toward the sound—a movement rather like a dog perking up its ears. It let out a little chittering sound that ended on a warbling garble.

Liena held her breath.

A chortle answered distressingly near. On her side of the bank.

And then—oh fathers, a third one!

She made herself as small as possible, hoping the tree she hid against would absorb her into its bark. So much for trying to kill a dragon. She had to get out of here.

But what if Zedong came back to look for her and couldn't find her? What if she got lost in the wilderness, and then she truly *did* become a snack for monsters?

Liena tried not to whimper as she scoured both sides of the riverbank for signs of the other dragons. If she could *find* them, then she could figure out the best direction to run.

A burbled grunt sounded far too close.

Moving slowly, trying not to alert any of the *mó guǐ* to her presence, she twisted her head to the bank next to her. Not even five paces away, with its forked tongue slithering out between its sharp teeth, was a ruby-red dragon.

She was going to faint.

Clutching her *jiaun* to her chest, she dared not make the slightest movement or sound. Even as the dragon stuck its nose into the air after drinking and sniffed, she refused to move.

Three dragons surrounded her. Three opportunities to slay a monster. Three chances to die.

She could scream. That would alert any nearby students to come to her aid. It would also alert the dragons. Perhaps if she could kill the one closest to her, and then scream, she would have a chance before the farther dragons chased her down.

They can fly.

Her heart sank, realizing she could never outrun them. It seemed her best bet was to hold still and wait. Pray that the dragons didn't notice her.

Zedong, please come back!

Suddenly, both of the dragons she could see shot their heads into the air, their noses angled upward. Slitted eyes darted every which way before landing uncomfortably close to where she clung to the shadow of her tree.

Finally, she heard it too.

A soft, swift gait.

She knew immediately that it wasn't Zedong's, but that didn't stop the hope from lurching in her chest. Maybe *now* she could scream—

A sharp whizzing sound broke through the silence, a burst of wind hitting dangerously close to her ankle. Liena couldn't help her squeak as a pair of arrows sank into the dirt, shot from a *jiaun*.

She leaned her head back against the tree, gasping, as another shot fired far too close to her. If she didn't move, she might be murdered by another student! But if she moved—

She glanced at the nearby dragon. To find it staring straight at her.

She froze.

The dragon rose up on its haunches, its wings outstretched, and hissed. Then it spat.

Sparks of fire shot through the air, landing by her feet. Liena was too frightened to even yelp as she scrambled backward, her hands trembling on her *jiaun*. She had to shoot now! Before it attacked!

Another arrow whizzed through the air, landing directly in the dirt by her feet. Not knowing what else to do, she cried, "Shoot the dragons! Not me!"

A hiss from the opposite bank made Liena glance toward the silver dragon, and found its eyes trained on her too. It reared back, standing upright on its hind feet, and flapped its wings.

It let out a loud, shrill cry.

She was gasping now, trying to scramble backward, but every movement she made elicited another hiss from the nearest dragon. Before she knew it, it started flapping its wings too, spitting harder at her. The sparks flew toward her. Two of them caught in the grass, smoking as a flame sprung to life and danced in the night.

"Help!" Liena cried, wondering where the student had gone. Would they not help her? The arrows had stopped, so they must have heard her.

From nowhere, the third dragon she hadn't seen leapt into the air, shrieking as it did so. It circled overhead, as the other two dragons scurried closer to Liena. Her hands trembled so hard she couldn't find the trigger on her *jiaun*.

At this point, she had to fight or die. She couldn't hope someone would come rescue her.

If she survived this, she was going to *murder* that Fang Zedong.

She took aim at the nearest dragon, squeezed her eyes shut, and pulled the trigger as she let out the loudest scream she could muster.

At first, she thought she'd hit the dragon because of the sudden cacophony of dragon shrieks that rent the air. But then fire burst everywhere, Liena was tripping over herself as she tried to get to her feet and *run*, and she had no idea if she'd hit it. Didn't even care.

She got to her two wobbly legs, turned to run, and stopped dead in her tracks.

The silver dragon had taken to the sky and swooped down toward her, its mouth opening as fire burned in the back of its throat. Liena screamed again, pulling a hard left, only to find another dragon flying toward her.

"Liena! Get *down!*" came a roar from behind her.

She didn't have a chance to before she was shoved to the ground by a heavy hand. Fire billowed everywhere, the heat of it blistering her skin. She screamed again, burying her face in the dirt. No matter how she covered her ears, the dragon shrieks tore through the fire, through everything, and Liena didn't know if it mean they were in pain, or furious. Or both.

The roar of fire soon swallowed all other sounds, and the world only grew hotter with each second. She twisted her face up, swiping her hair away from her eyes. Her heart still hammered, continued its unsteady racing, her lungs filling with smoke.

She pushed up on her elbows, coughing, only to realize there was a large foot near her face. When she craned her neck, she almost couldn't believe what she saw.

It was Nianzu, legs wide and braced on either side of her fallen on the ground, and fire was bursting from both open palms in an unquenchable stream. This was not like the other fire-wielders she'd seen, where they commonly created and threw fireballs. No, this was something entirely different.

The fire coming from his hands was like water bursting over a waterfall and beating the rocks below. It shot from his palms, from each of his fingers, unrelenting. His face was set in fury, those harsh lines cut sharper in firelight.

This was the most powerful fire wielder in history.

This was the Crown Prince and future Emperor of Zheninghai.

And he was standing over Liena.

Her head sagged back to the dirt in relief. She gasped, corrosive tears leaking out of her eyes, and tried not to choke on the smoke surrounding them. She was alive. She'd been saved.

A burning hand shook her shoulder. "Liena? Liena, answer me! Are you alright?"

She lifted her head again, managing a gasp of, "Thank you!" Then she sagged back down to the ground. She tried to gather her limbs underneath her, tried to find her strength again, but her legs and arms were like noodles. Utterly useless.

Two hands gripped her shoulders, heaving her into a sitting position. She blinked against the sting of smoke, coughing. She opened her eyes to find Nianzu's smoldering eyes staring down at her, his face fearsome.

"Hold this over your nose," he said, pressing a cloth to her face.

With that, another arm slid under her knees, and Nianzu swept her up into his arms and turned back toward the stream. Each step was purposeful, jolting through her quivering body, and his hands burned, but she couldn't be anything but desperately relieved.

He crossed the stream, walking straight through the icy current. His step never faltered once, his grip on her tight and secure.

She'd nearly died, but she had never felt safer in her life than she did now in the arms of the Prince of Zheninghai. She nestled her face deeper into his chest. Her heart ached even as her lungs burned.

This moment would be so fleeting. Before she would know it, she'd be set on her own two feet and made to walk on her own. And once that happened, would he ever take her into his arms again?

Best to savor this now, best to not let this moment of feeling *home* pass her by.

More voices and footsteps clouded her awareness, but she didn't want to face any of them. She gripped his tunic in her fist, breathing in one ragged breath after another.

"We need a river-bender," said Nianzu, his voice rumbling against her cheek. "Does anyone know where Master Shui is? Hanying or Jadaala?" He shifted his grip on her, hoisting her up so he held her more firmly.

"I saw Jadaala over—"

"Prince Nianzu!"

Nianzu turned toward several sets of pounding footsteps. When Liena peeked up at him, his face was so stern she immediately pressed hers back against his chest. There were scattered orders all around

220

to find the master or student with water magic powerful enough to put out the fire.

In the midst of this, there was a dry master's voice: "Well, young Highness, that is quite a fire."

She opened her eyes and twisted, enough to see the billowing fire that was now devouring the vegetation on the other side of the stream. Its smoke columned into the sky, blacking out the stars and moon.

"I overreacted," said Nianzu.

"A more targeted approach could avoid such widespread damage in the future," replied the master. "But I think they've found Jadaala and he'll be able to put the fire out."

"Liena!"

At the sound of that familiar voice, Liena's head jerked up. Nianzu glanced down at her, then up at Zedong as he practically stumbled over himself to her.

"Liena! Is she hurt?"

Fury as hot as the prince's raging fire burned in her gut. *Now* he was concerned about her? Now, after he abandoned her?

"I'll take her to the medics to be sure she's alright," said Nianzu.

"I can take her," said Zedong.

The prince's arms tightened around her. "No need."

With that, he brushed past Zedong and strode off.

Word came not long after that the fire had been put out. They had found two dragon carcasses in the aftermath.

One of the dragons had an arrow through its shoulder.

CHAPTER
27

THINGS WERE VERY silent the next morning at breakfast.
Liena was already eating by the time Zedong stumbled in,
bags under his eyes and hair disheveled and robes askew. He
said nothing to her as he took his usual place across from her and
began scooping rice into his bowl.

Liena didn't want to talk to him anymore than he wanted to talk
to her. She focused on eating and trying not to fall asleep at the table.

When Zedong finished eating and got up, his eyes met hers for
a brief second. They flashed with something she couldn't name.
Something strong.

He was striding away before she could read that look.

When she carried her candle into the library that night, yawning as she did so, she was surprised to find Nianzu already waiting for her in her corner nook. More surprising, he didn't have any studies set before him. He was just sitting there, rolling a tongue of fire around his hands. He snuffed it in his fist when she approached.

She smiled tentatively.

He didn't smile back.

Her footsteps flagged, but she blinked and forced them to keep moving. She set her candle down, then the rest of her supplies, and sat cross-legged on the mat across from him.

"We need to go to the beach tonight," Nianzu said.

Her gaze snapped up to his, her heart lurching even as her body groaned. "Tonight? But I have so much to study, and none of us got much sleep last night. Besides, I fulfilled my obligation to you, remember?"

He shook his head. "Combat is more important than your studies."

"It is one of my many classes, not my only class."

She *wanted* to go, wanted to have his attention all to herself. But how was it a good idea to keep getting her heart wrapped up in knots over a prince? Besides, she was absolutely exhausted.

"*Please* come?" he said.

Despite herself, her eyes snagged on his. She held his stare for a full five seconds before dropping her head. She was without will to dispute further. Too exhausted to protest, which didn't bode well for their training.

Once they reached the beach, Nianzu helped her down from the horse and tossed her one of the staffs he'd brought. The wind was especially strong, and especially cold. She shivered, her hair whipping around her face, her cloak barely staying attached at her throat.

Nianzu faced her, all business and completely serious. No trace of amusement creased the skin around his eyes. He braced himself across from her, holding his own staff. If he was cold, he didn't show it.

Her teeth chattered.

"Attack me," he said.

Every limb whined in protest, bubbling up to her lips. She barely clamped them shut and holed up her whimper. Instead, she closed her eyes for a brief second.

I can do this.

She darted toward him, aiming a blow at his left knee. He blocked, then blocked her second high strike.

"Faster," he said. "Don't give me time to think."

She growled, plunging her staff straight for his face. In swift, precise movements, he ducked, blocked, caught her staff in a circle and drove it into the ground. It only took one blow to knock her off her feet.

"Get up!" Nianzu said before she'd hardly even landed. "Defend yourself!"

The sand sucked her downward, her aching body pleading to stop, but she closed her eyes again. Found that core of determination and strength deep inside her.

I can do this.

She shoved up on her elbows, glaring at the prince. A twinge of a smile twisted the corner of his mouth. She dragged herself to her feet and faced him.

This time, he charged her. Muscle memory took over, followed by a thrill when she successfully dodged and blocked five consecutive attacks. The sixth, however, landed her flat on her face. She lay there, breathing in and out knife-cold air.

"Get up!"

She didn't *want* to get up anymore. Her body ached, and her mind was like a mushy bowl of rice. She tilted her head to one side, gasping as she stared at the lapping ocean waves. "I don't know if I can do this," she whispered.

"Get up, Liena!"

Fury rolled through her body. Why was he making her do this? She was exhausted. She'd been up half the night. How was this going to be effective training anyway?

She pushed up enough to fix Nianzu with her fiercest glare. "I'm done."

Nianzu's eyes flashed in response. "No, you're not. Get back up."

She didn't move, still glaring at him.

"You're angry with me," said Nianzu. "Good. Use that anger to get *up*. Use it to *fight!* You've got more in you than you know. You're stronger than you know."

"At the moment, I don't particularly care."

"*Get up!*" he demanded. "Quit acting like qilin-spawn."

Her jaw dropped open, her brows furrowing. She'd never heard the prince use language like that, and certainly never at *her*. "Acting like *what*?" she spat.

He fixed his chin at her, slamming the end of his staff into the dirt. "Like a dragon-eaten qilin-spawned phoenix face."

That did it. She was up, brandishing her staff and hurling herself at him. "That is ugly language!" she snarled, smashing her staff down on his shoulder.

"Oof!" he grunted, blocking her next attack. "Nice hit!"

It wasn't that she wanted to *hurt* him, but he hardly reacted to her hit. Couldn't it have hurt a little more? She struck again, only growing angrier when he easily evaded her.

"Block! Watch your left!" called the prince. "You should be thrilled to hear that I know much more *ugly* language. There are quite a host of ugly things I have yet to call you."

He darted beneath her guard, landing a smarting blow to her calf. She half-yelped, half-cried out in pain, stumbling. But did he stop? No, absolutely not. He came at her again, refusing to let her breathe or recover. His blows were harder, faster. Her knees buckled when she blocked.

"Stop!" she gasped. "It's too much!"

He only came at her harder, backing her into the frigid ocean. Fury ripped through her senses, shattering her exhaustion. She snarled, blocking and darting forward to land blows of her own until she pushed her way out of the ocean.

"You think this is enough?" he growled, not flinching as her blows grew faster. "Catch me by surprise! Use every bit of leverage against me! Each of your moves are as predictable as the sunrise."

"Predictable?" she snarled, aiming straight for his face. "Is *this* predictable?"

"Be angry!" he shouted. "Funnel it into your blows. Don't get careless now—use that anger to hone your strikes, to power your defenses. Yes, like that! Yes, yes!"

"You made me angry on purpose!"

"I'll keep you angry too!"

This time, when he knocked her down, her anger vanished like the dew on grass. She lay panting in the sand, the wind whipping at her hair, her cloak, her frozen, reddened skin.

"Excellent job!" cried Nianzu. "That was your best yet! Now get back up! One more round."

With each gasp, she sucked more sand into her mouth. But she couldn't move. Couldn't so much as twitch a finger. The weight of the sky above pinned her to the ground.

"Liena," he growled.

Even his string of curses could do nothing to rouse her. There was absolutely nothing left.

She gave him her all, but it wasn't nearly enough, was it? He'd still beaten her easily. Did it matter if her technique improved if she always ended like this, flattened on the ground?

I can't do this.

She squeezed her eyes shut, still gasping, as the tears began flowing. She heard the shift of sand as Nianzu came toward her, but she couldn't get up.

I can't do this. Any of this.

227

She was nothing but a girl playing at magic, at a life that wasn't hers at all. She was a fraud—a mistake. The limited success she'd had in the classroom was nothing against how woefully behind she was. She would never catch up. All of this work, this effort, this backbreaking strain—*not worth it*. She would give up. Go back home. Dig her furrows, plant her millet, harvest its heads, and beat them together until all those kernels were separated and ready for marketplaces and storerooms. She would go to the matchmaker, hope for the butcher's boy.

She would leave Ma, Pa, and Lao Lao exactly where they were in life: scraping to survive. But that would be fine because they were hearty people. They knew how to survive. She would survive alongside them.

This Academy thing, however? She couldn't do it anymore.

"Get up!" came the growl overhead. "I can't go easy on you because no one else will. You've got to get to your feet."

She ignored him, curling more into a ball, and pressing the back of her hand to her face as the tears came hotter, faster, pooling in the sand. His arm slid under her waist, and he hoisted her up to her feet. Except her legs wouldn't support her. She started to crumple, but he tightened his grip.

"Lock your knees," he said. "Stand up. You're never truly beaten until you stop getting back up."

But she *was* beaten.

"Liena," he growled, his arm still tight around her waist, holding her against him. "Stop crying. Stand up."

She shook her head, the tears coming harder. "I'm too tired," she whimpered. Too tired to stop crying, too tired to stand up.

"Do you think a dragon will stop for you to take a nap? Do you think an enemy will have mercy on you because you are weak?"

"There are no dragons!" she wailed.

He spun her to face him, keeping her upright with one hand as his other took hold of her jaw and forced her to look up at him. At the fury in his gaze. "You were almost *killed* last night. If I hadn't heard you scream . . . I *won't* have you be helpless. I *won't* have you freezing in the face of danger. Liena, I—" His voice caught, his throat bobbing. His grip on her face tightened, heated. "I *need* you to be strong."

She stared at him. "Why?"

A growl was the only response he gave before he bent and swept her up into his arms. She would be happy, except that his hot hands betrayed how angry he was. He marched to the horse.

Apparently they were done for the night.

She sagged with relief in his arms, closing her eyes as she leaned against his chest. *Safe. Home.* Just this last time. When she would later be held in the arms of some plain, nobody farm boy, she would have to fight to not remember this—what it felt like to be held in the arms of the Prince of Zheninghai when all her strength had fled her, knowing that he was strong enough for both of them.

But . . . was he?

She frowned, that niggling insistent voice rupturing her thoughts. Would the prince fight all her battles for her? Would he be her arena champion? Would he always be there to save her from *mó guǐ*?

What if he *hadn't* heard her scream last night? What if no one had?

Fire burst across her senses. Heat, but without all the light. She was scorching hot, lightheaded, falling, falling, falling—

Lavender light exploded around her.

She lost control of her own thrashing limbs, her screams, everything. The starry sky and the prince's warmth were all swallowed up in lavender.

Her vision clarified.

There was that girl again. The same one she had seen standing before Nianzu, the one who looked uncannily like Liena. Who definitely *wasn't* Liena. Now that Liena saw her for a second time, she saw the softened cut of the girl's face, the large and feeling dark eyes that weren't quite Liena's.

She was seated, her mouth pulled in a firm, straight line even as her knuckles whitened around her grip on her robes. Beside her, with three rows of black and gray braids running down his scalp, was . . . was . . .

Zedong?

The vision turned fuzzy, and Liena reached for it, grappling with rippling future. She needed to know more! Wanted a better glimpse of where he was, why he seemed so different, why he was dressed so unusually. Dressed like—well, shockingly similar to her mother's heritage.

He was dressed like a barbarian.

"Wait!" she cried. "Zedong!"

The lavender swallowed up the two figures, all-encompassing once again. The fire returned, so sharp and painful she screamed again. Had she ever stopped screaming?

As the light eased, the heat and the tension drained out of her. It left her like a puddle of water in its wake, ready to flow down the sand to join the sea and lose herself completely in oblivion.

She choked on a scream, swallowed it whole. Gasped. The air that flooded her lungs was ice sharp. She was lying down again, back flat on sand. The weakness she'd felt before was nothing compared to this.

She opened her eyes. Found herself staring up at another pair startlingly close. Nianzu's.

His mouth was open, all former anger replaced by wide-eyed terror. His weight pressed down on her, pinning her legs. He'd caught her wrists to the ground beside her head. She swallowed, found her mouth dirt dry. With monumental effort, she turned her head to the side and coughed.

Nianzu didn't move.

"Did you have a vision?" he asked.

She closed her eyes and nodded.

"That was . . . terrifying," he said. "Are you alright?"

"Sorry," she mumbled. "I'm fine, only weak."

"I'll take you back."

The prince slid his weight off her, bent, bundled her cloak around her, and picked her up again. "Now I have proof you're stronger than you know."

She let her head fall back against his shoulder so she could look up at him. "Hmm?"

"You were . . . I had a difficult time restraining you."

"Restraining me?"

"You were thrashing wildly and screaming, and whenever I came close, you hurled blows at me. Almost got me a few times."

She furrowed her brow. "I . . . Forgive me, Highness. I never meant—"

He chuckled and hefted her a little higher in his arms. "Sleep, if you can. You'll need strength when we get back to the Academy."

As she drifted off, as her awareness darkened and warmed, his deep voice rumbled through his chest, into her ear.

"I need you to be strong, Liena. So . . . so I don't have to be afraid."

Afraid? Afraid of what? What could possibly make a powerful fire-wielding prince afraid?

The night claimed her.

CHAPTER
28

LIENA DIDN'T EXPECT Zedong to acknowledge her the next morning. She assumed they were still mad at each other after the Hunt. Nevertheless, she passed by the other seated students, trying not to let her gaze wander too much to the popular crowd of students where Nianzu was eating.

The one time she did peek a glance, expecting to see him laughing and bantering with his friends, what she saw nearly froze her in place.

He was watching her.

She ducked her head, crimson flushing up her cheeks, and hurried to her typical spot where she awaited Zedong's sour and silent presence. Not long after she was seated, someone called out, "Arena battles have been posted!"

Everyone but Liena surged to their feet to check. She kept eating. Zedong would tell her, and it wasn't as if it mattered whom she would lose to tomorrow.

That thought made her pause mid chew. Had she truly given up?

She was sick of it all. Didn't want to keep sludging her way through this school year. Didn't want to get beaten again.

You're not beaten until you stop getting back up.

She hadn't gotten back up last night, had she? Nianzu had carried her back to the horse, wrestled her awkwardly atop it, and ridden them both back to the palace. She'd barely been able to wobble her way to her dormitory where she flopped into bed fully clothed.

She was *sick* of this. Sick of feeling like a failure.

Exclamations broke through her thoughts. Plenty of cursing, plenty of whooping and hollering as people saw who they were fighting. She didn't care about any of it.

That is, until she happened to glance up and find Shu, Nianzu, Lei, Mu, Jadaala, and Wan all staring at her with varying degrees of concern and elation on their faces. Liena's rice stuck in her cheek as she stared stupidly back.

Nianzu looked furious. She swallowed the sticky lump.

"Liena!"

She turned to see Zedong careening between the tables toward her. His hair was wild—not at all the tight braids she'd seen in her vision last night—and his face was a mixture of perplexity and worry.

Liena shot a glance back at Nianzu's group and saw him scowling with crossed arms as he watched his friends talk excitedly between them.

"What?" she said to Zedong as he skittered to a halt in front of her. "What's the matter?"

"Your—your arena battle!" he gasped. Apparently all was forgotten between them. "You're fighting . . . It's—"

She flung wide her hands. "What? It's *who*?"

His face curled into a wince. "It's Mao Shu."

Liena's jaw dropped, her gaze swiveling despite herself to watch Shu laugh at something Wan said, her face alight. Kang Lei clapped her on the back.

"That'll make perfect-but-one marks for your arena battles," she said. "You'll graduate with honors!"

"I can't believe they're just *giving* this to you," said Jadaala.

Was she wrong to believe that was smoke curling up from Nianzu's fist?

Shu glanced toward Liena, found her watching, and tossed a pleased grin her way, waggling her eyebrows as if they'd been assigned to work together to bake some culinary confection, not battle each other until one was pinned to the ground.

Liena glanced away but returned her gaze swiftly enough to see Shu's eyes shoot to Nianzu and his darkened expression. For a brief second, Shu's face melted into fury.

Then she was grinning again, sauntering up to him.

Lei, with her hair sweeping behind her in glossy waves, her rosy lips puckered to perfection, slid to his other side. "Why the long face, Prince?" she said. "Aren't you happy for Shu here?"

Shu gave him her best grin.

Nianzu spared her a glance, not even looking at Lei. "Congratulations, Shu, for being the advantaged warrior in your arena battle tomorrow."

Lei howled, slapping the prince's biceps and leaning her head into his shoulder as she laughed. "How dull you've become, Prince! You've offended Shu."

"My mistake," said Nianzu, pushing off the wall and striding away.

Liena watched him go, felt the eyes of those he left behind trailing to her. Zedong's strong emotion was practically leaking into her skin. She finally turned to look at him.

He was nearly snarling, one hand clenching the edge of the table as he stared down at the floor. "I hate, hate, *hate* them."

"I don't like them either," said Liena.

"*All* of them," said Zedong.

Liena said nothing. She stared down at her bowl, at the chopsticks that she still clutched.

"Does it matter if I'm sorely disadvantaged if I lose even when my opponent is younger than me?" she said finally, setting down her chopsticks.

"What?" he demanded. "You're going to just *let* her win? At least try to land a few blows to that smirk for me."

"And if I can't?" she shot back. "She has forcefields, Zedong. How am I supposed to land a blow on her?"

"I *know* she has forcefields. Don't talk to me like I'm stupid."

She bit back her barbed reply barely in time. Instead, she gripped her bowl with two hands and managed between clenched teeth, "I'm going to go to class."

Zedong caught her wrist. "Wait, Liena—"

"Let go of me! People are staring!" she hissed.

He let go, but his eyes blazed. "Now you care about what those qilin brains think? Perhaps you should stop sitting with me."

She didn't dignify this with an answer, storming off and leaving him to his breakfast.

She only paused once, at the entrance to the mess hall, staring down the beautiful halls before her. They closed in upon her, confining her. The brilliant blue, the sun shining through gold-edged lattice screens, the glint of light on the tips of a statue's nine silver tails made her wince. She was hot, so hot, but not at all like when she had a vision. Her hands trembled like fallen leaves, like Lao Lao's unsteady weight on her cane.

No matter where she looked, all she could see was a prison.

She was a magic-wielder of Zheninghai. She couldn't leave the Academy. This was her life—*failure* was her life. Her future.

Her choices were to graduate or be expelled. Live a lie or die. Because she wasn't *really* a magic-wielder of Zheninghai. She was just a girl, a nobody, who sometimes was overcome with nonsensical, unproductive visions of a future that was never going to happen.

It hadn't seemed important when she got her first vision. That had been a chance to escape the matchmaker, the dirt and millet. But now she realized how little choice she'd ever had in her life. She

236

was born to farmers. She worked, sweat, bled on that farm. Now she worked, sweat, bled at the Academy.

Would anything in her life be her own choice? Or would a matchmaker or magic make the choice for her?

It took everything not to burst into a run. Even though she could barely breathe, even though she felt like she was drowning alive, she forced her steps to be even, unhurried. Then she turned a corner, saw a darkened, unpopulated stretch before her.

She ran.

The tears flooded.

Never enough. Never enough. Never enough.

Not strong enough. Not strong enough.

Never strong enough.

The toe of her shoe caught on a lip of the paving stone, and she went sprawling. She landed hard on all fours, staring through blurry eyes at a mosaic of a fire-belching dragon. She crawled out of the open hallway into a dark corner, tucked into the shadow of a pillar with a character carved into it that read *Determination*.

She curled up into a ball, fitting her eye sockets to her knees and crying.

At some point, she fell asleep.

A pair of voices awakened her.

"I'm not sure I'm getting through to him."

Liena blinked to free her tear-crusted lashes. Her shoulder, hip, and neck ached, but she didn't move.

"He'll come around eventually. Don't give up on the experiment."

"What if it doesn't work?"

"Then we'll keep trying. We'll find another student if need be."

The first voice was distinct. *Master Gu.* The second she had only heard one other time, when she had stumbled upon Master Gu talking to him. Liena tensed, swallowing against the dryness in her throat.

"It's that Song girl," growled Master Gu. "She's the reason he's held out so long against the magic. If she'd never come, this would have been so much simpler."

"But you're getting rid of her tomorrow, right?"

"If all goes as planned. That Mao girl agreed to have a little *accident* happen during the arena battle. It was extremely difficult convincing the others to pit those two together, but in the end it'll be worth it. This should be what tips the boy over the edge and completes our experiment."

Liena didn't breathe, didn't move a muscle as they passed by her hiding place. Their long black robes swished dangerously near, and she squeezed her eyes shut, as if that could block her out of their sight.

Their voices trailed off as they disappeared around the corner. The last thing she heard were the clicking of their shoes on the polished floor. After counting to a hundred, she finally dared to move. Almost immediately, she winced, stopping, as she found a crick in her neck. She slowly maneuvered herself into a sitting position.

What had she just overheard?

Her mind spun, trying to fit the pieces together. Had Master Gu pitted Shu against her so that Shu could hurt her? But why? What did Shu have to gain from it? And what sort of *experiment* was this that involved Zedong?

Her arm hairs prickled, a chill racing down her spine. She had to tell someone. Had to get help.

Nianzu.

He would listen to her. He would help her.

She stumbled to her feet, wincing all the way, and glanced around to find her way out. That was when she realized the cast of the shadows around her.

"Fathers!" she gasped. "My classes!"

It was almost noon. She had missed half a day's worth of classes.

The thought made her almost return to her corner so she could curl up and die of mortification. Instead, she hurried back the way she'd come, straightening her disheveled hair and robes as she went.

Which class was she supposed to be in right now?

Panic similar to this morning's, though for an entirely different reason, clapped hold of her. *Oh fathers. Oh fathers.*

She turned another corner—

And found herself face to face with Master Zhong, Master Qing, and another master.

"Song Liena!" cried Master Zhong. "There you are! Half the staff has been looking for you!"

"Detention!" snapped Master Qing. "For skipping classes! Immediately!"

All the blood drained from her face. "Detention? I didn't mean to—I didn't realize—I wasn't—"

"This way," said the third master, face set severely.

Liena balked, casting a helpless glance at Master Zhong. "Please, I—"

"Move your feet, girl! Before your sentence increases."

Sentence?

Protests bubbled up, fighting for dominion over her tongue, but Liena bit them all back. She *had* skipped class, whether she intended to or not, and now she had no choice but to bear the consequences.

No choice.

Liena ground her teeth as she followed after the third master. Who was she, after all, that she thought she was entitled to choice?

An image of Zedong's pale face flashed before her mind, the horror that had struck him at the mention of detention. With wooden steps, she made after the third master toward the darkest reaches of the Academy.

CHAPTER
29

T HE MASTER PUSHED open a simply carved, heavy door, beckoning Liena to step inside the dim room and leave the windowless stretch of hallway behind her. For a split second, a wild impulse to run nearly overcame her.

Instead, gritting her teeth with force enough to crush them, she took those few steps. And then froze like a deer caught in lantern light. It was an empty room, with hollow wooden floors, bare walls, and paint-chipped screens covering every window. She hardly noticed the sparse room, however, because of the hunched figure standing with weight leaning on an unsteady cane.

"Lao Lao?" Liena gasped. She blinked, shook her head, expecting the vision to vanish from before her. This could be nothing but an illusion; there was no way in all the seven valleys Lao Lao would be here.

"Is that any way to greet your elder?" snapped Lao Lao. "Fathers, you wretched girl—what are you doing in detention? Your poor parents would be so ashamed!"

"I don't understand," Liena stammered. She whirled back toward the door only to find her escorting master gone, and the door shut and bolted.

"*You* don't understand? I'm the one who has just been informed of your detention. You're failing your combat class? You're behind in everything? For shame! Did you hear none of your parents' words about bringing the family honor? How could you have brought us so low? To be the laughingstock of the Academy!"

Those words cut deeply. So deeply, she almost forgot how impossible it was that Lao Lao was here. Her grandmother had always been harsh, but this? The worst of it was how true those words were.

"You are an illusion," said Liena. She would bet her life on it, that this was some twisted mind game the Academy used as punishment. Hadn't her masters taught her to look for inconsistencies? Lao Lao was wearing the exact same patchwork robes she'd been wearing when Liena had left, and there was no sign of a grueling journey on those garments.

For someone to know Lao Lao's personality, her clothes, even her existence . . .

"Get out of my mind!" Liena said, backing away and clamping her hands on her head. "Out of my mind! Get out!"

If a master found her suspicion about Zedong . . .

Lao Lao was shouting something, but Liena ignored her. She wasn't real. Liena had to protect her mind, her secrets, from whatever Academy master was digging around where they didn't belong. She had to think of something!

The sound *thwack* of Lao Lao's cane certainly stung as much as it ever had. Liena gasped, clutching her hand to her chest. She didn't have time to react before the cane fell again, hitting her shoulder this time.

How could an illusion cause so much physical pain?

Pain is in the mind.

Her mind was being manipulated by someone else. That was the only reasonable explanation for how Lao Lao's blows never failed to land, despite how Liena dodged and ran to avoid them. Making her feel pain that wasn't real, see someone who wasn't real, be rebuked for her failures by a loved one.

Cerebrally, this method of punishment made sense. It communicated the message without leaving lasting injury and was tailored to each student, while still training them to withstand pain.

But she hated it.

Rage consumed her, blinding her. She didn't care what grandiose things she'd said in the past about fairness. This *wasn't fair*. She didn't deserve to be flayed alive by her hobbling grandmother.

Liena gave up running, diving into a corner and curling into a ball.

Pain is in the mind.

The blow across her back—not real. The fire landing on her shoulder, her legs, her arms—*not real*. She sank deeper into herself, into her own mind. Into a place that was safe for her. She imagined herself wrapped up in Nianzu's arms, sheltered from everything. It was a bitter consolation, but she knew that no place would ever feel so safe to her.

At some point, the blows subsided into nothing. She gradually became aware of her body again, refusing to imagine the lingering pain of bruises and cuts. Instead, she steadily got to her feet, brushed off her garments, and turned around.

Lao Lao was nowhere to be seen. Instead, two masters in black faced her, their faces solemn. If Liena had to guess, one was an illusionist, and the other a mind-reader. She stared at them, the full weight of her hatred shooting into them.

She wasn't expecting them to speak.

"You have a strong mind," said the one on the left. "A resilient, strong, intelligent mind. Magic flows in blood, but yours . . . There's

243

magic in your mind. You may never be anything more than a low-magic seer, but there may yet be hope for something more for your offspring."

He dared compliment her after tormenting her? After using the memory of her grandmother against her?

No one moved to stop her when she strode out of detention and slammed the door behind her.

CHAPTER
30

T HE LIGHT WAS blinding to her dark-adjusted eyes. The last place she wanted to go was the mess hall, to face all of those students. To be the girl they pointed at and said, "*That's* the girl Shu is going to absolutely *demolish* tomorrow. That's the girl who was so scared that she went and hid during classes today!"

Liena trudged there anyway. The scraps of pride she still possessed refused to let her cower and hide. But before she reached the mess hall, a sharp, "*Psst!*" caught her attention.

Her head snapped up, glancing toward that sound, and her eyes widened at the sight of Zedong's head poking out from behind one of the screens by the windows. He motioned her to come.

She practically ran to him, ducking behind the screen.

Her eyes lighted on two bowls full of steaming food sitting on the floor. "Food! Oh, Zedong, thank—"

He cut her off, drawing her into his arms and hugging her tightly. She froze, too stunned to react.

"It's my fault," he murmured against her hair. "I did that thing you said I do, where I'm mad and I take it out on you. I didn't mean to."

She swallowed, her lungs suddenly tight. Everything constricted again, and when she wiggled in his arms, he only tightened his grip. Panic flared again across her mind.

Trapped. Trapped—

"Hungry," she gasped.

"Oh, here!" said Zedong, releasing her, sitting down, and gesturing at the two bowls of food. "We'd better keep our voices down, so they don't discover us here."

She nodded mutely and took up her bowl.

"You alright?" he asked.

She shook her head.

I can't do this anymore.

She ought to warn Zedong about Master Gu. But whenever she opened her mouth, she had to swallow back a sob.

Out, out, out.

She wanted out of here. Out of the Academy. Out of Zedong's life. Out of politics, of magic, of classes, of swords and staffs and *jiauns*—

She didn't want out of Nianzu's life, but that was probably the biggest thing she needed to free herself from. An overattachment to someone who could never mean anything to her.

"Liena?" Zedong prodded. "You know you can tell me anything."

"Can I?" she snapped, suddenly finding her voice. "*Can* I tell you anything, Zedong? Or will you get angry when I tell you things you don't like?"

"You can tell me."

She met his gaze, saw the wariness there, but also the determination to prove he wasn't the way she said he was.

Fine, let him prove himself.

"Nianzu has been taking me to the beach in the evenings while you're meeting with Master Gu," she said.

She might have punched him for the shock on his face. He stared, his mouth falling open, his eyes widening. His hands holding his bowl dropped to his lap as pain spread across his face.

"Every night?" he croaked. "And you never told me?"

Betrayal was written across every feature, and it stung her so deeply she nearly wept. *This* was why she needed out. Whatever Master Gu had planned for tomorrow's arena battle, if Liena stayed and let it happen, this would be the final straw for Zedong—whatever that meant.

Best to escape this place. Best to drive this wedge now and never look back.

Zedong's jaw clenched. His eyes flashed, and she could have sworn she saw blue in those depths. When he spoke, his voice was low and deadly.

"I'll kill him."

"See?" Liena said, throwing up her hands. "I can't tell you everything, now can I? But you don't tell me everything either, do you? What have you been studying with Master Gu? By this time, I know it's not reviewing your regular studies. What is she teaching you?"

Zedong let out a snarl, whipping his head to one side and glaring at the intricate designs on the screen they hid behind. "She's teaching me magic," he muttered.

"Magic? As in, she's teaching you how to better wield your magic?"

He shook his head, pupils dilating in and out.

Dread dropped into her stomach. Liena stared, watching his fists curl, watching him tense up like he was about to explode. "*What* magic is she teaching you?" she whispered.

His head swiveled back to her, incisors gleaming in his snarl. "What is *Nianzu* teaching you?"

The implication of that turned her face hot. She set her bowl down, blood pounding in her ears. "I can't do this," she said, standing. "Whatever magic you're tampering with, you've got to stop. You've got to stay away from Master Gu from now on. You've got to—" She stopped, choking on her own words.

Zedong stared at her, a mix of fury and concern.

She shook her head, swallowing back more tears. "Thank you . . . for being my friend."

Then she fled.

"Liena!" Zedong called from behind her.

She wasn't going to stop for him, or for anyone. She moved swiftly, quietly, as she'd been learning in her classes. To her relief, Zedong didn't follow her.

Out, out, out.

She knew she was emotional, worked up. Knew she was being rash, and probably very stupid. But she'd had enough, and for once, she wanted a choice. Wanted to prove she wasn't an animal on a leash to be guided about, fed, and beaten each time it disobeyed.

It might be a stupid and selfish choice, but it was hers.

Even thoughts of Lao Lao, Ma, and Pa couldn't deter her. They were survivors. They'd presumably survived this long without her. They could keep surviving. She shoved away the guilt, the responsibility, knowing full well how wretched she was being.

She just couldn't stay here a minute longer.

Winding through the hallways blindly, she followed her instinct. The library appeared to her left, and for the first time, she slowed. The tears she fought seemed to pause as well, giving her a heartbeat of rational thought.

She loved her studies here. Truly. As long and late and exhausting as those nights had been in the library, they'd been the best part. Her and Zedong, studying in companionable silence. Sometimes Nianzu too.

The moment passed.

She turned away from the library and slid into the opposite room.

It was a dark classroom. Night had fallen not long ago, and through the papered windows on the far wall, she could see the outline of the rising moon. It was large and full tonight. She paused just inside the doorway, staring at the rows of low desks and mats facing the master's desk. The moon cast an eerie half-light on the space, and though the windows were closed, it still felt cold.

This was the rashest thing she had ever done in her life. Then again, this was also the most desperate she'd ever been.

She strode down between the desks, past the teacher's mat, and approached the sill. With one swift shove, she unlatched the shutters and let them swing open. The dim light of night streamed in, unimpeded. She stared out the window, at the lotus pond gleaming below in the midst of the Academy gardens, at the expanse of winking city lights beyond it. Beyond that, the ocean.

There was nothing for her to bring. She called nothing hers but the clothes on her back and the necklace around her neck. With a deep breath, she climbed up onto the sill. Crouched, measured the distance to the ground.

A hand closed around her wrist.

Liena could only let out a surprised squeak before she was dragged down from the ledge and spun around until her back hit the wall.

"*What* are you doing?" Nianzu hissed, pinning both of her wrists against the wall.

She stared up at him, at the furrows bunched between his eyebrows, the downward tilt of his mouth. Planting her feet firmly and lifting her chin, she curled her hands into fists and said evenly, "I'm leaving."

"You leave, you die."

"I'll manage."

"No, you won't. They'll hunt you down and try you for desertion, and they will find you guilty."

A particularly sour, self-pitying comment jumped to her lips, but she withheld it. Instead, she fixed him with her most determined glare.

"You're not leaving," he said.

"Shall you keep me within your sight at all times to ensure I don't escape?"

His parted lips revealed gritted teeth. "I have many at my disposal to do that for me."

She lifted both eyebrows. "Oh, am I your prisoner now? To be kept under lock and key until you decide you want to bring me out to play?"

Heat flared in her wrists, and she sucked in a sharp breath.

"Where is this coming from, Liena?" he demanded. "This . . . this *bitterness* isn't you at all. If you're upset about detention, I understand. It's brutal. If you're upset about the arena battle, so am I—"

"Have you ever been to detention?" she snapped.

His gaze didn't falter for even one second, but he didn't answer.

"I didn't think detention was for princes," she said. "Just for—"

"Don't finish that sentence, Liena."

She bit her tongue, glaring at him, hating how her stomach still flipped when he said her name. Lowering her voice to barely above a whisper, she said, "You and I both know this place isn't for me."

"That's not true."

"I'm going back to where I belong, *Your Highness*. I'm going home. Now, if you would kindly let go of—"

He didn't let go. He tightened his grip and gave her a little shake. "Stop it! *Stop it!* You want out of this? I understand. Sometimes I want out too. But the only way out is *through*. You have to see this through to the end."

"I don't *want* to see this through, and I'm tired of having no choice in my life! Being born poor—do you know what my life has been like, Prince Nianzu? Do you understand that my only hope for raising my station was being matched with a boy better off than me? I would have been lucky to be matched with someone who ate meat on a regular basis. We eat meat with every meal here at the Academy! Then I got one vision out of nowhere, and now I'm stuck in this world that I don't belong in. Why can't I choose for once where I want to be? Where I want to go? Will you not let me choose for once?"

"You think you're the only one without choice?" he snarled. "Believe it or not, there's little choice when you're born the first son of an emperor. My life has been preordained for me. I am simply to walk in the steps laid out for me and try not to ruin everything. You say you have no choice, but you *do* have a choice, just like I do."

"Oh?" It came out far more biting and sarcastic than she meant, but she didn't care.

"You can choose to run, to hide, to give up, to *lose.* Or you can choose of your own free will to keep fighting, to be strong. Just like I can choose to give up on my people, my family, this empire, or I can choose them over me. I can choose their wellbeing over my freedom. I can choose to give my all. *You* can choose. You *must* choose."

Liena stared at him, at the fire burning in his eyes, unable to look away even if she wanted to. She scrabbled, searching for some argument, any means of defense. Finally, she found one. "Why do you care at all what I do? What choices I make? Don't say you need me to be strong. Me fighting or winning tomorrow will *not* somehow prove that you're capable of being emperor."

His face came suddenly closer, close enough that his nose brushed her hairline, close enough to make her flinch.

"Maybe that was what this was about once," he whispered, voice suddenly soft and near her ear. "But now it isn't."

She swallowed, all but gasping for air. Her attempts to scrap together her composure fractured further with every thud of her heart. "What's it about, then, Highness?" she managed.

He let out a great sigh, his shoulders sagging. He leaned forward, resting his bent head on the wall beside her. His breaths puffed warm against her neck, her shoulder. There was only a fraction of air separating them, but it felt like miles. Miles that she would drown in.

"Liena," he breathed.

"Yes?" she gasped, tilting her head back so she could catch a sip of air. Her eyelashes fluttered closed, open, closed, her chest heaving. Slowly, his head turned toward her. Something light as a feather and soft as a cushion pressed against her jaw. Her knees buckled.

He released his grip on her wrists, catching her against him. Her hands fisted in the front of his robes, clinging to that bit of solid in a world where she was melting.

The side of his face pressed against hers, his lips at her ear.

"I want to kiss you," he said. "Will you let me kiss you?"

Lightning struck her core, so sharp she let out a short, shuddering gasp. But she nodded, not trusting her voice for a second.

He didn't hesitate. He used his free hand to tilt her face toward his, tangling his fingers in her hair, and kissed her. It was a kiss made of magic, of flowers unfurling to the sunshine, of stars twinkling beside a full moon. She whimpered and, with a shudder, fell against his chest. He tightened his arms around her, and the sound he made into her hair was something like a sigh and a moan wrapped up together that said, *"I want you."*

"That's why I don't want you to leave," he said, his voice catching. "That's why I need you to be strong. That's why I want you to choose to stay."

Sobs choked in her throat, burning hotter than any fire. "But I'm not strong enough. I can't . . . I can't do it."

"You *can*," he said vehemently, holding her tighter. "I know you can."

She clung to him, weeping quietly. A thousand thoughts, emotions, and questions flooded her mind. So many things that she was afraid of, questions she needed answers to, worries about Master Gu, Shu, Zedong, and the arena battle tomorrow.

What came out of her mouth, however, was a trembling, "I don't understand."

"You don't understand what?"

"*This*. I don't know . . ."

He leaned back enough to look at her, tilting his head to one side. "This?"

How could she say what she was trying to say without being presumptuous and making a fool of herself? She chewed on her lip, sniffling back her tears, and tried to regain her composure.

"This—this!" she said helplessly.

"As in . . . us?"

She nodded vigorously, then blurted, "You're going to have hundreds of consorts!"

Whatever she was expecting, she wasn't expecting him to snort, wasn't expecting the lips she'd just kissed to spread in a smile, wasn't expecting that dimple. He pulled her closer and rested his cheek on the top of her head. "That certainly has been the precedent, hasn't it?"

"Don't tease me!" She wiggled in his grasp, trying to free herself enough to shoot him a glare.

He held her fast and chuckled. "I wouldn't worry too much about that."

"If you're trying to console me and soothe my worries, you're failing."

This time, he laughed outright as she scowled. But when he spoke, his voice was a soft murmur. A kiss of its own.

"I've always intended to have one wife," he said. "Call me a romantic idealist, but I've planned on that for nearly my whole life. Or you might just call me sick of harem drama and catfighting."

She stared at him.

His smile turned sad, and he sighed. "Actually, what convinced me was overhearing a conversation between my uncle and my father. My father was complaining about how several of his concubines were

253

always fighting and whenever he summoned them, all they did was complain about the others. He said to my uncle, 'It must be so much easier, keeping one woman happy.' My uncle responded, 'With one wife, I can spend less time placating and more time growing in love and friendship together.' Guess who is happier in his relationships? My uncle, not my father."

A weight fell off her heart, and the absence of it made her feel as though she might lift straight off the ground in flight.

"Only one?" she breathed.

He smiled, tilting her head back again so he could fix her with his dark eyes. She was caught in that stare, one so powerful that she couldn't look away. Could hardly breathe.

"Only one," he repeated, leaning down, and kissing her again.

"Liena! Liena!"

She jerked away from Nianzu, and he immediately released her. His eyes were wide with question, and she gasped. "Zedong! He's come looking for me! Quick, can you leave before he sees you?"

"Why?"

That was the question, though, wasn't it? "Because," she said, wincing, "he's in a bad place, and I don't want to make him madder."

"Are you certain you will be alright? I can stay—"

"No, no, just go! Zedong might get mad, but he won't hurt me. Now go before he sees you!"

He paused in the doorway, then said, "We need to talk again, before your arena battle tomorrow."

With that, he slipped out of the classroom and vanished. Liena, suddenly cold, wrapped her arms around her torso. It was like leaving the warm cocoon of her bed for the frigid dormitory air she faced each morning—the warmth and thrill of a first kiss, to whatever was about to happen with Zedong.

They hadn't exactly parted on good terms.

If he wasn't too overcome with his anger, he would realize that she had told him goodbye. She barely had time to sit down on the edge of the master's platform at the front of the room when Zedong burst in. His eyes were huge, his mouth open, his eyebrows pinched.

"Liena!" he gasped, sagging almost in half. "I was so afraid you'd gone, that I wouldn't be able to find you!"

She wrapped her arms tighter around herself and said, "I'm not leaving."

Her skin prickled with unease when he turned and closed the door behind them, approaching her purposefully. The relief and panic on his face was suddenly replaced by determination.

"I've been thinking," he said, each step echoing in the dark space, "and I think you're right. It's time to leave."

CHAPTER
31

L EAVE?" LIENA SPUTTERED. "*You* want to leave? I thought you
were turning over a new—"

"I'm done," he said, stopping in front of where she sat and
staring down at her. She had to crane her neck to meet his gaze.
Sometimes she forgot how tall he was.

"I'm done," he said again. "And I think you're done too."

Her mouth opened. She searched for any sign of hesitance, of
reluctance, of *anything* in his face beside that dogged determination.

He held out a hand to her, his mouth twisting up ruefully in the
moonlight streaming from the window behind them. "Run away with
me, Liena?"

This day couldn't get any more insane, could it?

"Why are you gaping at me like that?" he said, hand still
outstretched. "Weren't you about to run away? Isn't that why you're
hiding in this classroom?"

Her stupid throat wouldn't work. Her tongue was like a fat, dry slug in her mouth that she couldn't dislodge. Even if she could form the words, her mind stuttered on what to say, where to even begin.

She didn't take his hand when she stood. She found herself shaking her head, her hands trembling as one twisted in her sash and the other went to grip the beads at her throat.

"No?" Zedong said. "Why not? This place is a wretched, dragon-infested hole of arrogant qilin tails."

"Qilins don't have tails," Liena said numbly, stupidly.

"Yes, they do. They're long and ropey with a tuft at the end."

They stared at each other in surprise, both with furrowed brows.

Zedong shook his head. "Doesn't matter. This place is horrid, and it just keeps getting worse. It's unfair and everything's broken here. We can escape together, make a new life—"

"They hunt deserters." Was she Nianzu now? Throwing his arguments into the face of her friend?

"We can outsmart them. We can do it—I know we can. We can go north, to Butagin, and we can find a new life there. No more of this magic nonsense of Zheninghai."

All she could do was shake her head, wrapping her arms around herself yet again, as if they were protection against Zedong, his ideas, and the contrary tugs of her heart.

She could go with Zedong. Yes, it would mean leaving Nianzu behind, and that made every fiber of her being ache. But could she truly expect that she could have a future with him? He might say pretty things now, while holding her in his arms and kissing her, but what about in a few years? When he had graduated, and she was still slaving away at the Academy?

Would the emperor even sanction such a union? The notion was ridiculous. How could she have dreamed for even an instant that this was possible? Even if Nianzu believed it, she was an idiot for assuming he wouldn't change his mind. He would feel betrayed if she left, and if his words and actions were a true reflection of his heart, she might seriously wound him.

But he was a handsome prince. Some other girl would inevitably come along.

If Nianzu didn't keep her here, then what else was there?

Her family.

This was their chance at a better life. If she stayed, if Nianzu did follow through with his words, if that *only one* he spoke of was her, then her family's life could be so drastically different.

"How would we outsmart them?" Liena managed to ask amid the turmoil of her soul. "How could we possibly get past the trackers?"

Zedong's eyes flared, a wild smile spreading across his face. "With the new magic I've learned."

Her racing thoughts thudded to a stop with her heart.

"It's easy enough. I've learned so many spells, and one of them is a hiding spell. All I would do is—" He pulled aside the sleeves of his robes, revealing a small black bag. He opened the drawstrings, and Liena watched in horror as bits of black slid over the edge of the bag, like a trailing column of smoke but sinuous like a snake.

The smell of rot filled the room.

Black magic.

"That's illegal magic," she gasped, jumping away from it. "It's dangerous—"

"Yeah, well so is escaping the Academy," Zedong snapped, tightening the drawstrings. He stepped closer, his face so near. "Come with me, Liena," he pleaded. "Come with me. Let's go—together."

She stared at him, at her friend, at the world he opened up before her. A world of escape, of running, hiding, of forbidden magic.

Suddenly, free didn't seem so free as it once had.

She closed her eyes, the skin around them feeling dry and stretched after her earlier tears. She dug deep inside herself, remembering the feel of millet in her hands, like little beads, remembering the frantic trench digging when the land flooded, the water swirling around her calves as her toes sank into the mud, remembering parched and dusty earth clogging in her lungs. Remembered what an aching belly felt like, the smack of Lao Lao's cane, Pa's twinkling eyes, Ma's constant worried chatters.

If she was a fugitive, she could never see them again.

She remembered the thrill of dipping her quill in ink for the first time, the sweep of it across parchment, seeing significance in the formerly meaningless scribbles of characters on a page. She remembered the flickering candle whose light she worked so diligently by, trying to learn everything as though she were a soul drowning for air.

She remembered the race of her hot blood as she battled Nianzu at the beach, at his praise, at his demands to get up, to not give up. Remembered the press of his lips, so soft yet so fervent, so *wanting*.

Last of all, she remembered Zedong, that boy she'd seen in the corner all alone, who was about to be expelled—practically sentenced to death. When she opened her eyes, met the flickers of blue in Zedong's, she realized she wasn't looking at the same person.

She realized she wasn't ready to give up. Wasn't ready to give up on all the good in this world, in Zheninghai, in the Academy, because she didn't want to face what was wrong. When she spoke, her voice was firm, unshakable, and underscored with the passion of her soul.

"No."

Zedong blinked, and the blue vanished altogether. The blue that Liena now realized was *something* resulted from dabbling in illegal magic.

Illegal magic. Master Gu was teaching illegal magic.

Experiment.

Over the edge.

He swallowed. Jaw worked hard. Then he let out a vicious growl, his arms darting around Liena to drag her against him.

"Zedong—!"

"*Liena,*" he snarled, one hand reaching up and curling into her hair until his nails dug into her scalp. "*Come with me.*"

"No! Let me go! You're hurting me!"

"Don't you see?" Zedong continued, eyes flashing blue once again. His face twisted, contorting into something so unrecognizable she nearly screamed. "We're alike, you and me. Underestimated, misunderstood. But there is magic for us, Liena. There is power for us."

She shoved against his chest, gasping, as she angled her face away from him. His grip on her head was too strong, and he dragged her back so she was forced to meet his gaze. She could feel the breath from his mouth on hers, so close.

"I don't want black magic," she gasped, her voice cracking with frantic notes. "Let me go! I don't want this! I don't want this!"

He was too strong. Had he always been this strong? She couldn't fight him and doubted that even another several years of combat class could have given her the edge she needed to break away.

"You just don't understand, do you?" he said, breath huffing in and out of his mouth as he fought her struggles. "Your head has been turned by that prince, and now a rational thought can't compute in your mind."

"I am *very* rational!"

He let go of her so he could grab her face with both of his hands, dragging her toward him so their foreheads and noses touched. "Can't you see? Liena, I *love* you. I've loved you from the first day you walked into the mess hall. I've wanted you—I *want* you. I need you to come with me, to be my own, Liena. Together, we can do so much—"

"Love me?" Liena gasped, fighting, pushing, clawing at him. "Then let me go! Quit manhandling me!"

"Let me show you! Forget the prince. I'll show you how much I—"

She opened her mouth to scream.

Zedong smothered her cry with a searing kiss.

His kiss swept through her, burning and devouring. It was a raging fire. Unquenchable, never satiated. She tasted desperation, madness, and anguish on his lips.

She saw the truth now.

He had become a monster she couldn't tame.

She had thought she could save him. Instead, he dragged her down with him, clutching her hair in his fist, kissing her until she was empty. Hollow, weakened, desperate. She couldn't breathe; she was drowning. Drowning in madness and the death of dreams and rending heartbreak.

Her tears coursed down her cheek, burning as they flowed. She had played with fire and now it scorched every part of her soul, leaving her bleak and barren. If only she could be free of this guilt, this pity, this love. If only he would let her go, would listen to her reason. If only he would let her save him.

He was too far gone, she realized with sickening desperation. He was lost to her. But he couldn't be lost alone. No, he must destroy her too. She must be lost too. She must die so he wouldn't die alone.

Why did she care? Why couldn't she stop caring, run away, and forget him forever? Why hadn't she been able to leave him when he abused her verbally? When he guilted and manipulated her?

It hadn't just been because he was her friend, had it?

It was because she pitied him.

He pulled back enough to whisper to her, his grip still iron. "You want me. I know you want me. More than that prince. More than anyone you've ever wanted." His breath scorched her ear, his eyes blazing with madness. Insanity.

He was truly insane. She hadn't seen it until now.

"I don't want you," she whispered back. "I pity you."

She felt the change. It was immediate, and it was deadly.

He kissed her again, but it was a kiss of rage, of ruin, of revenge. She tried to fight, tried to pull back, but she was too weak, and he was too strong and too furious. Tears streamed down her face as panic surged in her breast. He would not let her go. He would crush her. His hands were claws, digging into her skull mercilessly. He was hurting her, and she was utterly powerless.

Helpless. Hopeless.

Yet again.

No. Never again.

She fought him. She gasped for air. Though her limbs grew wearier, though she was tired of fighting, she fought. This struggle might kill her, but she would fight with every ounce of strength she could muster until her dying breath.

She hadn't lost until she stopped fighting.

Bringing her knee up hard, she caught him in the upper thigh. He broke the kiss, cursing and struggling to regain his possession of her as she ducked under his arms. He caught her wrist, yanking her back toward him. She screamed, then twisted to drive her elbow into his ribs, like she'd learned in her class. He snarled, groping for a handhold. His fingers latched onto her beaded necklace, and one violent rip sent the beads scattering across the floor. Her head snapped back, but his balance was thrown off by the necklace, and she nearly pulled completely out of his reach.

"What are you doing? Let her go!"

Zedong whirled like a madman with his grip clenched around Liena's arm to see the intruder. His face contorted. "*You.*"

Nianzu's hands were almost bursting with fire. "Let her go *now* or so help me I will blast you to bits."

Zedong looked at Nianzu, then at Liena, and he snarled. With vengeful force, he flung Liena to the ground and jumped into the windowsill. His cloak fluttered behind him like a hawk. He turned deadly eyes on Liena, his profile framed by the huge moon rising in the night sky.

"I'm coming back for you Liena, and you'd better be ready when I do."

In a flurry of cloak, he turned and leapt out of the window, disappearing into the night.

CHAPTER
32

J UST LIKE HER *vision*. A tall, masculine figured, framed in moonlight, and caught in a deadly rage of emotion. Liena lifted her head slowly, almost ashamedly, to meet Nianzu's fiery gaze. His eyes bore holes into her.

"What . . . was . . . that?" he seethed between clenched teeth.

"Master Gu taught him black magic," she whispered. "And it took hold of him."

"*What?*" Nianzu demanded. "Black magic? Master Gu? Without the eye? Are you sure of this? Absolutely certain?"

She nodded, wanting to droop back down to the floor. But then Nianzu was there, helping her up. Even if his face hadn't been a thundercloud, his searing hands would have betrayed his fury. He immediately cooled them when she yelped, then apologized, and demanded, "Are you alright? Did he hurt you?"

She ached. Physically, sure. She imagined she would have bruises tomorrow. But it was her chest that ached the most as her heart throbbed like it suffered a physical wound. She pressed her hand to it, hardly able to draw breath.

Zedong was gone. If he wasn't caught and tried for desertion, would he ever come back? Did she want him to?

"Liena," said Nianzu, softer, knuckles tilting her chin up. "Are you hurt?"

"He was my friend."

"I know. I know."

It wasn't just grief that struck her so hard. It was betrayal. Guilt, too, as she wondered if there was anything she could have done to save him. If she had fought him harder to not study with Master Gu, if she'd trusted her gut, if she'd gone to Nianzu sooner, could he have been spared?

She didn't know.

When she planted a hand on the ground to push herself up to her feet, her fingers brushed something smooth and round. With a jolt, she realized it was a bead. Quickly, almost frantically, she began hunting the beads.

"It's just a necklace," she muttered to herself, even as her hands worked rapidly, scanning the floor and reaching under desks to pluck up the little beads. "Just a necklace."

Nianzu was there at her side, searching too. "Your family gave it to you," he said. "It's not just a necklace. We'll get a new cord for it."

Was this his life? Anytime something broke, immediately replacing it?

At this moment, she was only grateful when they finished scouring the classroom and Nianzu poured his beads into her palm. She set to counting them, making sure they were all there.

One was missing. The lotus bead was gone.

She ran her fingers over the small, rounded wood, and one of the remaining beads twisted, revealing a tiny painted flame.

266

"I'm going to find out what happened with Master Gu," said Nianzu, striding toward the doorway. "Go to the medic if you need to. I suggest you get plenty of rest before tomorrow. Meet me in the pits at fifth watch."

She should tell him what she overheard this morning. She should—

He was already gone.

Liena slid the beads into the pocket of her robes. She started to follow Nianzu, to do what he said and go to her dormitory. But she stopped, glanced back at the open window, felt the shiver of cold wind across her face and catching the ends of her hair.

The moon was smaller, higher now as it continued rising.

Zedong had made his choice. She had made hers.

Now it was time to act on it.

Practicing with Nianzu the next morning was productive, but also slightly overwhelming as he tried to tell her all of Shu's weaknesses, all the tips and tricks for getting past her forcefields.

"Her biggest flaw," he said, swinging his staff and making Liena block, "is that she sometimes pauses to gloat. Just for a second, or less. That can be enough, however. She also can't sustain a forcefield for longer than five seconds, which isn't much of a weakness because she can create new ones the instant the first dissolves, and she's gotten into a very good rhythm with them. What's more important to know is that her hands must touch in order to create a forcefield. To truly incapacitate her, you've got to pin her arms away from each other."

On and on he went, back and forth between correcting her movements and explaining Shu's flaws, which were so minuscule that Liena was beginning to think she didn't truly have any.

"One thing that you have to your advantage," said Nianzu, "is that she expects you to be terrible."

"Which is true."

"Which is *partially* true, but it's not the full story. You're capable of far more than she realizes. You need to play that to your advantage, even if it means purposefully making mistakes so she lets her guard down."

"I doubt that will be necessary," Liena said dryly.

When Nianzu was finally finished deluging her, and once she was breathless and sopped with sweat—despite how her fingers and nose were frozen from the cold—they headed into the mess hall for breakfast.

Immediately, she stopped. Zedong wasn't here.

"Come sit with me," said Nianzu, with a smile that didn't quite reach his eyes, as though he knew exactly what she was thinking.

"With *you*?" she gasped. "But all your . . ."

He flashed a lopsided grin. "I want to show off my girl."

With that, he ignored her protests and hearty blushes, neatly swiping her hand and pulling her after him.

Everyone was looking. Watching. Whispering.

What was the Prince of Zheninghai doing with *that* girl?

Her eyes trailed up from his hand holding hers to his shoulder, then his hard profile. She'd made her choice, and Nianzu had made his. He hadn't chosen the richest girl here, the prettiest girl here, or the most magically talented.

He chose *her*.

A slow smile spread across her face.

It was hard to fight the sudden rush of embarrassment when Nianzu pulled her down next to him at the table, even asking Lei to scoot over to make room for her. To make it even worse—better?—he began scooping food not into his bowl, but into hers.

Her face must be crimson.

"What's this?" Shu asked, a grin firmly plastered on her face. "Have you invited her because—"

"Because she belongs here," said Nianzu with an easy smile. Only the slight narrowing of his eyes betrayed his true feelings. "And because I want her here."

Liena hesitated, staring down at the bowl Nianzu had fixed for her of all the best things at the table. The portions were absolutely mountainous, as if he hadn't realized that someone as small as her wouldn't eat the same amount as he did.

Determinedly, she picked up her chopsticks and set to eating.

A place at the prince's side was his to give. He'd given it to her. She had nothing to be ashamed of. No reason to blush and duck her head.

She lifted her gaze, finding Shu staring at her with a smile that just kept wilting more with every passing minute. In an instant, Liena wondered why she had ever tried to justify Shu's comments. Shu had never intended to be kind—the *kindness* was a thin, false veil to protect herself from the people around her thinking she was too mean.

In reality, Shu was just a bully.

Mu cocked his head to one side, squinting at Liena. "Have we met? What's your name again?"

Liena smiled. "Yes, we have. My name is Song Liena."

CHAPTER
33

S HE TOLD HERSELF that there was no reason to be nervous, no
reason for her hands to shake. This was just another arena battle.
If she'd lost so many, it didn't *really* matter if she lost another.

But it did. More than ever. This arena battle mattered.

The battles commenced for the day, and as usual, hundreds of
students filled the pits, gathering around the erected arenas and
cheering for their friends, booing for their enemies. Her side was cold
where Zedong usually stood. She wondered if the dull ache in her
heart would ever leave, or if she was doomed to mourn her friend
until he returned or was killed. Even then, would the mourning stop?

There had been no public announcement of Zedong's desertion,
even though Nianzu had informed the masters. When it was his turn
for his arena battle, the master merely said, "Lian Delan will replace
Fang Zedong in the match."

It made sense why they would want to save face. If news got out that one student had successfully escaped, there might be more who would try. Liena highly doubted there were many, but she couldn't imagine she and Zedong were the only people who considered escaping.

She stood at Nianzu's arena, watching him fight Jadaala. They punched each other and Nianzu tried not to blast his friend to bits. Liena now fully understood what the other students had meant that he held back. It seemed pitiful now that Nianzu fought like every other student and limited his magic use when he could obliterate his opponent and all the spectators with the sweep of his hand.

He won anyway, even limiting his magic. She smiled, shaking her head to herself as she watched.

After his battle, Nianzu sidled up to her, sweaty and stinky, and gave her a grin.

"Excellent job," Liena said with a smile.

"What, that?" Nianzu said, waving his hand dismissively and trying to rein in his smile. "That was—"

"Let me guess, *nothing*."

His face split into a broad grin.

She rolled her eyes. "Has anyone told you how—"

"Arrogant I am?" said Nianzu. "Absolutely not. I'm the prince, remember?"

She couldn't help her giggle. She pressed her hand to her mouth to hide it, but he saw. He lifted his gaze back to the arena, a self-satisfied smirk playing on his lips.

Ma, you'll never believe.

Her smile faltered, however, when she caught a glimpse of a master in long black robes lurking on the edge of the crowd, silver-streaked hair falling past her hips and one eyeless socket fixed on her.

Liena's mouth went dry.

She tugged on Nianzu's sleeve. He pulled his attention away from the combat before them to look at her. She tugged again, and he bent down so she could whisper in his ear.

"Did you do anything about Master Gu?" she asked.

"I informed the headmaster, who gave me some grief, but eventually sent a few masters to scour her quarters and office for any sign of black magic."

"And?"

"They found nothing."

She blinked, mouth falling open. "Nothing? But then, how do we—"

"Mao Shu and Song Liena!"

Liena's eyes flew wide. Sudden terror struck her as her head whipped to her left, seeing Master Zhong in black, standing beside Shu with a grim expression on his face. Shu, on the other hand, was grinning sweetly. When she met Liena's gaze, she lifted one eyebrow.

And there was Master Gu, prowling not far away, in full view of the arena.

It wasn't just nervousness about a battle anymore.

Wasn't this about Zedong? If so, why did Master Gu still look so . . . devious?

Not that Master Gu had ever looked *not* devious.

Liena whirled and grabbed Nianzu's arm with both hands, turning frantic eyes up to him. "Nianzu, I—"

"You can do this," he said firmly, peeling her hands off him. "I know you can."

"No, you don't understand, I think—"

"Song Liena!" shouted the master again.

"Go on," urged Nianzu, squeezing her shoulder and giving her a little push. "I'm rooting for you."

She didn't have time to explain what she was afraid of! But she needed him to know! Catching his arm again, she said frantically, "If something goes wrong, you need to intervene."

His brow pinched, but he nodded. "Of course."

He didn't think he would need to intervene. Liena hoped he was right, hoped that she was afraid of nothing. After all, Zedong had already left, had already *gone over the edge*. There was no need for anything with Liena now.

Setting her shoulders, she walked to the arena as calmly and confidently as she could, even though she felt like she was walking to her own funeral. Shu just stood there grinning, almost triumphantly, as if she had already won.

Well, Shu *hadn't* won yet. Liena swung over the wall of the arena, landed with feet planted squarely in the sand.

"Good luck," said Shu with a wink.

"Let me guess," Liena retorted, not bothering to paste a matching false smile to her face, "I'll need it?"

Shu laughed. It was a laugh of fangs and barbs. "I take it that His Highness likes a sharp tongue?"

That's what this was about, wasn't it? The prince. Was that how Master Gu had convinced Shu to be complicit with her requests?

"I think he doesn't care for pretense," said Liena.

Shu's eyebrows lowered, her smile still firmly affixed. "I suppose barbarian rice farmers wouldn't have use for pretense."

"Millet."

"What?"

"Millet farmers," said Liena. "If you're going to insult me, you ought to do it with the correct information."

Her smile slipped as the whistle blew. Shu charged.

Liena leapt out of the way, almost as surprised as Shu when she dodged a forcefield blow. Shu frowned, then charged again. Liena ducked, darting under her side to land a blow of her own. Shu blocked it with enough force to send her hurling backward, but Liena had surprised her, had *almost* gotten her.

The first pounding of Shu's magic threw Liena straight to the ground. But just as quickly, Liena shot back up to her feet, blood throbbing, as Shu did exactly what Nianzu said—pausing to gloat instead of finishing her off.

Liena attacked before Shu fully returned her attention to her. Shu's training instinct must have kicked into high gear, because she whirled and hammered Liena into the ground before backing off to give her time to get to her feet.

You've only lost when you stop getting up.

Liena growled. Got up. Kept fighting.

This time, she was knocked down again even faster.

"I don't care who you think you are," Shu snarled in her ear. "But princes aren't for dirt like you."

"Isn't that for the prince to decide?"

"It's for the Glorious Emperor to decide, you phoenix-scorched idiot."

"Do you think the Glorious Emperor will choose you?" Liena asked.

Shu slammed her into the dirt. "It certainly won't be you. You're a failure, and you're going to keep failing as long as you're here."

"Oh?" was all she could manage as her mind grasped for any possible advantage or leverage she had in this situation.

"Because you're dirt. You're nothing. You came late to the Academy, you're behind, you came from nowhere. You have no connections, hardly any magic, and you are half barbarian. You have enemy blood in you!"

Shu slammed her face into the ground. Blood spurted as pain burst across her senses. Stars spun. Black closed in.

"But if I can do it," Liena grunted, "then so can anyone else."

You've only lost when you stop getting up.

"Master Zhong!" came a booming voice—Nianzu's voice. "This has gone too far!"

Shu wasn't trying to win. She could have won many times by now. She was trying to kill.

It just didn't make sense. *Why?* Why would Master Gu care about her now that Zedong was gone?

Oh.

Liena knew about Master Gu's illegal magic. She had sent Nianzu to investigate. It was Liena's fault that Master Gu was now under suspicion. And as long as she was alive, she posed a threat to Master Gu.

"I volunteer as champion!" Nianzu cried, his face a mask of fury as he swung himself into the arena.

There were gasps, as though no one thought the Crown Prince would stoop to being a champion for her. Shu raised an eyebrow as Liena gasped in relief.

"Here to rescue your helpless ladylove?" Shu taunted. "What a target she'll be—an emperor's consort who has weak magic! Who can't defend herself! Who will dilute the magical lineage! The thought!"

"Shu," Nianzu warned.

"Is this what you want?" Shu continued, furiously gesturing at where Liena lay bleeding on the ground. "*This*? Will you always be there to rush to her aid, Highness? Can you protect her from every danger she will face?"

Nianzu's hands were fists, smoke curling up from between his knuckles.

Suddenly, Liena's heart shifted in her chest. She looked down at the blood pooling around her, felt the ache of every muscle in her body. She looked up at the prince, standing ready to defend her. Ready to do anything to protect her.

Past him—Mao Shu.

This wasn't just about Shu. This wasn't just about arena battles. Shu was right. What about when Nianzu wasn't there? She chose to stay at the Academy instead of run away with Zedong. She chose to be here.

Right now, she chose not to give up.

She swallowed salt and blood, trying not to groan or wince as she pulled herself up. She wiped her nose on her robes, refused to balk at all the blood.

"No champion," Liena managed around a cough.

Nianzu turned, his face twisted into one fierce mix of anger and bewilderment. "What?"

She grabbed the edge of the arena and hauled herself up to her feet. "No champion," she repeated, louder.

"But—" Nianzu started to protest.

"No," she snapped. "I will do this. Succeed or fail. On my own."

Live or die.

Very hesitantly, Nianzu left the arena. But she couldn't mistake the pride mingling with the worry and fury on his face.

Shu had both eyebrows raised, a disbelieving laugh bubbling from her lips. "You want to keep going? By all means. Let's keep going." She cracked her knuckles, never once taking her eyes off Liena.

Liena didn't flinch.

"You can do this," said Nianzu from the side.

She didn't turn, couldn't spare any focus for him. Yet his words warmed her heart, bolstering her courage, fusing strength back into the fibers of her being.

This time, Liena was the one who charged first.

Surprise flashed across Shu's face. Instinct kicked in, however, and she threw up her forcefield. Liena anticipated it. She wheeled to a stop before she smashed into it, instead pounding with all the fury, all the blazing passion of her soul onto the forcefield, right where Shu's face was. Over and over.

Five seconds.

Shu must have realized what she was doing, because the forcefield vanished, and Liena's weight fell forward. Shu grabbed Liena's ankle, yanking to pull her to the ground. Liena caught hold of the fence, kicking backward so Shu had to let go or lose her teeth.

The cheers were thunderous, Liena realized distantly. Were they rooting for her?

She charged Shu again, refusing to give Shu a moment to breathe. The girl twisted, bringing her hands together to create another forcefield. Liena faked her out, luring her into trying to smash her with a forcefield. Liena took her narrow window, dodged to the side, and struck Shu square in the nose.

Shu stared, stunned.

Liena didn't stop. She landed a solid kick to Shu's knee and another to her ankle, forcing her leg to buckle. Shu flailed her arms to catch her balance, and that reprieve from the forcefields was enough for Liena to knock her to her knees, then leap upon her back.

Frantically, she yanked Shu's arm back, twisting it up hard behind her. She leaned all her weight on the larger girl, fought how Shu tried to get her hands together.

Just a few more seconds.

Sweat poured in rivulets down her face, mingling with her still-bleeding nose and Shu's blood. Liena ground her teeth, shifting her legs when Shu tried to buck her off.

If she could just hold her—

"Three, two, one—"

Shu gave a mighty shove, crying out in the effort. Liena gave her own cry as Shu wrenched her hand free, but Liena used her free arm to smash Shu's head into the dirt.

"Winner!" cried Master Zhong.

Shu and Liena both sagged, the latter on top of the former. Thunderous cheers split the air, so loud Liena almost couldn't hear the master's proclamation.

"The winner is Song Liena!"

She gasped, sliding off Shu, not believing her ears for a minute.

But then she was surrounded. Students in white jumped into the arena, running so fast toward Liena that she was suddenly terrified for her life yet again. They surrounded her, shouting and patting her back, shoving her shoulders like they were comrades.

"You did it!" they cried. "You beat Shu!"

"I've wanted to see someone beat Shu like that for years!"

"Best fight I've seen all term!"

Then arms swooped her up. She yelped, coughed, and then gasped in relief when she saw it was Nianzu. She wrapped her arms around his neck, glad as he swung them both out of the arena, out of the rushing throng of people.

Looking at his face was like looking into the sun—it was so bright she almost couldn't bear it.

"You did it!" he hollered, laughing and beaming. "You *did* it!"

Though her eye was half swollen shut, and she still tasted blood on her lips, she grinned. Her lungs felt like they might explode from the sudden rush, from the thrill that burst through her veins.

"I did it," she said, laughing incredulously. "Now, if you hadn't given me that little break—"

"Don't start making your victory anything less than what it was," he said sternly. "You won that fight, against all odds. Now I'm taking you to the medic because you sure took it bad. But first . . ."

He shifted his grip on her, leaning down toward her face.

"Wait!" she cried. Quickly, she swiped her sleeve across her lips, wiping away the blood. What an unromantic thing to do before—

Nianzu snorted, then spun so they faced the cheering throng of students, the masters trying to corral everyone back into the scheduled lineup. With a devilish grin at the watching students, and another at Liena, he leaned down and kissed her.

The cheers were deafening. Nianzu seemed to take that as encouragement to keep kissing her.

She made a little sound, trying to push him back. When he did, she pressed her sleeve to her nose. "It's bleeding again!" she shouted over the din.

"To the medics!" he cried.

CHAPTER
34

LIENA FELT LIKE her face was one huge bandage. It was especially awkward to be tended alongside Shu, who hadn't stopped scowling since she limped into the infirmary. The prince hadn't been able to wait outside the entire time, but he promised to come back the minute he heard she was done.

Now, with bandages around her ribs, face, and hands, she slipped outside. Her first thought was to sneak back into her dormitory, to try and get some extra rest before classes tomorrow. Her second thought was to hunt down Nianzu, perhaps convince him that they needed another celebratory kiss now that she wasn't bleeding. *Then* she would go rest.

But then she saw a gray and black head slip quickly into a side hallway.

Liena frowned. Had Master Gu been watching for the moment when she was done with the medics?

What was she to do?

Even though she looked ridiculous, even though the rational part of her mind told her she ought to find Nianzu, she darted toward the hallway Master Gu had vanished into. If she didn't go now, she might lose her. Perhaps she could find out where Master Gu hid her black magic.

Her body ached, needed to recover. Her nose, especially. But she couldn't miss this chance.

Sunlight streamed through the windows, casting on emerald green mosaics on the floor, the red-painted beams on the ceiling and pillars lining the hallway. The light refracted off chips of the mosaic, casting little rainbows on the opposite wall.

No sign of Master Gu.

Liena had to tilt her head extra far each way to get a clear view of the area, due to all her stupid bandages. She frowned, hurried forward softly. When the hallway intersected with another one, she peeked around the corner—and was rewarded with a shadow slipping away at the far end. Moving faster, she scurried along after, her heart's rhythm picking up with each step.

Down deeper into the less populated areas of the Academy, Liena followed Master Gu. Eventually, she realized with a mix of fright and thrill that this was the same place she had followed Zedong.

Her unease mounted with every step, leapt several paces ahead when she watched Master Gu head down the very same dark, stony corridor where the *mó guǐ* were held prisoner.

Heart in her throat, she crept up slowly to the corner, almost not wanting to peek around the edge. She was beginning to thoroughly regret her decision to not find Nianzu first. Mustering up her courage, she leaned forward, fingers gripping the plastered wall.

There was Master Gu, whispering to the tall, cleft-chinned master she'd overheard twice now. Liena's brow knit as she watched. Master

Gu was scowling, gesturing with her hands back the way they'd come. The other master stared back, his face very angry.

"Then we have to get rid of her another way," he said clearly. "Now that the headmaster has been tipped off, things could go south very quickly."

Her? As in, Liena?

She needed to get out of here. She pulled back from the hallway, turned, and broke into the fastest and quietest run of her life. It wasn't quiet enough, however.

"Hey!" came a shout from behind her. "Stop right there!"

She didn't stop. She would have been an idiot to stop!

Shock blazed into her leg. Liena gasped, buckling over her throbbing leg. She sprawled on the ground, and the moment she tried to get back up to her feet, another bolt of pain lanced her elbow.

A lightning wielder.

Liena cringed, trying to scoot away as she watched Master Gu and the second master stride toward her, the latter with two fingers pointed toward her.

"One move," said Master Gu, "and he kills you."

"Not ideal," coughed the other master. "Traceable."

Master Gu shot him a look, which he returned evenly. "She doesn't need to know that."

Liena stared, inching back with each breath despite how her arm and leg ached. How could she escape with them so near, so much stronger than her? And while she was injured, no less?

What pushed to the forefront of her mind, however, wasn't her own safety, but a desperate need to understand.

"What did you do to Zedong?" she seethed.

"We introduced him to black magic," said the tall, thin master without preamble.

Master Gu shot him a look of horror. "Why are you telling her?"

"She deserves to know why we need to kill her."

Liena pursed her lips. She tried to keep her hands from shaking too much, tried to keep her voice steady when she asked, "Why?"

"To see what it's capable of," he said. "Black magic is much more powerful than this sort of thing." He pointed the fingers of both of his hands at each other and a tiny bolt of lightning burst between them. "Our magic is limited, black magic is not."

"This has nothing to do with why we have to kill her," said Master Gu.

"But why Zedong? Why not just explore it yourselves?"

He scoffed. "Because it's *illegal*. Our lives would be completely upended if it was discovered that we'd touched black magic. But we haven't, only Zedong has."

That's what they had meant when they talked about an experiment. Liena was suddenly dizzy.

"What *is* black magic?" she asked, softly.

"It's a complex art that makes use of magical plants, spells, and other sorts of things."

"How . . . did Zedong get those things if you never used them?"

"Oh, we used the supplies, just did so safely, according to the textbooks."

Liena shook her head, her mind spinning far too fast. "But . . . but *why* do you want to know about black magic? Your lightning seems to work just swimmingly."

"It's limited," said Master Gu, snarling. Her eye socket looked especially garish in the weird play of sunlight and shadows in the hallway. "Some of us are tired of always being defined by our limits. Just think what we could accomplish if black magic became the standard! Zheninghai would be undefeatable."

There was an underlying tenor to those words. It almost made the unspoken ones even louder.

Then I will be undefeatable.

Liena stared into that eyeless socket. Then she screamed as loud as she could.

"Do it now!" said Master Gu to her companion, tossing him something.

Liena realized with horror that it was a ring of keys. He caught it and sprinted toward the *mó guǐ* dungeon.

"We may not be able to kill you," said Master Gu, already breaking into a run, "but we *can* ensure your death."

An explosion of bells rent the air, coming from the dungeon. The sound was so strange, so deep and musical yet so wild. Untamed. Liena had never heard that sound before, but she recognized it from her classes. Horror swept her from head to toe, and she was desperately scrambling to her wobbly feet before she could scream again.

But the second master rushed past her, sprinting faster on his two good, uninjured legs. He beat her to the entrance to the hallway, tossed her the *mó guǐ* keys, and slammed the two great doors in her face.

A thump sounded on the other side—the bar falling into place.

Liena threw herself at the door, screaming as loud as she could while pounding the ornate wood. No matter how hard she shoved, it wouldn't budge. Not even an inch.

She whirled just in time to see a mighty, four-legged beast clomp out of the dungeon. It was the color of sapphire, glittering scales lining its deer-like body. Hooves clacked on the mosaic floor, its antlers scraping the ceiling beams. Fire spattered out of its mouth, down its golden beard. Liquid black eyes scanned the room as the beast stomped one cloven hoof, shaking its molten mane.

A qilin.

Liena couldn't move. Couldn't breathe. Couldn't do anything except stare at the achingly beautiful monster that was about to kill her.

More fire came from the dungeon. The qilin snorted in irritation, the sound both horse-like and bell-like simultaneously. It stomped its hooves as a much smaller, much more sinuous monster burst into the hallway.

285

A ruby-red dragon. Just like the one she'd seen on the Hunt.

Her throat was dry, her entire body shaking. Her life flashed before her eyes as the edges of her vision darkened. She saw snatches of when she was a child, farming and Lao Lao and her parents, saw bits from the Academy, saw her last kiss with Nianzu.

No.

Did she beat Shu to die like this? Absolutely not.

She was scouring the room for an escape when a shrieking cacaw split the air and a firebird soared free. She didn't have time to process its terrifying majesty before she swept up the key ring and ran to the nearest window.

Her movement was all it took to make every pair of *mó guǐ* eyes land right on her.

She climbed onto the sill, fumbled with shaking hands only to discover there was no latch. The phoenix shrieked again, flying around the room as though trying to escape. It flames caught on the ceiling, smoke billowing as the fire grew.

Liena glanced back to find the qilin's eyes set on her, its antlers lowered as it pawed the ground.

"Phoenix scorched window!" she cursed.

She threw her entire body weight into the window. Her bandaged head rattled from the impact, and though she heard a crack, it didn't break.

"Liena!"

She startled, turning just in time to see Nianzu burst out from the dungeon hallway, the fire in his palms mingling with the blazes around them.

"Liena!" he cried.

He ran toward her, his handsome face soot smeared. She nearly wept in relief, gasping and sagging against the window.

The qilin charged. And realization hit.

"Fox spirit," she gasped. "Not Nianzu—fox spirit!"

MAIDEN OF CANDLELIGHT AND LOTUSES

She threw herself against the window again, choking on flames and smoke as two *mó guǐ* charged her.

It shattered, and she fell through.

CHAPTER
35

S HE ROLLED WHEN she landed, everything in her body aching. There was blood—she must have cut herself on the splintered wood. No time to worry about that! In a second, she was on her feet again, and that was the same second the phoenix burst through the window.

Smoke billowed out from behind her. She heard the roar of bells, the stamping of hooves, the shriek of the phoenix overhead.

The firebird dove for her.

She screamed and ran.

The garden. She was in the garden. The paths were twisty, cutting through cherry trees, gazebos, and lotus ponds. She needed to get help! Needed people stronger than her who could corral these monsters back into their cells. She still clutched the keys as she ran; clutched them like they were her only prayer for salvation.

The phoenix swooped low, diving in front of her. She skittered to a stop. Stared into molten eyes and saw her death when its beak opened, and fire burned in its throat.

She leapt.

Straight into the lotus pond.

Fire surged into the water, evaporating into a column of smoke above her. She held her breath, swimming as far away from the phoenix as she could get. When she had no more air, she shoved up to the surface, gasped, and ducked barely in time before more fire pelted where she had just been. The pressure and heat knocked her down to the bottom.

Under the water, its shrieks were so distant, so echoey. That didn't stop her heart from racing, her hand from clenching around the rusted keys. Her lungs burned with the need for air. The phoenix circled, circled, and she thought her lungs would burst in her chest.

Fire streaked across the sky, and Liena couldn't wait any longer. She swam to the top, gasping as she broke the surface.

A hand grabbed her arm and yanked her out of the pond.

"Liena!" cried Nianzu's voice. "Oh fathers, you're—"

She screamed, lurching out of his grasp. "Fox spirit!" she shrieked.

She didn't stop running, not until a hand caught her around the waist and pinned her sopping self against a dry, warm body.

"I'm not a fox spirit," he growled. "Are those the keys for the *mó guǐ*? Give them to me."

"No! I can't trust—"

In a flash, Nianzu pulled out a knife from his belt and sliced it across his finger. Blood welled at the wound, and he pressed it into her palm. The blood remained when he pulled away.

"Not a fox spirit," he said, breathless. "Give me the keys."

She handed them over, shivering in the icy wind. "What do I—?"

"Rally the other students!" Nianzu called over his shoulders as he ran toward the window she'd just broken out of. "This is what we've trained for!"

Gritting her teeth against the cold, she turned and ran toward the pits. Behind her, she heard the cacophony of bells, heard a swooping shriek overhead. Ahead, she saw fire. *Mó guǐ* fire.

Liena burst through the nearest door and found herself in the girls' dormitory. When she swung open the first door, she found a group of girls bunched together in hiding.

"Get up!" Liena cried, water dripping off her nose. "Arm yourselves! We must defend our home!"

She didn't wait to see if they followed. She raced through the dormitory, shouting at anyone she could find. It wasn't until she was racing down the next hallway that she heard footsteps behind her, that she realized there were actually students rallying behind her.

"Hurry!" Liena cried. When she wrenched open the library doors, she found a few students quietly studying. "*Mó guǐ* attack!" she shouted. "To arms!"

The pits were a screaming mess. The phoenix had already struck. Arena fences were in flames, students screaming everywhere and masters hastily arming themselves.

If Liena ever became queen, she would do whatever she could to set a better emergency protocol in place here. Growling under her breath, she ran into the billowing smoke of the pits. There was a boy no older than nine curled up in a ball on the ground, hands covering his head.

"Get up!" she said, grabbing his arm and dragging him to his feet.

He let out a cry, and she realized that his face was burned. Hissing, she shoved him toward the complex.

"Move! Don't stay in the danger zone!"

She found Jia next. The girl had a loaded *jiaun* in her grip, and she was trying to aim at the phoenix tearing across the sky.

"Get the wounded!" cried Liena. "We need to get the wounded out of danger!"

Jia's eyes turned to her, frantic and wide, with tears leaking. "I can't hit it!"

"Help me with the wounded!"

Something seemed to snap in place inside Jia's mind. Her gaze cleared, the panic shifting into determination. Wan ran by just then, and Jia tossed him her weapon. He caught it, saluting as he kept running.

"There's someone!" Jia shouted.

She and Liena ran forward, each hooking arms under the burned victim's armpits to drag her. But Liena almost froze when she saw the woman's face.

Only one eye.

"Is she dead?" Jia asked, the tears returned to her voice.

"Don't know," Liena growled. "Hurry!"

They ran, back and forth from the pits until they'd dragged everyone to safety inside. Several times they had to stop and take cover when the phoenix flew by again. But by now, the students had rallied themselves. Everywhere, archers stationed themselves and shot at the phoenix. When Liena ran back into the gardens—which were now demolished—more students and masters were fighting the qilin.

The dragon was already dead, a knife between its shoulders.

Nianzu had a rope around the qilin's neck, and Shu was at his side, fending off the beast's fire with her forcefields. Wan had caught its legs in vines, and as she watched, he sent more shooting up to clamp around the qilin's muzzle.

More masters ran forward, wrestling the beast through the garden. Nianzu grunted with effort, his face strained and the muscles of his forearms taut. Sweat slicked his jaw, and he let out a cry as he pulled *hard* on the qilin's bonds.

Wan had more vines wrapped around it in another minute, and nearly a dozen masters and final year students surrounded the monster as they pushed it back through a broken doorway to the dungeon.

Liena and Jia ran to help the wounded strewn around the garden in various stages of pain and injury. They didn't stop until each one was safe, and the medic team was tending their wounds.

When she came out, the wind frigid and merciless on her wet clothes, she was just in time to see Nianzu and Wan stumble back through the doorway, followed by more, including a battered and worn Shu.

Nianzu turned a rueful smile to Wan, both sweating hard and panting. They clasped forearms, Wan returning the smile with a gasp of relief. Nianzu turned and gave Shu a hearty pat on the back.

"Well done," he said. "I still have a head because of you."

Then his eyes lifted, scanning the area. They landed almost immediately on Liena, and he broke into a run, dodging around burned trees and straight up leaping over one of the ponds.

"And *you*," he said, reaching her and drawing her against his chest, wrapping his arms around her shivering body, "*Well done*. Best commanding officer I've ever had."

She laughed.

He pressed a kiss to the top of her head and growled, "You are going to tell me what in the seven valleys happened because I am *livid*."

Somehow, that only made her smile widen as she pressed closer to his warmth.

CHAPTER
36

THE CANDLE FLICKERED, sending shadows of her scribbling quill dancing along the wall of the empty library. Everything was peaceful at the Academy during festivals, and after the wild year, and the aftermath of the *mó guǐ* battle lingering for several months, Liena was glad to study in quiet.

"Missing my graduation? I'm quite wounded."

She gasped, pressing a hand to her leaping heart as she looked up from her studies. Nianzu was leaning against one of the bookshelves, arms crossed over his brilliant red graduation robes, candlelight playing on his smiling lips. A pang of sadness hit her at the sight of those robes, knowing they meant he wouldn't be here at the Academy with her anymore.

He had more princely duties to attend to now.

"I was there," Liena insisted, pushing those thoughts away. "I simply couldn't stay for all of the festivities. I have too much to do. This Magic Theory class is killing me!"

He glanced at the paper before her, raised an eyebrow, and then said, "Want help?"

She chewed her lip, opened her reference scroll and dropped her chin between her fists, propping her elbows on the table. In a few swift, long-legged strides, Nianzu was kneeling by her side and peering over her shoulder at the parchments.

"It won't make sense," Liena growled. "It doesn't seem to matter how long I study."

In truth, she was too distracted by the thought of going home next week, of *finally* seeing her family again. She could hardly wait to tell them everything that happened. The events of this last year crowded in her brain, filling every nook and cranny until she could hardly read the assignments before her.

Sometimes, it was also difficult to ignore the empty seat across from her.

Nianzu leaned closer, tugging the scroll more his way. "Oh, Dadong Theory," he said aloud, chuckling. "I struggled with this too. I think it's stupid that we have to learn this. It has no practical implications."

"Not unless it's proved true," Liena said. "If we can determine exactly how magic is transferred from generation to generation, it could change everything. It would reshape how people marry, which in turn would change many other things about our culture." Her voice grew softer and softer as she became aware of the smile on Nianzu's face.

"Indeed. But this"—He pointed at the parchment—"is nonsense. It's only the first iteration of the theory. I'd be surprised if they developed this into anything significant during our lifetimes. Technology simply isn't advanced enough."

"No," she agreed. "But if they don't teach us, then how will anyone know to research it further?"

"Hmm." He leaned closer, his chest almost touching her shoulder as he studied the page in front of her. Her vision blurred, her pulse kicking up several notches. His next words tumbled around in her brain, barely discernible over the hum of her own blood in her ears. "Which part are you struggling with?"

Belatedly, his words registered in her mind. Flushing, she picked her hand up and, with considerable effort, pointed at a random spot on the page. He made another low, "Hmm."

"You're struggling with . . . understanding the purpose of the Dadong Theory?" the prince said, amusement lacing his voice. "But it rather sounded like, a minute ago, you understood that part perfectly."

The blistering heat of her embarrassment sent her spluttering. "I . . . uh . . . That is, I was struggling with . . ." She trailed off as his hand, which had been planted on the mat behind her, slid to the opposite side of her.

Her breath caught. Just a tiny bit—and *very* quietly.

He heard anyway.

He stilled, one hand on the mat behind her, one on the table. Slowly, his face lifted from studying the parchment before her. She felt his eyes on the side of her face as she closed her own, heat flooding her cheeks.

A cool breath exhaled against her face. She shuddered as she felt the world grow warmer, warmer, *warmer* as he leaned closer. Close enough to brush his nose into her hairline in a soft and gentle nuzzle.

"Tell me to stop," his deep voice whispered above her ear.

She didn't. She couldn't. Not as he continued nuzzling her cheek, the skin just next to her ear, and not as he pressed a kiss to her temple.

Her throat was dry as the library around them, near ragged when she tried to summon her voice. She was certain her face was the reddest and hottest it had ever been in her life when she gasped, "Not in a thousand years."

His laugh was surprised. He tilted her face toward his and kissed her soundly.

"Just think," he said, pulling away with an impish grin, "in a few years, you'll be wearing the red robes, an Academy graduate yourself."

She gave a rueful smile. "Sometimes it feels like it's a thousand years away."

"It'll come quickly. And when it does . . ." He wrapped both arms around her and let out a contented sigh. "Then I will make you my queen."

Liena wasn't sure she would ever get over those words. Her mind almost didn't seem to fathom their meaning, accepting denial instead. But then she remembered her visions of that girl standing next to him. At the time, Liena hadn't wanted to admit it. She was too afraid her foolish heart would run ahead of itself. Yet no matter how much she denied it, she had always known the truth from that very first vision.

The girl in her visions had been her daughter. Her daughter, and Nianzu's daughter. Though most of her face was Liena's, her chin and the subtle strength of her jaw came from him. She would never forget the elegant robes the girl wore, or the way Nianzu had smiled fondly down at her.

It would happen. And if her other vision was to be trusted, her daughter would know Zedong.

"You're very certain the Glorious Emperor will approve? Of . . . of me?"

Nianzu waved his hand dismissively. "He won't care. He thinks I'm going to have a hundred wives, like he does, so he won't have a problem with it."

"That's devious!"

He laughed. "It gets even more devious! I'll refuse to marry anyone else, and then when my father passes on to the next life, when *I'm* the Glorious Emperor, I'll make you my queen. No one will be able to challenge it."

"Seems like you've got this all worked out," she mumbled, unable to help her blush.

"Oh, yes. I could think of nothing else until I worked out the plan. Which, by the way, was long before you noticed me."

"Before *I* noticed *you*?" she cried, scoffing.

He grinned. "How could I not notice the pretty new seer with her pretty accent facing off the entire Academy? I've been rooting for you since your first day. But let's get back to Dadong Theory, so you can graduate faster." He pressed one last kiss to the top of her head. "I'm ready to make you my queen."

CHAPTER
37

L IENA NEVER THOUGHT she'd nearly swoon at the sight of millet heads waving in the summer breeze, the hours of seemingly unending harvest beckoning. When that familiar hut came into view and she could make out the silhouette of Pa's form in the fields, she let out a sound that was something between a gasp and a squeak, and practically stumbled off her horse as she dismounted.

"Careful!" came the concerned voice behind her.

She didn't have time to be careful. She was *home*.

She ran as fast as she could, nearly twisting her ankle in several potholes along the way. "Pa! Ma! Lao Lao!" she shouted at the top of her lungs.

Pa straightened. After him, another head popped up above the millet heads—Ma. The door to the hut swung up from a cane thwack.

Pa was the first one to start running. He came hobbling out of the fields, limping on his bad hip. Ma was right behind him, shrieking something incoherent. And Lao Lao banged her cane against the doorframe in her own way of expressing excitement.

One minute, everyone felt so far away. The next, she was outside the door of her home, wrapped in warmth, dust, and the arms of her family. She didn't mean to cry, but *oh* she was so happy to be home! She wasn't the only one crying either; by the time she pulled away for a breath, she saw the only dry eye was Lao Lao's.

Of course.

"We didn't know when we would see you again!" cried Ma. "Tell us *everything*!"

"Well, a few months ago, a bunch of *mó guǐ* escaped their prison and rampaged the Academy! They were let out by two masters—one of them was killed in the battle, and the other was found out later because a feral wielder smelled his scent on the locks of the prison and then he went on trial—"

"What nonsense are you spewing girl?" said Lao Lao. "We don't want to hear about *mó guǐ*, we want to hear about the men!"

"Yes, yes, tell us about all the young men!" said Ma.

"*I* want to hear about the *mó guǐ*!" said Pa. "Were you safe? Are you alright?"

"I was fine, Pa. There were Hunts and Night Games and I had this friend—"

"*Who* is *that*?" said Lao Lao, her gums parting in a gape, white eyebrows rising high.

They all turned.

Nianzu strode toward them, the leads of their horses in hand. He wore his armor, his long cloak billowing behind him with each confident step. He grinned; one eyebrow quirked. Liena immediately flushed with embarrassment, realizing she'd completely forgotten him in her excitement to be home.

Lao Lao, Ma, and even Pa gaped at him.

"Oh fathers bless us," whimpered Ma.

"*Who* is *this*?" demanded Lao Lao again, eyes round as saucers as they traveled up and down the prince, taking in his broad shoulders, his height, and the fetching military garb.

Liena got to her feet, shuffling with a scarlet face to Nianzu's side and ducking her head. "Ma, Pa, Lao Lao, may I present the Crown Prince of Zheninghai, Prince Nianzu."

The shocked stillness permeated the air outside the hut, punctuated only by one of the horses snorting.

Then Lao Lao fainted.

Nianzu darted forward, catching her with Pa as the cane hit the floor. They lowered her gently to the ground, and he lifted horrified eyes to Liena. "Seven valleys, I didn't mean—I hope I didn't—"

"She's fine," said Liena.

Ma and Pa dropped to their knees beside the passed-out grandmother, but instead of tending to her, they were bowing to Nianzu. He didn't notice, however, because he was too busy lifting the tiny, frail Lao Lao to carry her inside.

"Where should I put her?" he said.

Liena stumbled between her bowing parents into the hut. "Over there, on the bed by the fire."

He looked around the room, stopping short for a split second. She could almost feel his shock as he registered the one bed her family had shared—except Liena, who had slept on the floor—and the dirty, tiny abode that had been her home. But he overcame his surprise so quickly she almost doubted she'd seen it at all.

Lao Lao groaned, coming to just as Nianzu knelt to lay her in bed. Her eyes opened wide again, and she lifted one knobby-fingered hand up to touch his cheek. "Now I can die happy," she murmured.

Nianzu's flush was so bright it was even visible in the dark hut. He turned away and coughed as Liena pulled the threadbare quilt up over her grandmother while trying not to giggle like an idiot.

303

"Rest," she said to Lao Lao with a smile. "I have much to tell you later."

Continue the saga with a new cast of characters in Guardian of Talons and Snares. *Can Kai and Aranya stop almost killing each other long enough to save their empire? Or will his secrets destroy them both?*

MORE FROM
ANASTASIS BLYTHE

THE ZHENINGHAI CHRONICLES

Guardian of Talons and Snares
Warrior of Blade and Dusk
Princess of Shadows and Starlight
Captive of Twilight and Treachery

ABOUT THE AUTHOR

Anastasis Blythe makes her home in central Texas with her husband and their two adorable but rather whiny cats. When she's not writing, she is reading an unhealthy amount of fantasy novels, daydreaming about future books, and trying to keep up with the laundry.

If you would like free novels, regular behind-the-scenes updates on her writing, and an early peek at new book covers, join her community at Patreon.com/AnastasisBlythe.

CONNECT WITH ANASTASIS ONLINE AT:

Website - AnastasisBlythe.com
Instagram - @AnastasisBlythe
Facebook - Anastasis Blythe
Goodreads - Anastasis Blythe

Milton Keynes UK
Ingram Content Group UK Ltd.
UKHW041844291223
435208UK00014B/260/J

9 781960 6060